# WITH LOVE

# *With Love*

JENNIFER BLAKE

KRISTIN HANNAH

LINDA LAEL MILLER

BERKLEY BOOKS, NEW YORK

This is a work of fiction. Names, characters, places, and incidents are either the product of the authors' imaginations or are used fictitiously, and any resemblance to actual persons, living or dead, business establishments, events or locales is entirely coincidental.

A Berkley Book
Published by The Berkley Publishing Group
A division of Penguin Putnam Inc.
375 Hudson Street
New York, New York 10014

PRINTING HISTORY
Berkley trade paperback edition / August 2002

Visit out website at www.penguinputnam.com

Library of Congress Cataloging-in-Publication Data

With love / by Jennifer Blake, Kristin Hannah, Linda Lael Miller.
p. cm.
Contents: Pieces of dreams / Jennifer Blake—Liar's moon / Kristin Hannah
A midsummer day's dream / Linda Lael Miller.
ISBN 0-425-18495-1
1. Love stories, American. I. Blake, Jennifer, 1942–
II. Hannah, Kristin. III. Miller, Linda Lael.
PS648.L6 W57 2002
813'.08508—dc21                     2002022348

PRINTED IN THE UNITED STATES OF AMERICA
10  9  8  7  6  5  4  3  2  1

# Contents

❦

# PIECES OF DREAMS

*Jennifer Blake*

# One

Amelia Bennington glanced up from her stitching as the steam whistle of the *J. B. Cates* blasted one last time from the landing at the end of Main Street. The steamboat was leaving, finished with the stop for Good Hope on its regular run from New Orleans to St. Louis and beyond. It had made a fairly long halt this evening. There must have been a team of Missouri mules to be loaded, or maybe a passenger to be put off.

None of the other young women sitting around the quilting frame suspended from the ceiling by grass ropes was paying the least attention to the boat. As Melly looked around at her friends in the glow of the lamplight and listened to their low, laughing voices, she felt the sudden rise of emotion. They were all so dear. She wanted to remember this evening for the rest of her life, every last detail: the steamboat's musical warning, the bumbling of moths and gnats about the hot lamp globes, the smell of the fresh-made lemonade served by Aunt Dora to ward off the late August heat, the scents of thyme and basil and roses wafting from the front garden through the open windows.

Soon it would all change. She would become Caleb's wife, and nothing would ever be the same again.

The waves of her thick, dark hair caught the lamplight as she allowed her gaze to rest on each of the four friends who had been such a large part of her life, the four who would be her bridesmaids. Green-eyed Esther Montgomery, with her strong face softened by incredibly long lashes and her forthright, common-sense views on everything from female suffrage to the best way to make wax posies. Lydia McDougall, tall, auburn-haired, with her tendency toward the dramatic, her warm temper, and her warmer heart. Barbara Zane of the doll-like china-blue eyes and ash-brown curls, known to all as Biddy because she was as petite and aggressive as a bantam chick. And Sarah Franks, Melly's second cousin, statuesque as a goddess, with silvery-blond hair and deep blue eyes, always doing for others, especially her father and three brothers. Of all the friends she had known since childhood, these four were truly special.

It had been a blessing to be near them over the past few years, Melly thought, sharing their problems and heartaches as they had shared hers. Three near spinsters and a widow, they were all over twenty and without husbands, a fact that had made them unusually close.

It was the natural order of things that they would marry, change, grow apart; Melly knew that. She was anxious to be wed, to go with Caleb to the farm he was building for the two of them outside town, of course she was. But at the same time, she could not help feeling a little blue, and even a tiny bit fearful.

Leaving her needle standing upright in the thickness created by two layers of cloth on either side of fluffy cotton batting, she smoothed slender fingers over the silken surface of the quilt top on which they were all working. There was so much love, so many hopes and dreams sewn into it.

The center square was in a starburst design that she herself had pieced over the winter and spring just past. Put together with the scraps left from her wedding gown of pearl-colored Oriental silk, it also incorporated pieces of silk and satin in various shades of blue remaining from the dresses made for her bridesmaids. In the center of the starburst was a Greek cross with four arms of equal length. Across the center Melly had used gold thread and looping Spencerian script to embroider her wedding date: *September 10, 1843*. Her initials had been inscribed in the arm above it, with Caleb's in the one below. The squares set around this focal point, in a star design with a diagonal cross, had been pieced from the silk and satin dress scraps by Melly's aunt Dora, the woman who had raised her after the steamboat accident that killed her parents. Then each of the four corner squares had been done by a bridesmaid, and featured diagonal bars embroidered with their names and a small sentiment or token of remembrance.

Though they all called it a Friendship Quilt among themselves, it was far more to Melly. Wedding present, housewarming gift, treasured keepsake, it was a shimmering work of art and a lovely reminder of her friends and everything they had meant to each other. More than that, it was a symbol of everything that she would soon become.

Two weeks from this very night, she would walk down the aisle of the church in her gown of rich, flowing silk. Afterward, she would drive away with Caleb. In the house he was building for her with sweat and the toil of loving hands, the two of them would truly become man and wife.

How strange to think that it would be upon her in just a matter of days. The waiting of their three-year engagement had been so long it sometimes seemed it would never end.

"Melly's daydreaming again, girls." Esther Montgomery, seated at the lower right corner of the frame, made the accusation with a quick glance from her soft green eyes. "Just look at her blush. Two guesses what's on her mind!"

"Nothing of the kind!" Melly said in laughing indignation, though she could not help the now even darker flush that invaded the creamy skin of her face.

What would it be like, really, to be a wife? What would she and Caleb say to each other, what would they do, once they were alone together? How would they find their way past the embarrassment of undressing and getting into bed?

Yes, and what precisely would happen then?

Melly thought she had a glimmering from the few comments she had overheard between Aunt Dora and her bosom cronies. It seemed all too likely that this physical union would be awkward. Yet from it would come the mingling of their two souls, hers and Caleb's, as well as the birth of their children. Caleb was a good man, levelheaded, kind, gentle; she would have to trust that his love and her own common sense would see her through the ordeal.

"And why shouldn't she be thinking about it?" Sarah Franks asked with her usual protective instinct. "Caleb Wells is handsome enough to make anybody's heart beat faster."

"As if she would dwell on such a thing!" Biddy, used to making herself heard above the hubbub of a one-room school as a teacher, had no trouble speaking over the other girl's voice. "Melly's more likely contemplating how to decorate her new parlor."

Esther made a disparaging noise, but Melly seized on the suggestion. "That's exactly what I was doing, thinking how nice it would be to display our quilt for visitors to see. I could fold it over a bench—or maybe hang it like a tapestry if I can persuade Caleb to make some kind of support for it."

"If?" Sarah said with lifted brows. "You know Caleb would cut off his arm and hand it to you if he thought you wanted it."

"Oh, Sarah, don't be disgusting," Biddy said.

"Well, he would!"

"Sarah's right," Lydia McDougall joined in with a nod that made her auburn curls dance. "Do you recall the time Caleb took off his coat and laid it across the mud so Melly wouldn't get her new shoes muddy? That was years ago, when she was hardly more than twelve or thirteen."

"I thought that was Conrad," Esther said, referring to the twin brother of Melly's fiancé.

"I'll have to say it sounds the kind of thing Conrad would do," Sarah Franks said with a thoughtful look in her eyes. "He did have a flair about him."

"Still does, I'd say," Esther agreed. "Just look at the way he sent the silk for Melly's wedding dress. Amazing to think that he picked out such lovely stuff in far-off Cathay and sent it all the way across the sea."

"It would have been more to the point if he had brought it himself," Biddy said. "And come to his brother's wedding."

"A sea captain in the China tea trade can't do just what he wants, Biddy," Sarah said in tones of quiet reason.

"Anyway," Lydia said, "I know Caleb gave Melly his piece of apple pie at the last church homecoming because I saw him."

"Yes, and he gave her his hat to use for a fan last Sunday when it was so hot we were all about to swoon."

"I forgot my fan," Melly said. "And Caleb said he didn't care for the apple pie."

Sarah laughed. "Well, that was a bold-faced lie, because I saw your aunt Dora put a piece big enough for two men on his plate not ten minutes before."

"No wonder he was so generous, then!" Lydia's golden brown eyes sparkled as she spoke.

"Anybody who works as hard as Caleb needs a lot of nourishment," Sarah said. "It was still good of him to give up a treat for Melly."

Esther waved her needle in Sarah's direction. "You ask me, he works too hard. He used to be a lot of fun, back before Conrad went off to sea. Now he's turning into a drudge without two words to say for himself."

"Don't you think that's natural?" Melly looked across the quilt with an earnest smile in her dark eyes. "Caleb has a lot on his mind with the farm, the new house, and the responsibilities ahead of him."

"All I'm saying is, you'd think he'd act happier about the whole thing."

Melly had to agree that Caleb had been rather solemn of late. Still, he had always been known as the steadfast, dependable twin; that was his strength. She said, "He's happy in his own way, I'm sure of it. He's just quieter about it than . . . well, than Conrad used to be."

"Who wants cookies with the next round of lemonade?"

That cheerful call came from the doorway leading from the back of the house into the front parlor where they were working. It was Aunt Dora, bustling in with a platter of gingersnaps in one hand and a new pitcher of frothy lemonade in the other. Her gray-streaked blond hair curled in wiry tendrils from the bun on top of her head, and her round face was flushed from the heat of the outdoor kitchen where she had been baking in the relative cool of the evening. She set her burdens down on a side table and wiped her hands on her apron, then began to refill glasses.

"Did I hear somebody mention Conrad? Mercy me, but that boy was a scamp! Enough to give trouble a bad name, he was, but such a charmer that a body really hadn't the heart to scold. I recall the time he put a bucket of water up the apple tree outside my window so Mr. Prine got a regular drenching when he came prowling around on Saturday night. Dampened the man's ardor for a good two weeks!"

Mr. Seymour Prine was a longtime resident at the boardinghouse run by Melly's aunt. He was also a suitor of many years' standing. But as the Widow Bennington had a fierce dislike of the indulgence in strong liquor, while Mr. Seymour got drunk every Saturday night, the pair seemed destined to remain apart. It was a shame, really. Mr. Prine was as quiet and pleasant-spoken a gentleman as anyone could expect from Monday through Friday: neat and clean in his habits, with upright posture and a fine head of silver hair, highly respected as a teller at the bank just down Main Street. But on Saturday night he wended his way to the riverfront saloons. There he had a few, then a few more. By midnight he was back at the boardinghouse outside Aunt Dora's window, where he stood with his hat held over his heart while he spouted stanza after endless stanza of *The Rubáiyát of Omar Khayyám*—with special emphasis on those concerned with wine and amorous dalliance. Aunt Dora was scandalized, or pretended to be.

"Poor Mr. Prine," Sarah said.

"Poor Mr. Prine, my eye!" Aunt Dora set a fist on her ample hip. "The idiotic man just stood there dripping and moaning about drowning his glory in a shallow cup!"

Esther winked at Melly as she joined Sarah in teasing the other woman. "But only think how faithful he's been."

"Yes, and think of how convenient it is that his bed and his ladylove are in the same place."

A wicked smile tilted Esther's wide, mobile mouth. "Dear me, Aunt Dora, you don't mean—"

"I do not," the older woman fumed, her blue eyes snapping, "which is a fact you know very well, Miss Priss! It will be a cold day in Hades before that whiskey-soaked gallant winds up in my bed. The very idea! I've a good mind to take my gingersnaps straight back to the kitchen."

"No, no, don't do that, dear Aunt Dora," Lydia cried. "You know she didn't mean anything."

"What Lydia is trying to say," Melly interpreted with a laugh, "is that she's starving, as usual. I'm sure everyone will be nice as you please in return for a cookie."

"Well, that's all and good, but it's a man she should be trying to please, along with all the rest of you."

"Like you?" Esther inquired, all innocence as she met the older woman's gaze.

"I had a man once, God rest his soul, and don't need another one."

"Nor I," Biddy said in near inaudible tones.

There was a brief and sympathetic silence. They were all well aware that Biddy's young husband had been struck by lightning as he plowed in the field only months after they were wed. That had been over two years ago, but she still wore black.

Then there was Sarah. Though she never spoke of it, and did not now, she had also lost her man. She and a young carpenter named Theodore Frazier had been engaged a few years back, but Theo had stepped on a nail while repairing a barn and died, agonizingly, of lockjaw. Since then, Sarah had devoted herself to her father and brothers, and to nurturing her roses and herbs and her flock of chickens.

"Yes, well," Aunt Dora said, clearing her throat. "You're all still young and prime for loving, regardless, and there's no reason you shouldn't find it like Melly here." Her eyes took on a sudden brightness. Abruptly she turned and set down her pitcher. "Hold on, now. You've just put me in mind of a way to maybe help things along. I'll be right back!" Her skirts jerked and swayed as she hustled off in the direction of the kitchen.

The young women looked at each other, mystified and a little wary. Melly pushed her chair back from the quilting frame and rose to fetch the cookie platter. "I don't know what Aunt Dora's up to," she said as she began to pass them around, "but we can't let good gingersnaps go to waste while we find out, now can we?"

She was back in her chair, brushing cookie crumbs from

her mouth while leaning carefully away from the quilt top, when her aunt returned. As she saw the kitten in the older woman's arms, her brows lifted. Aunt Dora paid no attention.

"All right, ladies, gather close around the quilt now, and push all the needles through and underneath out of the way," the older woman called with a wave of her free hand. "What we're going to try is a tradition handed down from my grannie, one that maybe came from the old country in years gone by. The saying goes that if you drop a cat onto the quilt frame at a quilting bee, then the girl it runs to will be the next to marry. Yes, and the first man through the door will be her groom."

"But that's not a cat, only one of Vanilla's kittens," Melly protested.

"Looks mighty like a cat to me," Aunt Dora said, holding the mewling kitten up to her face and rubbing noses affectionately. "Besides, a big one like Vanilla might claw the silk, and we can't have that. Now, ladies, are you ready?"

Esther tilted her head. "What if the first man through the door should be Mr. Prine?"

"Then I pity the bride," Aunt Dora said shortly. "Enough sass. Here we go!"

Stepping to the frame on the side opposite Melly, she held the kitten above the center of the half-finished quilt, letting it dangle bonelessly for a few seconds. Then she dropped it.

The small cat landed spraddle-legged, looking startled and annoyed as the quilt bounced and sagged in the middle. Gathering itself with immense dignity, it patted the starburst under it, then took a tentative step.

"Call to it, girls," Aunt Dora directed. "Come on, now. You have to do your part if you want it to be a fair trial."

"Here, kitty, kitty," Sarah said, obliging as always.

"Over here, cat," Esther said, trying not to laugh.

Biddy eyed it askance. "Don't let that creature come near me, or I'll start to sneeze and won't quit till doomsday."

"Sweet little kitty," Lydia crooned with a grin and a competitive glance at the others. "Come here, darling bitty kitty. Over here. Come to Lydia."

The cat sat down and started to lick a paw.

A gust of giggles and half-smothered jeers greeted the performance. Melly looked toward her aunt, humor flashing bright in the black-eyed-Susan brown of her eyes. She made no effort to coax the kitten herself, of course, since she knew perfectly well when she would be married, and to whom. "Now what?"

"Call it again," Aunt Dora urged the others as she placed her fists on her hips. Her frown was earnest, as if she actually expected the kitten to reveal the future happiness of at least one of their number.

They did as suggested, except for Biddy, who made shooing motions in the direction of the others with her small hands. The kitten looked up from its ablutions and pricked its ears, but made no move to leave its seat.

"Oh, dear," Lydia moaned in mock dismay. "Does this mean we're all hopeless?"

"Don't be ridiculous," Melly said bracingly. "It's my belief you're all trying to avoid your fate. Call him as if you mean it!"

At the sound of Melly's voice, the kitten blinked and turned its head in her direction. Then, as if executing a tiresome duty, the small animal rose and glided into a dainty walk, picking its way over silk and satin and the gold featherstitching that outlined the connecting seams of the squares. At once, the bridesmaids renewed their giggling, cajoling efforts.

The kitten paid no attention. It did not hesitate, but made its way straight to Melly. Dropping into a crouch in front of her, it launched into a graceful leap. As she caught it in her arms, it climbed up to snuggle into the tender curve of her neck. Immediately it began to purr.

"Hey! No fair!" Lydia cried.

Biddy made a sound of mild disgust. "What can you expect? The silly thing belongs to Melly, after all."

"She is definitely going to be married, you'll have to give the cat that much," Sarah pointed out in a throaty chuckle.

At that moment, the front door swung open. The young women turned as one to see who had arrived. Their lively chatter died away into sudden, breathless silence.

The man who stepped into the room was tall and broad and bronzed, with hair so bleached by the sun that it had the color and sheen of spun gold. Standing relaxed and four-square in the doorway, he appeared as sure of his welcome as a conquering Caesar. As he saw the women staring at him, his blue eyes took on a brilliant sheen of merriment while a slow grin curved his mouth.

"Caleb!" Melly cried. Driven by amazement over the opportune arrival, she lowered the kitten to the quilt, pushed back her chair, and sprang up. Then, laughing, she ran to fling herself into her fiancé's arms.

A soft grunt of surprise left him as he caught her against his chest. An instant later, his blue gaze turned smoky with the rise of desire. His firm lips parted for a quiet oath, then he lowered his head and touched his mouth to hers.

It was like stepping into a whirlwind, a spinning fury of the senses. Melly's lips tingled, heating with the contact. Her heart seemed to stop. She felt buffeted, storm-tossed, lost in a delirium of sheer, pulsating magic. Dimly she was aware of the parlor, her aunt, her friends, but they did not seem to matter. All that had being or reason was the warm, hard arms around her and the sweet, tender taste of the man who held her so close to his heart.

"Melly!"

That voice. Her name, resounding in heavy syllables that held accusation, disbelief, disapproval. And pain.

It was the last that reached her. The pain.

She pushed free, stepped back, though she had to hold to the arms of the man she had just greeted for balance. Turning her head slowly, she stared at the person who had called to her, the man who now moved from behind the first to enter and then stopped at his side.

It was like seeing double. There were two of them, two men of devastating power and appearance, two men dangerously alike.

And the second, the latecomer, was Caleb, her future husband.

Melly's heart sank, shivering inside her, as she saw what she had done. The first man through the door had been Conrad. The second had called her name.

She had kissed the wrong brother.

# Two

"I'm sorry," Conrad said in husky tones as he gazed down at Melly. "I-I didn't mean, that is, I just—" He stopped and took a deep breath to prevent himself from stammering like a schoolboy. "It was the surprise."

The apology was a sham, and Conrad knew it. He had taken shameless advantage, though he didn't regret it for a minute. He wasn't a man to turn down a taste of heaven when it came his way.

And it had been heavenly. He would never forget the intoxicating taste of Melly's lips, that fresh and tender assault on his senses. Not if he lived to be a hundred.

He hadn't seen it coming—how could he have? For a single instant he had thought it was just plain surprise that caused him to react with such stunning intensity. But that wasn't it at all.

Melly, that was what had shook him, left him wanting more. Melly herself—the rich welcome and joy in her eyes as she came toward him, the entrancing shape of her face, the slender curves of her body pressing against his in a fit so right, so perfect, it was as if he had been born to hold her. She had stolen his breath and his common sense, knocked his notions of proper behavior for a loop. For a single instant she had made him forget who she was, who he was—had made him forget that he was not his brother.

He had kissed Melly, his twin's promised wife. God, how stupid could he be?

Caleb, he saw, was mad as hell, and who could blame him? If Melly belonged to him and he had seen Caleb kissing her, he would be ready to wear the mark of Cain right square in the middle of his forehead.

That was, of course, one of the major curses of being a twin. It was too easy to put himself in his brother's place. Far too easy.

"Come in here, you rapscallion!" Aunt Dora cried, stepping forward to envelop him in a quick, well-padded hug. "Have a seat, both you boys. Have a cookie while I bring two more glasses. Mercy above, Conrad, if it's not just like you to drop in out of the blue!"

"Not quite," he offered with a grin. "I only stepped off the steamer like anybody else."

"Which is still enough to give a body heart palpitations when we thought you were on the other side of the world. You might have let us know you were coming! Though I expect we should have guessed you'd not let Caleb marry without you."

"So you should have," he said promptly, his gaze bright.

"Cheeky as always, Conrad. But maybe we should be calling you *Captain* Conrad now?"

He shook his head and tried to look doleful. "Not when you'll probably have me swabbing the deck before the night's done."

"When did I ever do such a thing?" Aunt Dora demanded, setting her fists on her hips in mock irritation.

"Often!"

The older woman laughed. "Maybe so, but I'll let you off tonight, seeing as how you're the prodigal. But mind you, I make no promises about tomorrow."

Conrad was grateful for the teasing welcome masked as scolding. It was exactly what was needed to ease the strained atmosphere and return things to normal. More than that, it made him feel as if he had come home.

As the older woman trundled off in the direction of the kitchen, Melly reached to take Caleb's hand and give him a swift peck on the cheek that made his stodgy brother blush scarlet. Falling back on her role as hostess then, she directed Caleb to draw up the single chair that sat against the near wall. As that was being done, she turned back to Conrad.

"You remember everyone, don't you?" she said with careful politeness. "That's Lydia there on the end, of course. Her father owns McDougall's Mercantile. And my cousin Sarah, seated there next to her?"

He smiled, responding easily to the greetings as Melly continued quickly around the sewing circle. He was glad of the reminders. The ladies had changed out of all recognition since he'd left Good Hope. Except for Melly.

The introductions done, Melly resumed her seat and drew Caleb down next to her. Conrad, left to fend for himself, dragged a chair closer to the group of females, though not quite near enough to be a part of it. That was always the way it had been for him, or so it seemed—outside the charmed circle.

"Well, I have to say Melly's mistake seems perfectly natural to me," tall, blond Sarah Franks declared as she looked with raised brows from him to his brother. "I think I might have trouble telling the two of them apart if we met on the street tomorrow."

"Maybe," tall, auburn-haired Lydia McDougall said with a sly and laughing glance at her friend, "but Melly never kisses Caleb hello like that."

Now that was interesting, Conrad thought, his gaze on Melly's flaming face. Why? he wondered. No cooperation? But the answer ceased to matter as he caught the fleeting glance she flung in his direction. That look reproached him, castigated him for his presumption—and sent a shaft of pure yearning winging through him.

"Yes, and maybe it's just that we've never seen her do it," Esther Montgomery said.

Conrad didn't care for that idea, didn't care for it at all.

"She used to be able to tell Caleb and Conrad apart with a single glance, the one person in the whole town who could," the little one, Biddy, commented. "Seems she had better start practicing that trick again."

They were all looking at him and his brother now. Conrad shifted uncomfortably, feeling the tips of his ears grow hot. At the same time, he knew that Biddy was right. Melly had usually been able to recognize him on sight back in the old days. He could fool her sometimes, if he tried hard enough, but not often.

Aunt Dora came scurrying in again. Taking charge without effort, she steered the conversation into safer channels, demanding to know where he had been and all the things he had done in the long years he had been gone. Conrad obliged with a version that was considerably more colorful than the reality in some cases, considerably less in others. Mustn't disappoint the ladies, he knew, but heaven forbid that he should shock them.

Even as he spoke, however, his mind was busy elsewhere. Melly had been—what?—all of thirteen when he left? He remembered her as a princess in pigtails, one of those girls who never seemed to go through an awkward stage. Smart, sweet, tenderhearted, though she had her temper, maybe from being a little spoiled after what she'd gone through in the steamboat explosion, being thrown into the water and half drowned, losing her parents. She had ruled the play yard with a high hand, ordering all the boys around like so many hired hands. He had not been among them, of course, being nearly ten years older, but he had enjoyed watching her antics and always felt a warm spot for her in his heart.

All the signs had pointed toward Melly being a beauty one day, but he hadn't been able to stick around to see it. The sea had called to him—or so he had thought. Mostly he had just needed to get away from his old man and Good Hope, Missouri, to see the world, be on his own, make something of himself.

Conrad hadn't gotten along with his father at all. His greatest failing, he sometimes thought, was that he wasn't Caleb. Caleb had been the good twin, a fine son, steady, hardworking, obedient, good with animals, especially horses. In short, he had been everything that Conrad was not.

Conrad had cordially disliked anything that ate grain back then, still did if the truth were known. Since his father owned a livery stable and acted as the town blacksmith, that had been the ultimate sin.

The old man had expected his sons, both of them, to follow in his footsteps. Caleb had seemed content for it to be so; Conrad couldn't stomach it. The punishment for that rebellion had been unremitting. He had escaped it finally by stowing away on a river steamer heading down to New Orleans. There he had found a ship that agreed to take him on as a seaman.

And the sea had embraced him with its siren arms and treated him well. He had learned a lot about himself from it, had grown up with it. Over the years, the roving, deep sea life had taken a strong hold on him, one almost impossible to break, even for a visit home.

He had managed to pull away this time because he felt the tug of something stronger, some need he didn't fully understand but had been forced to heed.

It had begun when news of Caleb's engagement to Melly had reached him, by means of a water-stained letter left waiting in a letter box in a distant port until he picked it up. Not long afterward, he had come across the bolt of pearl-colored silk in a tiny shop in Hong Kong. He had held the heavy, fluid material in his hands, captivated by its smooth texture. In that instant, he had seen Melly's face, seen her with his twin who had looked so much like himself, might even have been himself. The silk had been bought and shipped as a wedding present, but the damage had been done.

Nights without end, he had stayed awake in his bunk,

thinking of Good Hope, of the simple life in the little river town, of Caleb and Melly and all the good, decent people he had known as he was growing up. Mr. McDougall at the mercantile who handed out licorice whips when he wasn't drinking. The fire-and-brimstone preacher who harried his flock like a sheepdog, keeping the strays in line. Gandy Jack, down at the riverfront saloon just across from the livery, who used to give him two bits now and then for sweeping out the place. And especially Melly's aunt Dora, who, with no children of her own, had taken pleasure in feeding half-grown boys who were always starving.

His restlessness had ended when he'd decided to start homeward. His ship, the *Queen of the Sea*, had needed to go into dry dock to have the barnacles scraped off her bottom anyway; a ship needed to be clean to compete in the China trade, where every ounce of extra weight meant slower time and therefore less money for the captain. He had left his ship in Baltimore while he continued on to Good Hope by steamer.

Now he was here, and Melly had kissed him. Funny, but it had not seemed like a mistake. Rather, it had felt like a homecoming.

Melly could not stop staring at Conrad. He looked so familiar: the broad forehead and thick, gold-dusted brows, the straight line of his nose, the rugged planes of his face. She knew precisely the way his hair grew in a wheat-straw whorl of a cowlick on the back of his head, and the angle where the strong column of his neck merged with his wide shoulders. He was so very like Caleb.

Yet he was also different. His eyes were a more brilliant blue, his hair bleached a shade lighter by an equatorial sun;

his skin carried a darker golden-oak glaze. The way his firm lips shifted into a smile was not the same, nor were the lines that bracketed his eyes. He had seen more, done more, felt more, and the experiences had etched themselves into his features in ways that baffled and intrigued her.

Caleb's fingers tightened on Melly's hand where he still held it. She glanced at him and saw what appeared to be a warning in his eyes. She gave him a reassuring smile. An instant later, her gaze dropped to his mouth, and she remembered the kiss he had given her two evenings ago as he said good night. It had been brief, circumspect, pleasant. The contours of his mouth had been smooth and gentle. But her heart had not tripped into a hammer beat, her head had not spun, or her body shivered as if with fever.

"What's this?"

It was Conrad who spoke from the other side of the quilt, leaning toward one corner where Lydia had been making arabesques of stitching around the square she had inscribed. With a long, brown finger, he touched the small motif embroidered there.

"It's a ship, of course!" Lydia answered with mock indignation. "Can't you tell?"

"Indeed I can, but it seems a bit unusual." His smiling glance held inquiry.

Lydia gave a small shrug, even as she sent a quick look at Melly. "It's to remember the times when Melly and I used to fancy ourselves taking a steamer down the Mississippi to New Orleans, then sailing away, maybe living in places with strange, foreign names like Tahiti."

"I've been there," he said softly.

"Oh, I know—we both knew, because you wrote about

it to Caleb. Which is what brought it on, I expect." Lydia's lips curved in a faint, disconsolate smile. "It was just silly make-believe to pass the time. Of course we outgrew it."

"Too bad," he said, and looked straight at Melly.

She wanted to look away, to deny that she had ever thought of him while he was gone, that she had ever indulged in make-believe.

It was impossible.

She wasn't quite that good at pretending.

# Three

The trees that shaded Good Hope's Main Street made islands of coolness on either side of its arrow-straight length, stretching from the church at one end to the riverboat landing at the other. Great oaks and elms, they had been left standing when the town was laid out soon after being established by French trappers and traders. The searing heat of the last two days had made their leaves droop, sucking the moisture from them so they rustled in the warm wind.

It was not a particularly good evening for a box social at the church. But that didn't matter much, since it was also too hot for anything else.

The basket Melly carried was heavy. A large part of the weight was Aunt Dora's fault; she had kept offering additions, such as a jar of pickled peaches to go with the pound cake and yeast rolls that accompanied Melly's fried chicken and potato salad. But Melly had added things as well, as if she intended to feed two men instead of one.

The very idea was silly beyond words, of course. Conrad was perfectly capable of finding another young woman to feed him. In any case, she wasn't sure her future husband would be there tonight, much less his brother.

Across the street, Biddy and Lydia emerged from the mercantile and started toward the church. They waved and called, then began to pick their way across the dusty street to join her. Like her, each had a basket on her arm. Lydia's, done in bronze straw, was a nice match for the flamboyance of her iridescent bronze-green twill. Biddy's basket, like her widow's clothing, was perfectly simple, being of woven white oak covered by a black-and-white-checked cloth.

"Your mother and father aren't coming?" Melly said to Lydia as the two women gained the sidewalk.

"Mother will be along as soon as she decides what to wear. Daddy isn't feeling well this evening, so he won't be able to make it."

Melly made sympathetic noises, though she was not at all surprised. It was understood that any excuse of ill health on the part of Mr. McDougall was to be taken as an indication that he had been drinking. As for Lydia's mother, that fading, dithery lady was always late, being congenitally unable to make up her mind until the last possible second. Though the polite fiction was that the older couple ran the mercantile store that bore the McDougall name, it was Lydia who kept the place going.

"Where's Caleb?" Biddy asked, glancing toward the boardinghouse then back down the street behind them in the direction of the livery stable.

"I'm not too sure he's going to make it, either," Melly said with a wry grimace.

"I thought I saw him heading out early this morning in a wagon."

Melly nodded. "He drove out to the Bedgood estate sale. He said he might run late, especially if they parcel out the house furnishings before they get to the tools and animals."

"You should have gone with him," Lydia put in from Melly's other side.

"I did suggest it," Melly answered with an unhappy shrug. "But Caleb thought it might cause talk if we were caught on the road together after dark."

"Yes, I suppose," Lydia answered.

Biddy did not look convinced, nor was Melly herself. It was sweet of Caleb to be concerned for her good name, but she would have enjoyed the outing, not to mention the opportunity to find things she would need to set up housekeeping.

It might also have been more flattering if her bridegroom had been less insistent on avoiding gossip. He was supposed to be anxious to be alone with her, wasn't he?

No, she told herself, she must not think that way. It was not that Caleb did not want her with him. He just always knew the right thing to do and did it no matter the cost to himself.

Melly gazed down the street toward the river. She could see the front of the livery stable at its end, near the landing, with the house just this side of it where Caleb and Conrad had been brought up. There was no sign of Caleb's wagon, no movement anywhere in the vicinity if you didn't count the hound scratching its fleas near the stable door.

Nor was there any sign of Conrad.

On the other side of the street, a couple of men sat shooting the bull, balancing on straight chairs that were rocked back against the wall of the steamboat office. Just back this way, the milliner, Miss Tate, was pulling down the blinds on the front windows of her shop next door to the mercantile. Farther along, past the turning for Hickory Street, the elderly doctor came out of the frame building that served as his office, hospital, and home. He waited until his wife joined him, then escorted her in the direction of the church with a hand in the middle of her wide back. As the two passed, they called a pleasant good evening across the street.

The three young women returned the greeting, then turned by common consent and followed along after the older couple.

The church that marked the opposite end of Main Street was of white clapboard with windows of stained glass and a steeple surmounted by a lightning rod. The young bachelor preacher, who had taken the place of their previous pastor back in the spring, stood greeting his parishioners on the steps. He could not be considered particularly handsome, having craggy features and the stooped shoulders of a scholar, but was so kind and possessed such dry, self-deprecating humor that he was universally well liked. Some of the congregation would have preferred more fire and brimstone in his sermons, but Melly enjoyed his erudite expositions on good and evil followed by polite benedictions.

As they paused near the steps to allow elderly Mrs. Pollack, who had a crooked back, to mount slowly ahead of them, Lydia leaned to whisper, "Did you know Esther has been walking out with the reverend?"

Melly gave a quick nod. "I saw them strolling along the river levee last Sunday afternoon. Isn't it lovely?"

"Oh, do you think so?"

"Don't you? It was what I was hoping for when she started teaching Sunday school after her mother died. She would make a grand pastor's wife."

"Well, she adores children," Biddy said, frowning, "but don't you think she's had enough drabness in her life?"

Melly bit the inside of her bottom lip as she considered that point. It was true that Esther had never had much fun. Her father had stepped out for a mug of beer when she was a child and had never come back. Her mother had taken to her bed, becoming an invalid. Esther had cared for the older woman for years while her youth slipped away.

"Yes, but Esther is firm in her faith," Melly said. "She's really a good person, much better than I am."

"Oh, don't say that!" Lydia exclaimed. "We all know you're as good as gold."

"No, I'm only saying I don't believe it would be a sacrifice for her to marry the Reverend Milken if she loved him."

"But she might marry him just to have somebody—or else to keep from hurting his feelings," Biddy said with a shake of her head.

Melly saw what she meant. Neither the need for companionship nor compassion seemed likely to lead to a happy wedded life. It seemed some stronger emotion was necessary to make marriage worth the risk, some greater heat required to fuse a lasting union.

"Ladies," the Reverend Milken said politely as they climbed the steps. "I see Miss Esther and Miss Sarah aren't with you. I trust they will be along presently?"

"Oh, I'm sure of it," Melly said, carefully avoiding looking at Lydia or Biddy. "You needn't worry."

"I wasn't worried; it's only that the five of you have

been so much together of late that I never see one without looking around for the others."

Melly felt her lips twitch as she suppressed a smile over the reverend's grave demeanor. "Indeed we have, with all the preparations for the wedding." She leaned a little closer, adding in low tones, "But if you'd like a little time alone with Esther, you might remember her basket has an apple-green bow."

"Does it truly?" he murmured with a twinkle in his eyes. "I'll bear that in mind."

Melly and the others moved on into the church, where they were joined shortly by Esther and Sarah, carrying baskets. The five of them circled the church's meeting room, with its gay paper decorations and its table piled high with baskets, exchanging greetings and stopping now and then to talk. There were any number of questions about Caleb's whereabouts, of course; everyone had watched their courtship and was looking forward to attending their wedding. Unwilling to keep constantly explaining and making excuses, Melly only smiled and said she expected him to be along eventually.

Conrad's activities in the last day or two were also a subject of interest; somehow they all seemed to think Melly must know the latest. Actually she had barely seen him, and was happy to learn of his various visits to old friends and neighbors.

The purpose of the box social was to bring in the money for new hymnals. The baskets brought by the unmarried ladies would be put up for bids. The gentleman who was top bidder for each would be privileged to eat its contents, in company with the lady who had prepared them. It would be a blind auction; no names would be announced. A large part of the fun was watching the shenanigans as some of the young men tried to gain inside information about the offerings of the prettiest belles. The ladies, of course, were not above swapping baskets and trims with their friends to add to the confusion.

Melly had not bothered with such elaborate precautions. The unattached men in town, she figured, would most likely leave her basket for Caleb's bid out of common courtesy. If he did not appear in time, she would simply take her chances, as it was for a good cause.

The oldest of the deacons, a bent fellow with a white beard that hung halfway down his chest, wielded the auction hammer. Melly and the other girls smiled at their excitement as they waited to see what their fate would be.

Esther's basket was among the first to be presented. She turned pink with pleasure as the reverend placed the winning bid. There was much good-natured kidding from all sides, which he and Esther took in good part, as he picked up his prize and came to claim his lady.

Biddy's basket went next, claimed by the bashful young giant who worked as printer's devil at the newspaper office. She seemed pleased enough as she went off with him.

Mr. Seymour Prine, to no one's surprise, carried off Aunt Dora's basket and meekly presented himself to his vexed partner. A few moments later, Sarah's basket was bought by Sheriff Telford, a tall, dark-haired man with wide shoulders and a swagger in his walk.

One by one, then, the baskets of the young unmarried

women vanished from the table where they were on display. There were still several left, however, Lydia's among them, when Melly's basket was brought forward.

She looked around one last time for Caleb, but there was no sign of him. Nor had Conrad put in an appearance. From the advantage of her greater height, Lydia peered over the crowd as well, then grimaced and shrugged. Melly gave a resigned sigh.

The elderly deacon made a show of staggering about with her basket, joking about its weight. Melly flushed, but joined in the general laughter. Bids were slow in getting started, however, as people glanced around for some sign of her intended. Finally the sheriff's deputy, Leamon Stotts, a nervous, gangling man with a thatch of red hair and only a vague acquaintance with soap and water, yelled out, "Five dollars!"

Lydia giggled behind her hand. Melly gave her a quelling look in spite of her dismay.

"A hundred dollars!"

That firm call came from the back of the room. A murmur spread around the crowd. Five dollars was a fair sum for a basket, ten was generous indeed, and twenty was wildly extravagant. People craned their necks to see who was crazy enough to throw away so much hard-earned gold on a supper.

The deacon also squinted in the direction of the bidder. Abruptly he gave a crack of laughter and brought his hammer down with a solid thump. "Sold!"

"Oh, it was Caleb!" Lydia said, standing on tiptoe to catch sight of the winner. "What a sneak, hiding away like that to make you think he wasn't coming. You'll have to make him pay for that."

"I think he already has," Melly said dryly as she began to move forward.

She saw his golden head as he threaded through the crowd to collect his prize. He moved with such confidence; exchanging greetings, shaking the offered hand here and there, fending off the comments that came his way with laughing ease. An odd feeling shivered down the back of her neck. She slowed her footsteps as suspicion brushed her.

A hundred dollars. And Caleb had been hoarding every penny to buy farm equipment and livestock.

Then he was stepping up, taking her basket, pretending to need both hands to heft it. He exchanged another quip or two with the men gathered around before turning in her direction. His stride was free, his gaze a bright, rich blue, his smile brilliant as he gazed into her eyes.

"Well, love," he said as he stopped before her and offered his arm, "and where shall we go to enjoy our feast?"

*Conrad.*

She had not the smallest doubt. It was not Caleb, but his brother. Why was he pretending?

She opened her mouth to accuse him, then closed it. It was possible Caleb had sent him. It could also be, she mused, that he meant to save her face, to prevent people from knowing that his brother had failed her. Or it could be that he felt sorry for her and thought she might prefer sharing her basket with him than with Leamon Stotts. In the last, at least, he was perfectly right.

But if he was trying to fool her, then he deserved to have the tables turned on him. Didn't he?

# Four

The town park was a tree-shaded space sweeping in a wide apron from the cemetery behind the church to the river. At its center was a pavilion where the local brass band played on Sunday afternoons. Radiating from this central point were walks set with rustic benches. During the long days of summer, the older men gathered in the park to play checkers and pitch horseshoes. Elderly matrons came to crochet and gossip, while young mothers spread picnics under the trees and watched their babies nap as older children bowled hoops or used the fallen acorn shells as cups for tea parties.

For the box social, a long line of tables knocked together from scrap lumber had been set up behind the church. It was there that the married ladies spread the food they had brought in their baskets. Most of the unmarried couples joined them, for the sake of both convenience and propriety.

Caleb would have headed at once for those long, crowded

tables, with their chattering and neighborly congregation of folks. Conrad had other ideas.

Melly gave him a quick glance of surprise as he led her off down the path of packed sand that wended deeper into the park, but raised no objection. So far, so good, he thought.

Or was it? Could it be his brother was not always as circumspect as might have been expected? Conrad frowned as he considered that possibility.

The sun had set, and the blue-twilight of evening was deepening, the shadows under the trees growing thicker. Faint smells of dust and smoke and food drifted on the air, along with a hint of dankness from the river. The sounds of voices and laughter faded behind them as they strolled.

"So," Melly said, releasing his arm and snatching a leaf from a tree branch hanging low over the trail. "Did you have a profitable trip?"

"Trip?"

The smile that she slanted him had a vivid gleam. "To the estate sale, of course. Did you find what you wanted?"

Conrad thought quickly of how a fiancé might answer. "One or two things. It would have been much better if you could have come with me."

"Oh?" She gave him a wide-eyed look as she shredded her leaf, dropping the pieces.

"You might have found something for the house—besides which, it would have been a pleasant outing for the two of us. But I suppose you had other things to do, cooking and so forth."

"If the sale had run late, we might have been caught on the road by darkness."

He gave her a long, slow smile as he reached to take her hand. "Would that have been so bad?"

"I—possibly not," she said in low tones as she veiled her gaze with her thick, dark lashes, "but only think what people would have said."

"Why should I do that," he said, his own voice husky, "when it makes not a particle of difference?"

He could have sworn her fingers trembled in his for an instant. Could she be as affected as he was by the mental picture of what might have taken place between them during the homeward drive in the dark? He hoped not, since he was supposed to be Caleb.

Abruptly she snatched her hand away. "Caleb Wells! What has come over you?"

"You," he said, allowing the warmth inside him to surface as he smiled down at her. "Is that so strange?"

"Downright astonishing, I would say."

Her stringent tone made him think he might have overplayed his hand—or rather Caleb's. A wry smile curved his mouth as he attempted to bottle his ardor. "It's been a long engagement, love."

"Yes," she agreed. "But it was you who refused to think of marriage until you had bought and paid for land and could build a proper home."

"Did I say that? I must have been an idiot."

She gave him another slanting glance. "I'll admit I thought so. Even if you didn't want to live with your father, Aunt Dora would have loved having you around. Of course, I understand that you want to be able to provide for me, but we could have been together so much sooner."

He reached for her hand again and tightened his grip to

draw her closer against his side. "Has the waiting been so bad, then? As terrible as for me?"

"You—you've found it hard?" she said with a slight catch in her voice as the curve of her breast brushed his arm.

St. Elmo's fire seemed to dance along his body every time she touched him. His voice tight, he said, "You've no idea."

She pressed more fully against him and rested her head an instant against his shoulder as she spoke in a low, sultry murmur. "It won't be long now until the wedding. We will be together then—alone in the dark."

"Melly—" The single word was strangled as forbidden images sprang full blown into his mind.

*Melly with her hair down, swirling around her in a silken curtain as she came toward him where he waited in the bed. The look of love and sweet anticipation in her face as he drew her nightgown away to reveal lovely, tender curves. The moment when their bodies were joined, and she was his inescapably, eternally.*

Not his. Never his.

Caleb's. His brother's bride. Conrad dragged air into his cramped, aching lungs.

"Caleb?"

She was on to him. He knew it with sudden and positive instinct.

Or was it the faint quiver of laughter he felt where her chest still pressed his arm? The hint of diabolical teasing that laced her use of his brother's name? Or maybe just the simple fact that he recalled, belatedly, how Melly had once been able to tell him and his brother apart when no one else could manage it?

The witch. The conniving, enticing little witch!

"Darling," he whispered as he leaned over to set the heavy basket on the path. Straightening again, he snaked a hard arm around her narrow waist. With smooth and easy strength, he swung her into the shadows under the low-hanging limbs of an ancient oak and pressed her back to its trunk.

"Caleb!" she gasped as he moved in so close her swinging skirts piled against his booted feet.

He chuckled deep in his throat as he cupped her face in his free hand. "My sweetest love, why should we torture ourselves? There's no need at all to wait. . . ."

On the last word, he lowered his head and took her mouth in a searing kiss. At the same time, he trailed his fingers down the curve of her neck and over her collarbone to cup the gentle globe of her breast.

For an endless, aching moment, Melly was completely still, stunned into immobility by the onslaught of sensations that whipped through her at gale force. A rippling of purest pleasure ran along her nerves, tightening them as it went. She had the insane need to cling forever to the man who held her. Then his tongue touched hers, retreated, plunged boldly deeper.

Caleb had never done such a thing, not in quite that way. She had never felt this warm presentiment of what physical union might be like, never known such an abrupt and reckless rush of her entire being toward heated fulfillment. She wanted to feel the power of his male strength against her, inside her. She needed to have him teach her the power and mystery of love between a man and woman so she would not fear it.

Want. Need. Such foreign words to her. Until this moment.

She stiffened on a sharp gasp. Spreading the fingers of her hands, which were trapped between them, she shoved him away, dragged her mouth free. She shuddered, then breathed deep once, twice. Her voice low and not quite steady, she said, "Conrad Wells, what do you think you're doing?"

He laughed, a rich yet strained sound that she felt in his chest against the palms of her hands as he caught and held them against him. "Playing along. Isn't that what you wanted?"

"No! I never expected—" She stopped and drew a quick breath before she brought out the thought uppermost in her mind. "Your brother would never have tried such a thing!"

"Wouldn't he? Poor Caleb. Or maybe I should say poor Melly."

Anger boiled up inside her in a red-hot tide. Without conscious thought, she jerked loose and lashed at him with the flat of her hand.

The slap never landed. He caught her wrist and forced it down. And the humor disappeared from his face as if it had never been there. He stared at her while a muscle corded in his jaw and the blue of his eyes went dark as night there in the gathering shadows.

Her fingers turned numb from his grip. She could feel his anger, and something more, beating around her like storm waves. She lifted her chin and tightened the corners of her mouth to prevent them from quivering.

His gold-tipped lashes flickered. All expression was wiped

from his face. Opening his fingers in abrupt, complete release, he stepped back, well away from her. "I apologize— something that looks fair to becoming a habit. I meant only to pay you back for stringing me along. I may have gone too far."

"Indeed you did," she said, dropping her gaze to her wrist as she rubbed it to restore the circulation. The blame was not all his, however, and she knew it. "I suppose I shouldn't have led you down the garden path—or the park path, in this case."

He tipped his head. "Here I was, thinking I was the one doing the leading."

A brief smile touched her lips. "You were so sure you had me fooled. I wanted to discover just how far. . . that is . . ." She trailed off as she realized where the thought was leading her.

"Unfortunately you found out that I'm not so noble as Caleb. My impulses sometimes lead me to do things I regret; I'm not called the wicked twin for nothing. But if I promise it won't happen again, will you still let me share your supper?"

The quiet words were a release. She breathed easier as the tension between them faded. "Certainly. I-I expect Caleb asked you to see after me if he didn't make it back. It was kind of you to go to the trouble."

He was quiet so long that she looked up to search his still features.

"Yes, it was all Caleb's idea," he said in a rush. "Shall we see what goodies my good brother missed out on in that two-ton basket of yours?"

Melly pushed away from the tree, and Conrad stepped

back to allow her to regain the path. But he did not offer his arm, did not touch her in any way. As she passed him, she glanced once at his set face. And she was suddenly certain that his brother had played no part whatever in Conrad's showing up this evening.

As Melly brushed past him, Conrad caught her warm, sweet scent. It was astonishingly familiar beneath the overriding soap-cleanliness, starch, and sunshine. Involuntarily a crooked smile touched his lips, and he inhaled deeper.

He felt the tenuous rein he held on his more base inclinations slipping, and he closed his right hand slowly into a fist, cursing silently as he sought control. God, but he was an idiot.

Regardless, he did not turn back toward the church and its crowd. He knew he should, for Caleb's sake as well as Melly's—not to mention his own. But it was a sacrifice he meant to avoid unless the lady insisted.

She didn't. As he picked up the basket and turned in the direction of the band pavilion, she followed. She seemed to be almost unaware of their direction as she walked beside him, kicking her skirts away from her feet in moody and pensive silence.

To ensure her continued distraction, he said after a moment, "I'm sure Caleb will be sorry he missed the social."

"I suppose." She sent him a brief glance, then looked away again.

"He's working like a demon, trying to have everything finished in time for the wedding."

"Yes, I know."

"Everything has to be perfect—the house, the sheds, the barn. He's been trying to get his crop in so he won't have to worry with it. I think he's happy to have me around now, because I'm another pair of hands to help."

"Which is not exactly what you expected to be doing while you were at home, I would imagine," she suggested.

He shrugged. "Frankly, it's not what I expected from Caleb either. I never thought he'd make a farmer."

"You thought he'd wind up a blacksmith? He didn't care for it much more than you; he was just less outspoken about it."

"More diplomatic, you mean? I have to say, the old man seems to have taken it well enough."

"You broke the trail for Caleb, I think. Your father didn't want to lose him the way he lost you. He—cares about you, you know, and worries when you're so far away."

Against his will, Conrad was touched by her attempt to mediate the old rift between father and son. He said quietly, "It can't be helped. As for how he feels, well, distance and time, not to mention a little more maturity on my part, has shed a little light. We've actually managed to say a few words without fighting since I've been back."

"I'm glad." As they reached the pavilion, she turned toward the wide steps, indicating that she would set out the food there. She settled onto the top step in a sighing of skirts and reached for the basket as she went on. "Tell me about the places you've been, the things you've seen."

Her suggestion was a bit more than just polite conversation, he thought. Something in it reminded him of his old yearning after things new and different. Recalling what Lydia had said of her and Melly's urges to roam, he said, "There was some mention of Tahiti the other night. I was thinking about the islands this evening when the sun was going down.''

''About going back, you mean?''

He shook his head. ''The ways the sun sets there, actually. It's huge and turns blood red as it drops into the sea. Then it washes the whole world with paintbox colors: vermilion and orange, rose madder and pink and gold. The ship's deck and rails, the sails above you, the water—everything is so drenched with color it almost hurts your eyes. You can't look away, don't even want to move because you're afraid you'll make it fade. I don't know how to tell you—it's almost as if the sun sets inside you, warming and coloring your heart.''

''Oh, Conrad,'' she said with a catch in her voice as she sat with a napkin-wrapped chicken breast forgotten in her hand. ''It sounds glorious.''

It had been, but not nearly as glorious as the woman sitting there beside him in the dusk. Watching her face, seeing the longing in its pure, perfect lines, he felt a savage need to snatch her up and spirit her away with him, to show her all the wonders he had seen and then to find more to spread in front of her. The ache of it was like a knife turning in his soul.

Impossible.

He had to remember she was Caleb's, that nothing he could do would change that. That nothing should.

He had lost his chance years ago. He had gone away and left her to Caleb.

Caleb was the better man, always had been. Soon he and Melly would become man and wife. Then he would drive away with her to his farm, carry her inside, and close the door.

Caleb would bungle the wedding night. It was inevitable. What did he know of women and the tenderness they required? Caleb wasn't too strong on imagination, mistrusted the instincts that might guide him. How was a man like that to know what Melly needed? How could he touch and hold her with the required patience when he had not even understood how she might feel about being left alone tonight?

Or maybe Caleb would be fine. Maybe thinking his brother was wrong for Melly just made him feel less at fault for what he was doing now.

Caleb deserved better from him. So did Melly.

He didn't want to attend this wedding.

No. But he must.

Afterward, the sea would call him back, and he would go. He would rove the world, testing nerve and daring, building his fortune. And never come home again. Never.

But not yet.

# Five

"I never did!" Conrad said with indignation.

"You did, too! Just because I ran through the spot where a horse had been standing. You whispered that odious name plain as day. *Smelly Melly*. I'll never forget it!"

"It was Caleb, I swear." Conrad crossed his heart with a swift wave of the chicken leg he had been nibbling. They had eaten their fill long ago and were only pretending now as an excuse to linger. And a good thing they had finished, too, considering the subject under discussion. Not that it bothered him a bit, but Melly's straight little nose was wrinkled in such a comical expression of distaste that it made him long to kiss it.

"It was not Caleb!"

He pointed the chicken bone at her. "You just don't remember. You were only five years old; you said so yourself. You didn't learn to tell us apart until you were at least six."

"And you were almost fifteen—old enough, surely, to

have some consideration for the feelings of a little girl. I was so mortified by the experience that I cried for hours. And I still check my shoes every time I come in from the street."

"Oh, Melly," he said softly, his chest tight. "I'm so sorry."

"There! You did do it!"

He gave a definite shake of his head. "I meant I was sorry it happened, not that I take responsibility."

"Well, Caleb would never have done such a thing."

"My brother may be a paragon, but he's still human. And he's never been above pretending to be me when it suits him. Anyway, it had to be him, since there's only two of us and it wasn't me! I would never have dreamed of saying such a thing, because I used to think you were the sweetest-smelling little thing—"

He stopped abruptly as she swung her head to stare at him in the dimness.

"You what?" she demanded.

"Absolutely. And I still do." He folded his lips over the words, stubborn and unrepentant, though he shielded his gaze with his lashes. "Lavender and roses and spice. The scent is always with you; it's one of the things I remembered most when I was on the other side of the world."

"I—it must be Aunt Dora's potpourri. She puts it in the dresser drawers, the wardrobe, everywhere," Melly said, apparently at random.

"Don't ever let her stop." Avoiding her gaze, he reverted to the previous subject out of sheer self-protection. "Anyway, I've done enough in my short life that I deserved a good hiding for without taking the blame for things I didn't and don't do. It plain wasn't me who called you names."

She watched him a moment, then took another pickle slice on the end of her fork, popped it into her mouth, and slowly chewed it. After she'd swallowed it, she shook her head. "I can't believe it. All this time I thought . . ."

"Don't be too hard on old Caleb. It was only a tiny slip of the halo."

Melly watched the crooked smile that curved Conrad's mouth, heard the trace of bitterness and old pain in his voice. With their families living so close together on Main Street, they knew a great deal about each other's lives. She could remember Conrad always being in trouble of some kind, could remember people calling him a scamp and worse, while Caleb was known for being polite and staying out of trouble.

She could also recall angry scenes when Conrad had shouted at his father in protest over being blamed for everything. Once, she had come upon him crying after a terrible quarrel that had ended in a visit to the woodshed. She had wanted to put her arms around him, to help ease his awful grief. But he had been older, and she knew he would not like knowing she had seen the tears in his eyes. She had crept away without a sound. Yet she had felt a special sympathy for him afterward, even when everyone else in town shook their heads over him.

She said now. "Caleb doesn't claim to be an angel."

"No," he agreed on a sigh, "a body can't even hold that against him."

"Still. . ."

"What?" he said when she did not go on.

"It makes me wonder what else there might be that I don't know about him."

He watched her a long moment before he tossed the chicken leg away and began to wipe his fingers on his napkin. "Not a thing," he said deliberately. "Or if there is, all you have to do is ask, and he'll tell you all about it. He's a good man, the best."

"I know that," she said simply.

"Yes, well, I wouldn't want you to think I was suggesting otherwise."

She nodded her understanding of his loyalty. "On the other hand, I don't believe that you're exactly Satan's second in command."

His gaze touched her mouth and lingered there. Then he said, "I wouldn't bet on it."

Looking away, he began to pick up their picnic and pack it back into the basket. Darkness had fallen while they ate, and it was time to be returning to the others.

They cleared everything quickly, working together with an economy of motion and little need for words. Melly tucked the tablecloth they had used over the last of the food. As she reached for the basket handle, Conrad beat her to it. Rising with the lithe flexing of taut muscles, he transferred his burden to his left hand. Then, extending his right, he closed her fingers in his warm grasp and drew her up to stand beside him.

It was just then that they heard the soft scrape of footsteps on the sandy path. Caleb loomed out of the dark, square-shouldered, wearing his displeasure like a Greek mask.

"How cozy," he said. "And how incredibly dumb. I guess you know you'll have the whole town gabbling like a flock of geese."

"Not if you'll keep your voice down," Conrad said in stringent censure.

"Keep my voice down? Why, when most everybody else has gone home? Good God, Conrad, this isn't some free-and-easy heathen land. What were you thinking of when you led Melly way down here? Or need I ask?"

Conrad stiffened. As Melly tried to pull her fingers free, he tightened his hold. His voice carried a warning note in its deep timbre. "I suggest that you think carefully before you say any more, brother. All I was doing was enjoying Melly's home cooking, since it didn't look as if you were going to show up to appreciate it. As for the rest of the fine citizens of this town, I doubt they'll say a word—unless you want to keep shouting until they realize I was the one who ate the pound cake she made for you."

Caleb jutted out his chin and put his hands on his hips. "You mean you let everybody think you were me."

"More or less. I had this notion your reputation could survive an hour alone with your bride-to-be."

"And just what did Melly think?"

Caleb appeared to be speaking to his brother, but Melly thought his words were for her as well. She said tersely, "I knew exactly who he was."

"Good," Caleb said on a hard-drawn breath. "That's good, since it means Conrad couldn't take advantage."

Melly glanced at the man who stood protectively at her side; she couldn't help it. Not only *could* Conrad have taken advantage, but he *had*. And she had encouraged him, in a way. By the same token, she thought he had meant nothing harmful; it was just his way to be forward.

In any event, she resented being forced to stand there while Caleb glowered in righteous indignation. It gave her a vivid idea of what it must have been like for Conrad all those years, accused with little to say in his defense, always facing someone so certain of moral superiority.

Voice taut, she said, "I would remind you, Caleb, that this whole thing would not have come about if you had been here. Or if you had taken me with you on today's outing."

"I've already explained what I was about," Caleb said brusquely.

"So you have," she took him up, "but if my reputation can survive tonight's small indiscretion, I'm sure it would have weathered the short time we'd have been alone together on the road."

"It isn't just that," he said.

"Oh? Are you saying you don't trust yourself to be alone with me any more than you do your brother?"

"Melly," Conrad said in soft warning beside her.

"No, I want to know," she insisted. "Because if that isn't it, then I can only assume that I'm the one Caleb expects to misbehave."

"Oh, for heaven's sake!" Caleb said, running a hand through his hair. "You can't expect me to take this business lying down."

"I 'expected' you to be here. Or I thought you might join us before we finished eating. It even crossed my mind that we might all laugh about the joke. I never dreamed you would come storming up in a rage because I shared a few pieces of chicken with your twin."

Caleb was silent for long moments. Then he sighed and shook his head. His voice low, he said, "You're right, I shouldn't have flown into such a lather." He lifted a hand to rub the back of his neck. "It's been a long day, and I didn't find any of the things I wanted. Then to come back and see you and Conrad out here—well, anyway, maybe you can overlook my temper?"

It was as near an apology as he could come, Melly knew, and a fine reflection of the generous man she had always known, the Caleb she had agreed to marry. Stepping forward, she took his arm, smiling up at him. "I'm sorry, too; I know we shouldn't have wandered so far. But I was glad Conrad was here, since otherwise I might have had to eat with Leamon Stotts!"

Caleb smiled with the easing of facial muscles that indicated a return to his usual even temper. "I suppose you'd have been even more aggravated with me then."

"Indeed I would!" she agreed, and went on in that rallying tone. The two men joined in, if somewhat stiffly, and the moment passed away.

As they were nearing the church and the last of the buggies gathered around it, however, she realized an important fact. Caleb had absolved her of blame, but the courtesy had not been extended to his brother. In fact, he had hardly spoken to Conrad other than to condemn him.

Conrad was well aware of his brother's displeasure, but it was not a matter of grave concern to him. Though he felt sure he would hear more on the subject of his sins once they had seen Melly home.

He did not wait while Caleb walked her to the boarding-house door. With a polite good night on the sidewalk, he jammed his fists into his pockets and continued in the direction of the livery stable and the river. If his brother was going to kiss Melly, he had no desire whatever to stand and watch. Self-torture was not his pleasure.

He must be mad. What had possessed him to pretend to be Caleb this evening? He should be past such juvenile tricks.

Yes, but Melly had been so lovely, so lovable, and so apparently accessible, that he had lost his head. And he'd be lucky if that was all. Not that it mattered a sailor's damn.

She wasn't for him. Soon, she would be his brother's wife, a tired drudge of a farmer's helpmate. Caleb would plant a child in her belly that she would bear in agony, and he would keep on doing it until her glorious body was a memory, until she was exhausted and faded, with lines in her face and gray in her hair.

She would become exactly like his mother—and Caleb's—had been before she died. His brother might care, but would feel no more blame than their father had before him. If Melly died in her early middle age, Caleb would miss the clean house, the good food, the convenient female body. But he would never miss the woman, because he would never have bothered to know her. Worse, he would think that was the way it was supposed to be, since it was all he had ever known.

"God," Conrad whispered, staring up at the nightblack sky with its silver dusting of stars. If he had Caleb's chance, he knew, he would learn every thought and need and dream that Melly possessed. He would discover everything she had ever done or felt, her sorrows as well as her joys. He would take endless delight in sparring with her to find out her views on everything under the sun. He would tempt and tease until she had no secrets.

Nor would her pleasure be hidden from him. Nothing, nothing would stop him from exploring her lovely form inch by careful inch, while using every wile he had ever learned from foreign females, ever heard, ever imagined, to delight her. He would protect her from the ravages of endless childbearing, serve her rather than expect to be served, and it would be his greatest pleasure.

That was, of course, if he was intending to take a wife and settle down in Good Hope. But he wasn't. Couldn't.

"*God*," he said again.

"Blasphemy, brother?" Caleb inquired with heavy irony as he caught up with him again. "I can't say I'm surprised. Maybe cursing like a sailor will help you feel more like a man."

"The problem," Conrad said with succinct precision, "is not how much of a man I may be."

"Oh, I think it is," Caleb said. "Or have you forgotten I could always beat you in a fistfight?"

"You could once, thanks to fifteen pounds' more weight and hours spent hammering iron on an anvil. Things have changed."

"I doubt it. But we'll find out if you ever take my place again with Melly."

Conrad gave him a laconic look. "If you don't want it filled, then don't leave it vacant."

Caleb put out a hand to bring him to a halt, then squared off to face him. "Meaning?"

"Don't take Melly for granted. Don't disappoint her. Don't leave her alone."

"You're telling me how to treat my future wife?" Caleb's stance was belligerent in the dark.

"You could use a few pointers from somebody." The words were even, hard.

"Melly and I were fine until you came along, and we'll be fine again when you're gone. In the meantime, don't forget which twin you are."

Caleb, his warning given, turned on the heel of his heavy farm boot and stomped away. Conrad propped his fists on his hips as he watched him go. He didn't much care for ultimatums, never had. They brought out the devil in him.

For two cents, he'd show his brother exactly how to go about taking care of Melly. It would be a cheap and much-needed lesson.

Hell, he might even do it for free.

## Six

The drive out to the new house with Caleb was, Melly considered, the direct result of events at the church social. That he had asked her was a surprise; that the two of them went alone was nothing short of amazing.

She had ridden out once with her aunt, driven by Mr. Seymour Prine, just after Caleb bought the land. Her many hints since then that Caleb should show her how the house was progressing had never borne fruit. She had come finally to believe he really didn't want her to see it until it was completed.

She did not expect a great deal. Caleb could not afford anything grand, and the two of them had agreed that it would be best to start small and add on as their family grew. The house, then, was to be a simple cottage made of vertical boards with a porch across the front and an attached kitchen on the back. There would be a proper parlor, however; Melly had insisted on that. They would need someplace other than the kitchen to entertain their guests, particularly in the heat of summer.

It was certainly hot today. Melly, jostling on the wagon seat, blotted her face with her handkerchief and slanted her parasol to block a little more of the sun's rays. The wind felt as if it were blowing from the devil's own forge. It swirled the plume of dust that boiled up behind them, enveloping them in a gritty fog that gathered in the folds of her skirt and settled on the tired weeds and sunflowers edging the road. Sweeping onward, it spun drying milkweed silk and thistle down across the road, and the drying cornstalks in the fields they passed rustled with the touch of its hot breath.

Following the wind's path across the picked-over cornfields, Melly caught sight of a landmark hill looming on their left. "We're almost there, aren't we?" she said, turning to Caleb with a smile. "I was woolgathering, I suppose. But I didn't know you had finished gathering your crop."

"Conrad has been giving me a hand this week. It made a difference."

Conrad. A small tremor ran over her at the unexpected introduction of his name, though she did her best to ignore it. "That was good of him. Did you get a fair yield?"

"Better than expected," Caleb answered with a nod. "It's been a fine growing summer, with the rains coming at the right time."

The corners of her mouth turned down. "We could still use a shower to settle the dust and cool things off a bit."

"Wouldn't hurt," he said in laconic agreement, adding, "but not this afternoon. We don't want to get wet."

Melly felt so hot and grimy that the thought of being rain-washed sounded like a wonderful thing, though she didn't say so. "Maybe it will rain and get it over with before the picnic on Saturday. You mean to come, don't you?"

"Picnic?"

"To celebrate our quilt, which should be finished by then. I told you about it at the social, remember?"

"You must have told Conrad," he said in hard tones.

He was right.

"Oh. Yes," she said as color rose in her face. "Anyway, it's nothing elaborate, just a simple outing down by the river. We thought first of a fish fry, but it's too hot to hover over a fire. Mostly it's just a chance for my friends and me to enjoy each other's company, since it's the last time we'll be together before the wedding."

Feeling as if she had been babbling, she stopped abruptly. Her explanation seemed to mollify him, however, for his frown relaxed, and a teasing light rose in his eyes.

"My dear Melly, you can still see your friends after we're married. It's not as if you're going to be shut away like some female in a harem."

For a brief moment he looked and sounded so much like Conrad that she blinked. The next instant, she wondered if he was not repeating something his brother had said. But that was uncharitable and she knew it.

Flustered, she said, "I realize that, but things won't really be the same. We won't be running back and forth, in and out of each other's houses a dozen times a week. And I'll be different. A married woman has different concerns, different ideas and—and feelings."

"I should hope the last at any rate," he said, leaning closer with warmth in his eyes and his shoulder pressing hers. She smiled, though she hardly knew how to answer.

Still, rolling along with their bodies touching and the rattling of the wagon in her ears, she thought she caught a glimpse of how their life together would be, its shared understanding and quiet pleasure. It was comforting, yet disturbing at the same time. There should be something more, it seemed. How was it that she had never felt the lack before?

The wagon topped a slow rise and started down. Turning to glance ahead, Melly saw the farm that was Caleb's pride and joy.

The cottage was charming, a white-painted doll's house with scrolled brackets at the tops of the two posts that supported the porch and dark green shutters on the windows. It was perfectly placed, facing the road beneath a great oak tree, yet convenient to the barn and other outbuildings.

Regardless, Melly was disturbed. Her gaze was drawn to the barn. Spreading wide and deep and tall, it was a massive structure that overwhelmed the farmhouse, making it seem puny and insignificant.

"What do you think?" Caleb's voice was rich with satisfaction.

"I think—well, it's a dear little house. Just—just perfect." She could not stop looking from it to the barn and back again.

Caleb gave her a fond and approving glance. "Just wait until you see inside."

"You've been busy. It looks ready to move into."

"It is. I meant to show it to you on our wedding day, sort of bring you home to it, but—well, I couldn't wait."

"And you finished the barn, too?"

He gave a firm nod. "Working with Conrad is like having four hands; I hardly have to think what I'd like to do before he's there with it half done. And he's a demon for keeping after things until they're perfect, I'll say that for him. The responsibility of being a ship's captain has been good for him. There was a time when I could work circles around him, but not anymore."

It almost sounded as if he had tried. She wondered if the two men had spent the last few days competing with each other. If so, they had certainly accomplished miracles in the process. With some care, she said, "Where is Conrad today?"

"Resting, I hope," Caleb replied with a wry laugh.

It was good to hear the respect and even affection in Caleb's tone. She hadn't liked to think of the two brothers being at odds because of her.

Looking toward the outbuildings again as they drew nearer, she said, "I didn't think about the barn being so much bigger."

"Didn't you? That's the way it is, you know—lot more animals on a farm than people."

He had a point. The crops and animals the barn would have to shelter would be their livelihood. Yet looking at the barn overshadowing the house gave her a peculiar suffocating feeling, as if it was she who was being overpowered.

As they drew up in the yard before the house, Caleb climbed down and came around to help her from the wagon.

She leaned to put her hands on his shoulders, and he caught her waist, lifting her free of the wagon bed with easy strength before setting her on her feet. Her body brushed his, but he did nothing to prolong the contact, seemed not to notice. The disturbance inside her increased.

With a hand on her elbow, he guided her toward the porch steps. They reached the front door and he flung it wide, then stepped aside for her to enter ahead of him.

The house was simple but well designed. The walls were painted white except for the parlor, which was given some interest by a rose-patterned wallpaper. The kitchen was large and convenient to the back garden area. There was a fireplace in the parlor as well as the bedroom, and both wood mantels had been painted to look like gray-streaked white marble.

It was a pleasant house, everything considered, but it lacked color, had little character or warmth. Then again, these things could be added, Melly thought. She could paint flower and ribbon designs on the bedroom door and stencil the floors to look like rugs. She could make curtains and cushions and antimacassars, frame the needlework samplers she had done as a young girl and hang them on the walls. Of course, her precious Friendship Quilt would have to go in the parlor. Then there was the furniture. She would choose chairs and tables with some life to them, and a pretty oil lamp as well.

"I think," she said as they returned to the front of the house, "that I would like to buy a parlor set first."

"Not bedroom furnishings?" Caleb asked with the lift of a brow.

She colored a little as she moved ahead of him into the

parlor. "We will have my bed and wardrobe. They are good quality, my mother's and father's set that Aunt Dora kept after the accident. She sold most everything else and put the money in the bank for me. I don't mean to spend all of it, but I saw a model for a rosewood parlor set brought to the mercantile by a drummer. Mr. McDougall could order—"

"There's no hurry for such folderols," Caleb said with a decided shake of his head. "What we really need is a good hay rake if the money's on hand."

"A hay rake." She heard the flatness of her tone, but could do nothing to prevent it.

"The better our machinery, the more I can do and the better things will be for us. We've talked about this before, Melly."

"Yes, I know," she said in some distress. "I understand that you want to build a good life for us, and it's not that I don't appreciate all your hard labor in building the house and trying to make it nice, the way you've worked in the fields out here as well as helping your father at the livery. But I would like something of my own, and this is my money—"

"Your money?" he said, face grim. "What I have is yours, Melly, and I expected you to feel the same way. That's what being married is all about."

"I do feel it!" She flung out a hand in a pleading gesture as she sought words to explain. "But you're making all the decisions for our future. You bought the land, chose the house design; you picked out the paint and wallpaper and arranged the kitchen. You aren't letting me be a part of what you're doing at all. Is this what marriage is supposed to be?"

"You don't like the house?" he said, his voice tight.

"Of course I like it! That's not the problem."

"You want to change the kitchen?"

"The kitchen is fine!"

"Then I don't know what's wrong with you. We want the same things, Melly. We have the same dream of a good, solid life here on the farm, working the land and watching our crops and our children grow and prosper year by year. It's all we've talked about, all we've ever felt was worthwhile."

"I still want those things," she said in desperation. "But don't you see that it isn't all I need?"

His face hardened. "I see you've changed since Conrad came home."

Had she? Or had she just remembered the way she used to be before she'd agreed to marry Caleb? Before she'd learned to be practical. Before she'd been forced to accept the fact that the things she'd conjured up in her mind, the places she yearned to see and the things she longed to do, were impossible.

It was not really so much that she and Caleb had the same dream, she thought with sudden insight, but rather that she had given up her own so that only his was left.

That was often the way of it, she knew; she had seen it before with her aunt's friends. So many women became faded shadows of their men, without a view or opinion that was solely their own. And yet she had not expected it with her and Caleb.

The hardest thing, however, was not giving up all the things that made her different, but knowing that her future husband had no idea she had ever thought of anything else. Or that if he did, he actually felt the sacrifice was natural, the way things should be arranged.

He was wrong.

He wouldn't accept that, she knew, would never believe that their disagreement wasn't really over furniture or money. It didn't matter, she told herself. It was necessary to make a stand somewhere, and it might as well be here.

She stared at him, her eyes dark and a little bleak. Lifting her chin, she said plainly, "I am going to have the parlor set."

She turned away without waiting for an answer. Walking through the open front door, she crossed the porch toward where the wagon stood with the horse cropping at a patch of dry grass. She climbed unaided to the seat, then settled her skirts and sat staring straight ahead.

Caleb came out of the house, secured the front door behind him, and crossed to the wagon. The vehicle rocked as he gained his seat. He unwound the reins from the brake handle and sat holding them for a few moments before he turned his head to look at her.

"Does it seem I'm putting the farm ahead of you, Melly? Is that it?" he asked in low tones. "I didn't mean to. It's just that there's been so much to do. I wanted it all perfect for you when you came here as a bride. There's a lot I'd like to give you someday—another room or two on the house, a nice organ for the parlor, all the pretty doodads and gewgaws that you deserve. It's just that first things come first, to my mind." He transferred both reins to his left hand and reached out to place his right on the fists clenched in her lap. "But I want you to be happy. If you've got your heart set on parlor furniture, then that's what I want you to have. I do love you, Melly."

"Oh, Caleb," she said quietly, but could not go on for the lump in her throat. He was trying his best to be reasonable, and to show her he cared.

She looked up at him, letting her gaze roam over his strong, regular features, meeting the straightforward devotion in his eyes. There was so much fondness between them, so many years and memories, so many good times. She had danced her first dance with him, shared her first grown-up kiss with him behind the door of the livery stable. He knew her so well, knew that she loved blackberries and cream, kittens and Christmas, but despised yellow squash and baying hounds. He knew she was fearless when it came to snakes and spiders or thunder and lightning, but terrified of deep water after having nearly drowned in the riverboat disaster that killed her parents. Surely that was a firm enough foundation on which to build a life?

"I love you too, Caleb."

A soft exclamation left him. He leaned closer and pressed his mouth to hers.

It was a kiss of warm and careful affection. The dry smoothness of his lips was pleasant. She felt the abrasion of his beard stubble at their ridges as he caressed her mouth with gentle movements. Then he drew back and sent a quick glance around, as if checking to be sure no one had seen them. They were safe. He lifted the reins and slapped the horse into motion.

He looked down at Melly once more and smiled. She felt her lips curve in a faint response.

Yet all the while she was distracted, almost fearful. It was wrong to compare the staid embrace of her future husband with the wild, reckless kisses of his brother, but she could not help it.

# Seven

The day of the picnic dawned breathlessly hot. The air was still and heavy, with a sulfurous scent to it. The molten sunlight that poured over everything had a metallic, brassy sheen.

The very idea of building a fire in the cookstove to fry chicken, roast corn and make apple pie was enough to make Melly feel light-headed. To actually do it was like descending into the pits of hell.

She was all for calling off the outing. There was a thundery, oppressive feeling in the air that she did not like. Moreover, the chance of any enjoyment being gained from sitting beside the river seemed remote if they would have to send the whole time fanning themselves or swatting at heat-drugged flies.

Aunt Dora laughed at Melly's misgivings. This little spell of heat, she declared, was like a breath of spring compared with the ones she had endured in her younger days. The only problem might be if the hot weather broke with a cloudburst. Anyway, it was bound to be better beside the water.

It was, indeed. The site chosen for spreading the picnic cloths and pallets made of old quilts was a couple of miles out of town. It was an oak-crested ridge that merged with the river's natural levee to form a wooded platform higher than the water. A hot breeze wafted over their vantage point now and then. It ruffled the glassy surface of the water below so that it sparkled in the sun like millions of glass shards. Whispering in the leaves of the oaks overhead, it stirred the leaf shadows that patterned the quilts where they sat. The touch of it fanned their moist faces, sifted through their hair with delicate, cooling fingers, and lifted the light summer skirts of the young women in indolent billows.

A steamboat churned past, spreading a froth of foam over the water, the *Cincinnati Star* on her way down to New Orleans. It gave them a blast of its steam whistle that startled a nearby flock of crows into flight. Passengers on the boiler deck and deckhands and chambermaids on the deck below waved and called across the water. The steamer's wake rocked an old piece of raft tied up just along the way, causing it to thud against the levee's bank with a sound like distant thunder.

Still, nothing could banish the heat-induced lethargy that held them in its grip. When they had eaten, they all sat around in a kind of daze, talking in fits and starts and staring out over the endless glide of the river.

"Oh, I ate too much," Biddy said, pressing her hand to her abdomen.

"My, yes, we can tell." The wry comment came from Esther as she surveyed the other girl's tiny, corseted waist and slender shape under her full black skirts. "You really should get yourself right up and walk it off."

"Good idea," Biddy returned with alacrity. "Let's stroll along the levee a way." She waited expectantly for volunteers.

Esther rolled her eyes at her. "Don't be daft."

"Melly will come," the smaller woman said as she turned in her direction. "Won't you?"

Reaching up to smother a yawn, Melly said, "Maybe. In a little while."

Biddy glanced around at the others lounging here and there on the quilts, her gaze hopeful. "Doesn't anybody want to walk?"

Aunt Dora groaned as if even the suggestion were excruciatingly painful. No one else answered.

They were eleven in number. Besides Melly, her aunt, Caleb, and Conrad, there were the four bridesmaids: Biddy, Esther, Lydia, and Sarah. Aunt Dora's boarder, Mr. Prine, had somehow attached himself to the party. Esther had invited the Reverend Milken as well, since he was at loose ends and always looked in need of a homecooked meal. Sheriff Telford rounded out the group; he had happened by as Sarah was leaving the house, and she had asked him to come along.

The extra men had been more than welcome, since Aunt Dora never skimped on food. The only problem, or so the older woman claimed with mock seriousness, was that the few poor souls remaining in town were left with no one to keep the peace or pray for them—assuming, of course, that anybody found the energy to get up to mischief. But that wasn't likely, Aunt Dora pointed out, since they had the worse mischief-maker with them.

She was referring to Conrad, though he appeared unlikely to cause trouble of any kind. He was stretched full length on the edge of the quilt near Melly. His eyes were closed, his gold-tipped lashes meshed, his head turned toward her so that his cheek rested on the hem of her skirt. He looked for all the world as if he were fast asleep.

Caleb, on the other hand, was talking quietly with the preacher. Melly wondered if the discussion had to do with the wedding ceremony. The impulse to join them nudged her, but she couldn't quite make herself move. Besides, she didn't want to wake Conrad.

A faint, far-off booming, different from the rocking of the old raft, caught her attention. Glancing toward the southwest, she asked of no one in particular, "Was that thunder?"

"Too far away to do any good even if it was," her aunt allowed with a sigh.

Caleb glanced over at her and smiled a little, as if in agreement. As his gaze fell on the long form of his brother, however, a muscle tightened in his jaw. A moment later, he turned back to listen to something the Reverend Milken was saying.

Sarah appeared to notice the byplay from where she sat idly braiding a long silvery blond tress that had fallen forward onto her breast. Her gaze lingered on Caleb, and her face softened in a way that startled Melly for an instant. Then the fleeting impression was gone as her cousin glanced her way and shook her head with a look of comical sympathy.

The tall blond girl flung the strand of hair she was toying with back over her shoulder as she asked, "Did you get the binding sewn on the quilt?"

"Yesterday afternoon," Melly answered. Covering the edges with bias binding made from strips of blue material had been the final step. "I brought it, of course, since the picnic is in its honor."

Aunt Dora waved in the general direction of the pile of cushions behind Melly. "It's in the pillowcase there, I think."

Moving cautiously so as not to disturb the man sleeping so near, Melly reached for the stuffed pillowcase, then pulled the quilt from it and spread its silken folds. "Didn't it turn out well? I'm so proud of it."

"Lovely," Biddy said. There was real feeling in her voice, and it was echoed by the others in turn, each in her own way.

"It's the most beautiful thing I've ever laid eyes on, is what it is," Aunt Dora said in downright tribute. "And I've seen plenty, believe you me."

Melly flushed at the praise. Still, the quilt really was quite glorious as it lay with its soft fabrics gleaming in the muted light falling through the tree canopy overhead and its fine stitching tracking over it in regular and precise patterns.

The motifs of the bridesmaids' squares made lovely corner accents. The rich aquamarine blue of the sea waves beneath the clipper ship in full sail that Lydia had stitched. The shades of pink and rose which her cousin Sarah had used to embroider a rose wreath to indicate the bouquet of late summer blooms she would make for Melly to carry up the aisle. The sweet simplicity of the daisy Esther had cross-stitched on her square along with the Shakespearean phrase *Love comforteth like sunshine after rain.* The swirls of silver-gray embroidery in a running chain stitch of Biddy's eloquent and moving Biblical fragment, *Whither thou goest . . .*

Each of her friends had adorned her square according to her own taste and personality; therefore each square was a vivid and unique reminder of the person who had sewn and initialed it. Melly would have cherished the quilt for that reason alone, but the exquisite workmanship and fortuitous blending of colors and fabrics made it a treasure to be cared for and handed down through the years.

"I'll need to be careful of it," she said with a misty smile. "But I will be, always. And I'll never, ever part with it, not for anything."

Caleb, glancing over at it, shook his head. "I give it five years. After that, the babies will be spitting up on it while they use it for a napping pallet."

"Caleb Wells! What a thing to say!" The rebuke came from Biddy.

"That's right," Lydia said with an indignant glance. "You hush your mouth."

"Five years," Melly's fiancé repeated with an unrepentant grin. "Mark my words."

Conrad roused himself from his somnolent enjoyment of the sound of Melly's voice and the pleasurable torment of breathing in her unique fragrance while feeling the silky softness of her dimity skirt against his jaw. He didn't care for Caleb's superior tone or the suggestion that eternal motherhood would leave Melly too tired and harassed to care about fine things. More than that, he was curious.

Levering himself to one elbow, he cast an eye over the finished quilt, then gave it a closer look. The squares were pieced from scraps of the silk he had sent to Melly; he recognized the goods. Strange he had not noticed earlier, but then he'd had other things on his mind.

A crooked smile tugged at his mouth as he said, "What you need is a special box to protect it. I have a small chest on my ship made out of carved teak that I picked up in Hong Kong to keep moisture and bugs out of my papers. I'll send it to you, if you like."

"She won't need it," Caleb said, cutting into their quiet exchange. "I can build Melly a box out of cedar."

Melly sent her future husband a quick look. "What I would really like is a rack of some kind to display the quilt in the parlor, if you—"

"Sketch out what you want," Caleb said brusquely. "I'll see to it."

There was a small silence during which Conrad very carefully did not look at either his brother or Melly. He had wanted her to have the chest, and couldn't see that offering it to her violated any rules about presenting personal items to unmarried females. Caleb apparently felt otherwise. Or maybe it was just that he didn't want Melly accepting anything from him.

Did Caleb know he had provided Melly's wedding gown? Somehow Conrad doubted it. The groom wasn't supposed to see the thing before the wedding, after all.

Conrad hated to think of the way his brother might find

out. It could easily be on his wedding night as he stepped close enough to his new wife to see the small Oriental figures in the brocade, to touch the heavy silk, to slide it from Melly's slender body. His hands closed slowly into fists as he pictured it.

It was Aunt Dora who filled the lengthening breach in the conversation. Turning in his direction with lifted brows, she said, "And just what do you know about boxes for the fine things women like to keep anyway, my lad? I thought you'd been at sea these many years, far from the company of women."

"Don't know a thing, Aunt Dora," he said, giving her a bland look from under his lashes.

"Go on with you. I'll just bet there's been a woman or two traveled a few miles on your China tea clipper."

His amusement faded. "Not my ship."

"If you say so. Still, you must've consorted with them somewhere, because you didn't learn your tricks in Good Hope. Not that I'm blaming you, mind. A man's a man wherever he may be, and a bear don't pass a honey tree without trying to climb it."

"Good Lord, Aunt Dora!" He drew back in a pretense of shock.

"Now don't go trying that innocent stuff on me, boy, because it won't work. I expect you'd just rather not take females to sea."

"I might take a wife if I had one," he said in tentative tones. "Some captains do; I know a lady who always sails with her husband. Once when he was laid up in his bunk, half out of his head with fever, his ship ran into a hurricane.

His lady took charge, giving orders she claimed to be re-laying from her husband. The ship sailed right through the storm, when every man jack on board had thought she'd surely go down. The captain laughed himself hoarse when he heard, because he hadn't been able to give a sensible order for five solid days."

"Sounds like a woman with a head on her shoulders to me," Aunt Dora commented with a notable lack of amazement.

"A man of sense, rather, for marrying the right one in the first place."

The older woman pursed her lips. "Still, not every female is cut out for a life afloat."

"Nor every man."

"No, but most of the ones who take to it become sea rovers who can never settle down to one woman or be satisfied with a quiet life tending hearth and home. I think you're one of them, my boy. What do you say to that?"

He met the woman's wise eyes, saw the purpose there and also the anxiety that forced her to it. His gaze flickered to Melly, then returned to her aunt. Grimly he said, "You may be right. Or close to it."

"I thought so," the older woman said, then sighed. "You always were about half pirate."

Caleb said, "More like three-quarters."

"Humph," Aunt Dora said, giving Melly's fiancé a brief glance. "And the other quarter of you both was always two-year-old brat."

Conrad had to laugh. At the same time, he glanced at Melly again. She was staring out over the river, her teeth set in the softness of her bottom lip. Caleb, on the other hand, showed no signs whatever of regretting his brother's future absence.

It was a short time later that Biddy finally prevailed on Melly to go for a stroll. As he saw Melly gathering herself to rise, Conrad sprang up and pulled her to her feet. Once upright, he decided he might as well amble along with the two ladies as escort. That got Caleb moving. Then the Reverend Milken elected to join them. Next thing they knew, everyone was meandering off along the levee in the hot afternoon sun as if it made perfectly good sense.

Everyone, that is, except Aunt Dora and Seymour Prine. Melly's aunt watched them with openmouthed incredulity before lying back on the pile of cushions and closing her eyes. Mr. Prine shifted his position so that his body blocked a shaft of sunlight falling on her face. Then, taking a small book from his pocket, he settled himself for guard duty.

The group of picnickers turned downriver, talking in fits and starts, rambling with no real destination. The breeze off the water was stronger than earlier, and carried humid promise in its breath. Conrad sniffed the air and lifted his gaze to scan the heavens. There was a bank of clouds creeping above the trees from the southwest that quickened his weather senses.

As they neared the old abandoned raft that lay at the water's edge, Sheriff Telford detached himself from the others and stepped down the slope of the levee, digging in his heels for purchase. He put his hands on his hips as he surveyed the sorry craft. Glancing at Conrad as he came to stand beside him, he nudged the water-soaked logs with a booted toe. "We ought to sink the thing before some kid takes it out and drowns himself."

Conrad cast a practiced eye over the raft. Its logs were beginning to rot on the ends, and the ropes lashing it together were black with mildew. But the majority of the center logs, where it counted, were solid. The hemp fibers of the ropes seemed strong enough, and the knots were firm and tight. The rough steering oar attached at the stern appeared fairly new.

He said, "Whoever put it together knew what he was doing."

The rest of their band were straggling down the slope. As Caleb caught their exchange, he said, "The whole thing looks rotten to me. Sheriff's right, the best thing would be to chop it into kindling."

Conrad sent his too-rational twin a frown. "Some kid must have spent hours building it."

"Time that he should have spent helping out at home, I expect," came the unsympathetic reply. "I'd rather not be responsible when he winds up floating facedown in the river." He looked around at the other men. "Anybody bring an axe?"

The preacher looked dubious, but Telford nodded. "Might have one in the toolbox of my buggy."

Caleb and the two other men swung around and started toward where the buggy was tied up next to Caleb's wagon and the rig rented by Mr. Prine.

Conrad knew he should back off. This was no longer his town or his people. He wouldn't be around if the boy who built the raft should drown one fine day. But he remem-

bered too well the things adults did to young boys in the
name of saving them from themselves—the lectures, the
whippings . . . There had even been a raft, once, that had
disappeared. He wondered suddenly if Caleb had helped dis-
mantle that one, too, for his brother's own good.

The raft was tethered to a stake pushed into the ground
only inches from Conrad's right foot. A basic seaman's knot
held it fast.

It only took an instant to jerk it free, toss the line onto
the logs, then shove the raft off. As he straightened, he was
caught and held by Melly's wide gaze.

She was watching him, her face a little pale and her lips
parted. She looked toward Caleb, as if deciding whether
she ought to call out and tell him what his brother had
just done.

It might have been the reminder of the past that roused
the devil in Conrad, or just the fact that his brother was so
determined to override him. Maybe it was being forced into
a public avowal of his need to roam that did it. Or perhaps
it was the perverse determination to live up to what everybody so obviously expected.

Then again, there was a lesson he had vowed to teach.

The distinct possibility existed that he needed no excuse,
however. The urge toward outrageous action was simply
there, and he succumbed without a qualm.

One moment he was untying the raft, the next he was
at Melly's side. He bent to thrust one arm under her knees
and the other behind her back. She gave a low cry as he
lifted her against him.

Swinging hard, he splashed to the craft that was easing
out into the current. He hoisted her to the wet, uneven

surface, then pushed farther from shore with a strong surge. As she wrenched over, clawing at the slippery logs, he pulled himself up beside her and swung his legs on board.

Lydia screamed. Esther yelled. Sarah called Melly's name in horror. The sheriff, the preacher, and Caleb swung around, then pelted to the water's edge. The first two stopped, but Caleb kept coming, cursing as he plunged in waist-deep and began to swim.

It was too late. The river current caught the raft, swung it around and away from the bank, and sent it skimming downstream.

"Don't worry!" Conrad called across the water. "We'll be fine! I'm three-quarters pirate, remember?"

Chuckling at his own mordant wit, he reached for the crude steering oar at the stern and put his back into swinging it, helping the dipping, gliding raft along. He reached the main channel, let it take the rough craft. The yells and cries died away. Caleb, never a particularly strong swimmer, began to fall back.

Within a few short seconds, the raft was rounding the next bend. A half dozen more strokes of the steering oar and all trace of the others vanished.

Water and trees, all around. Nothing but trees and water.

Conrad felt the rise of fierce exultation.

He had the river to himself.

Yes. And he had Melly.

# Eight

For the next several minutes Conrad concentrated on putting distance between himself and any possible pursuit. His blood was up, the rising wind was in his hair, and he was sliding smoothly over the river's surface, guiding the raft with a rhythmic play of the stern oar that was as natural to him as breathing.

He had escaped, and the woman he loved was with him. His satisfaction couldn't last; he knew that. But for this small piece of time he was a contented man.

The woman he loved.

God, yes, beyond doubt.

He had not meant it to happen. But then, he had learned early in his ventures at sea that things seldom went as planned. A crooked smile curved his lips as he glanced down at Melly.

His pleasure vanished. She was huddled on her side in the center of the raft, knees drawn up, eyes tightly shut, face white as death. He remembered her cry as he'd hauled her aboard the raft, the stiffness of her body against him, the way she had clung to him before he'd set her on the wet logs. He had thought her reaction only surprise and revulsion at being on the dirty, waterslicked craft.

That wasn't it at all.

Melly was afraid to the point of terror of deep water. The old, half-forgotten knowledge bloomed like a fiery explosion in his mind.

Releasing the oar, he plunged to his knees beside her. The movement rocked the raft with a violent tilt, and he heard her soft moan. The small sound cut deep, sliced into his heart. He caught her shoulders and dragged her up, folding her into his arms.

"Oh, Melly, I'm sorry, so sorry. I should have remembered. I'm an idiot, a criminal idiot, but I've been gone so long, and you seemed so— No, I should have remembered. How could I forget? God, how could I?"

He was jabbering, but couldn't stop in his bone-deep remorse. She was so cold and racked by shudders, and her pretty dimity dress was stained and wet where water was washing through the logs. His fault, all his fault.

"Please, Melly, open your eyes. Look at me. Please . . ."

She heard him, for she burrowed closer, but that was her only response. He lay back, braced against the support column for the oar, pulling her against the length of him. His hands shook as he rubbed her arms in an attempt to warm her chilled flesh. She pressed her face into his chest, and he felt her warm breath through his shirt. She moved nearer to fit the curve of her hip more firmly into the cradle of his legs.

Conrad sucked air into his lungs and stifled a groan at the sudden stir of fervid heat in his lower body. With wide unseeing eyes, he stared at the clouds mounting in massed darkness overhead:

*Dear God, but he wanted. . .*

He couldn't. No. What kind of bastard was he to even let it cross his mind? This was not what he had intended.

Or was it?

A shudder of denial rippled over him. No. His needs and desires were not important. He had to help her. There had to be a way.

"Oh, Melly, sweet Melly, it's only water," he murmured in low and unsteady supplication. "It's cool and wet and deep, but not evil. Men are evil; they'll take your life and maim your soul and mangle all your pretty dreams. You must not trust any of them, ever—least of all me. But water is life, just life."

She seemed to grow more still, as if she was attentive to his words. Dragging air into his lungs, he went on, giving her his hard-earned knowledge of the thing he loved most, after her.

"Water quenches our thirst, cleans us, comes raining down to save the parched green things of this earth, to save us. And it's beautiful. It holds all the colors of the world— yellow, brown, gray, blue, yes, and green in tropic lands. It gleams and sparkles like liquid sapphires far out to sea, and like emeralds and aquamarines close to shore. Sometimes it's as clear and still as the finest mirror; other days the waves billow and roll, riding as high as the sky. Water can take a man down, hold him, drown him if he isn't careful. But it's a gentle death compared to most. And no harm is meant, ever. The river, the sea, the ocean is only there. Wild or calm, deep or shallow, it's only as nature made it."

She was shaking less, he was sure of it, though fine tremors still coursed over her. Was there a little more color in her face?

At least her breathing was no longer so frantic. It was surer, deeper, so deep it flattened the firm globes of her breasts against him, threatening his sanity.

His voice not quite even, uncertain what he was saying in his need to reassure her, he continued. "The sea to me is siren and mistress and all the other things that men who love it call it. The sound and feel and look of it is inside me, a part of me. Yet it's just water all the same. It can harm us if we let it, yes, but also serve us. This raft floating along on the river can carry us to all the wide, free reaches of the world. If we let it, it could carry us past all the towns and right on out to sea, steadily taking us wherever we wanted to go. I wish it would. . . ."

He trailed off, his breathing ragged as he fought for control of the ache that had filtered into his voice.

Melly stirred and sighed, her warm breath fluttering across his throat. "So do I," she whispered.

The words were so soft he might not have heard them if he had not been straining so hard for some sign, some sound. But he did hear, and his heart kicked into a hard beat.

At the same time, he was unbearably moved that he could reach her with his words. That he could banish her fears even for a moment was a gift beyond price, one that helped ease his guilt for having forced her to face them.

Holding her in his arms seemed to fill the emptiness in

his soul, to soothe the loneliness he had carried with him for years. It was as if they belonged together, as if he had always known it. Still, the fierce grip of possessiveness he felt inside stunned him.

The top of his head felt on fire. The muscles in his arms corded. He lay perfectly still while he fought impulses too dark to be named.

*Safe.* Melly felt so safe within the strong, confining circle of Conrad's arms. The horror in her mind receded, drifted away to nothing. Her last small shiver faded, along with the goose bumps on her arms. The core of warmth remaining inside her began to radiate outward again, leaving languid weakness in its wake.

The rocking of the raft and its steady glide were oddly soothing. The firmness of the shoulder under her cheek, the planes and ridges of muscles against her breasts gratified her in some way she did not care to consider. The need to lie as she was forever, happen what might, was astonishing.

Then the internal echo of the words she had spoken half in delirium reached her. As she recognized their startling truth, she opened her eyes and lifted her head to look at the man who held her.

There was torment in the rich, sea blue of his gaze, and something more that made her draw a strangled breath through parted lips. Suddenly every fiber of her being was awake, alive, and aware.

She felt the quick rise and fall of his chest, the thud of his heart under her breast, the taut muscles of his abdomen and the sheer, hard strength of him. His scent, made up of starched linen, bay rum, fresh air, and heated male, assailed her, inducing such mind-swimming pleasure that the muscles of her belly contracted. The river gurgled and slurped around the raft. The wet logs rubbed together with a steady rhythm, rocking her against the firm apex of his thighs.

Warm, she was so warm. Somewhere deep inside a rich, languid urge stirred, stretched, tingled along her nerves. Her lips felt swollen, sensitive. She was sinking in the deep-sea darkness of his eyes, buffeted by the storm she saw brewing there, drowning in its fury. And she didn't care.

Then Conrad's thick, gold-tipped lashes came down to shield his expression. He turned his head to stare at the passing shoreline.

"Hell and damnation!"

He shifted to sit erect. Then he cursed again in soft, foreign fluency.

"What is it?" she said, her voice husky and not quite even. She dragged the black, wind-whipped silk of her hair out of her eyes as she stared toward the featureless green shore. A brisk wind had sprung up, ruffling the water that lay between them and the land.

"We've drifted past Good Hope. I meant to pull in there at the landing, be waiting when the others got back."

"How far past?" Her question was punctuated by a rumbling sound of thunder that was much closer than earlier.

"I'm not too sure, though I recognize that big dead tree over there from the trip upriver the other day. I should have been keeping track, but—" He stopped, folding firm lips over whatever he had meant to say.

Melly had always stayed as far away from water craft as she could get. Still, she knew there was a big difference between traveling upstream and down on a raft, even with a steering oar. The crude paddle at their stern could guide them but would not propel them upstream against the river's strong current.

She said, "We'll have to land and walk back."

"No other choice," he agreed with a nod as he disentangled himself and rose to his feet. Squinting against the rising wind, he scanned the bank some distance ahead of them for a suitable place to put ashore.

In that instant thunder boomed again. Lightning crackled immediately afterward, streaking down toward the water in a crooked line like a crack in the overturned bowl of the sky.

Melly flinched. As the brightness faded, a sharp, almost singed odor drifted on the wind.

Clutching at a knot in the binding ropes, she stared around her, frowning as she noticed how the weather had changed in so short a time. Dark clouds blotted out the sun, leaving the sky almost as black as night. Whitecapped waves dotted the wide river's surface. A fog of mist torn from their crests made it difficult to see the distant shoreline. Water slapped over the logs on which she lay, wetting her to the skin.

"Conrad—" she said with a shading of alarm.

"Right," he said in grim agreement. "Whatever we're going to do, we'd better be quick about it." Then, swinging with strong grace on the pitching square of logs, he reached for the rear oar.

She shuddered, feeling exposed and bereft without Conrad's protection. Her old terror hovered, threatening to swamp her just as the river seemed intent on swamping the raft. Yet at the same time she could sense the slow unfurling inside her of something near excitement.

There was a peculiar beauty in the gathering storm, a

majesty in the fury of the elements. And the man who stood over her was part and parcel of these things. Feet braced, he rode the raft as if it were a living thing. With his hair whipped into a wild golden tangle and his shirt plastered to the hard sculpting of his body, he was fearless as he faced the late summer gale. With him there was the assurance of security, and intimations of a consummate glory that pounded in her blood, swelled like a storm tide in her heart.

Conrad pulled with teeth-clenched effort at the steering oar, but they made scant progress toward the west bank. The wind was too strong from that direction; it was holding them off. The yellow-brown river surged and frothed around them, threatening to upend the raft. The ropes lashing the shifting, rubbing logs together creaked under the pressure. The air was thick with spray and laden with the scents of ozone and ancient effluvia stirred up from the river bottom.

As they rounded the next bend, lightning pitchforked down the sky again, hissing as it struck in the water beside them. Melly heard Conrad's low oath. A bare moment later, he shouted, "We've got to get out of this!"

The raft changed directions. Melly swung around, narrowing her eyes to gaze ahead of them. There was an island looming ahead in the middle of the river. The dark green mass was much closer than the western shore. Conrad, she could see, was going to attempt to land on it.

It was then that the rain began, sweeping toward them in a thick, gray curtain. It peppered down around them as the raft grated over the sandbar that angled out in front of the island.

Conrad ignored the hissing clatter as he leaped over the side and splashed ashore with the rope tether in hand. He dragged the waterlogged craft higher, grounding it on the bank and lashing it to a willow that leaned down from the stand of trees along the water's edge.

Melly struggled to her feet, staggering against the blowing rain, half blinded by bits of flying bark and leaves. Conrad swung to scoop her up in his arms. Head down, he waded ashore, then fought his way through weeds and willows, emerging beneath the sheltering canopy of maple and sweet gum trees.

The rain rattled down through the leaves, fragmenting into a fine mist. The smells of wet earth, bruised greenery, and musty lichen rose around them. Conrad pushed deeper, not stopping until he reached the center of the isolated spit of woodland. There he set Melly on her feet under the spreading limbs of a great oak.

The sound of the rain beating the river surface to a froth came plainly to where they stood, yet at the same time seemed remote. The tops of the trees above them swayed and groaned, moaning with the wind, but Melly and Conrad were protected from its force. Sheltered by the great umbrella of oak branches, they were out of the worst of the storm. The thunder and lightning had subsided, making it unlikely they would be struck dead where they stood.

Conrad looked down at her. For long moments, they stood still, lost in the perilous moment and the currents of emotion that shifted between them.

Then wry amusement crept into the brilliant blue of Conrad's eyes, pleating the skin at the corners into tiny, endearing fans. Melly felt an answering smile curve her own mouth. They stared at each other, at their wet hair plastered to their heads, their sodden, mud-stained clothes, the raindrops spiking their lashes and dripping from the tips of their noses.

Suddenly they were laughing, holding each other in the relieved aftermath of peril—and the certain knowledge that, beyond all logic or sanity, they had not only survived their adventure, but enjoyed it.

Then just as abruptly they were silent. The rain splattered and sang, whipping in gusts. It dripped around them, wetting the ground beyond the oak's edge, forming runnels that oozed and spread and became freshets heading toward the river. The cooling air brushed Melly's wet skin with coolness, beading it with goose bumps. Against that chill, she could feel the intense body heat of the man who held her. The need to move toward it, toward him, was so strong that she felt light-headed with it.

She inhaled in sharp dismay and stepped away from him. He let her go. Turning from her, he braced one hand on the trunk of the oak while he raked his hair back with the other. She thought his stance relaxed—until she saw the bark crumble under the pressure of his white-tipped fingers.

Whirling away, Melly dropped down to crouch at the base of the tree. She rested her head on her drawn-up knees and clasped them with her arms. Closing her eyes tightly, she did her best to hold her treacherous impulses at bay while keeping body and conscience together.

Time became elastic, stretching and contracting until it ceased to have meaning. It might have been twenty minutes later, or two hours, when the sky began to lighten. The wind dropped. The pounding rain slackened at last, became a drizzle, a sprinkling. Thunder grumbled still, but it was fading away to the east. High overhead, a bird called. The trees dripped, clouds remained to dim the light and threaten another small shower or two, but the worst appeared to be over.

Conrad left the oak's shelter while the last raindrops were still pattering down. She thought he meant to check the river to see if it had settled down enough to chance the raft again. The day was waning. They would need to get going soon if they were to cross to the bank, then land and walk back to Good Hope before dark.

He returned almost immediately. There was a taut set to his shoulders and grim irony in his face as he stopped a few feet from where she sat.

"Better make yourself comfortable," he said, his voice flat.

"What do you mean?" She tried to decipher his closed expression.

"The tree I tied up to was undercut by the river and washed away."

"I don't see . . ."

"The raft went with it."

It was an instant before his words penetrated, before her befuddled brain made sense of the laconic syllables. Then she saw what he was saying, and an odd, fatalistic horror shifted through her.

The raft was gone.

They were stranded.

# Nine

Marooned by the river like the rawest greenhorn. Conrad silently castigated himself with a few of his more choice seaman's epithets.

There was no question of how he had come to make such a stupid mistake; the answer was all too clear. It was sitting across from him, on the other side of the signal fire he had kindled in this willow-circled clearing near the river's edge.

It would be some time before the others found them. They had also been caught by the storm, so would have slow going on the muddy river road back to town. Everyone would expect him and Melly to be waiting for them there; it was the logical solution. How long would it take before they realized the two of them weren't there and weren't coming?

Thank God for the oiled pouch of sulfur matches that he had stuffed into his pocket. Such preparedness was second nature rather than planned, but was no less effective for that. The fire would not only alert whoever came in search of them, but would dry their clothes and help keep the mosquitoes and gnats at a reasonable distance.

Melly had taken down her hair to dry it. Watching her comb the tangles from the long, waving strands, staring at the way the soft, night-dark mass gleamed in the firelight, made his guts twist with pure, aching need. He wanted to gather her hair in his hands, bury his face in its warm, damp silk, and breathe the essence of her into his very being.

The bonfire crackled, leaping higher in a small explosion of sparks that spiraled into the purple twilight sky. Melly looked up at the sound, then glanced over at him across the flames. Her eyes reflected their red-hot glow, while the pure planes and angles of her face were enameled in blue and gold like some exquisite, fabled mask of enchantment. He held her gaze, absorbing it, and for a single instant there was nothing between them except smoke, wavering heat waves, and the aching mystery of desire.

Her throat moved as she swallowed. She lowered her lashes and bent her head. Picking up a small stick, she gouged absentmindedly at the dirt beside her. After a moment, she asked, "Do you remember the time we were walking along the levee and we saw that man throw a grass sack into the water?"

It was an effort to redirect his thoughts, but he nodded as he recalled the incident.

"There were kittens in the sack; we could hear them crying as it started to sink. I wanted to rescue the little things, but the water was too deep—and I was so afraid. You dove in and brought the kittens out to me. Vanilla, Aunt Dora's boardinghouse cat, was one of them."

A reminiscent smile creased one lean, sun-bronzed cheek. "You always were tenderhearted."

"And you always knew it. But do you remember that you were pretending to be Caleb that day?"

So he was. He looked away from her. "Maybe."

He lifted a shoulder in a moody shrug. "You were so young, only six, maybe seven. You wanted to go with me, and I—well, I wanted the company. Your aunt trusted Caleb." He heard the old pain in his voice, but could do nothing about it.

"That was the day I learned to tell you apart," she said softly.

His heart took on a trip-hammer beat. "How?"

"Some of the kittens drowned. You held me while I cried. From then on, all I had to do was touch you."

"But you never said a word . . . so I figured—"

She gave an emphatic shake of her head. "Caleb picked me up once to put me in a wagon, and another time he'd helped me into a rope swing. When you held me that day, it felt . . . different. Later on, I could see the difference in your eyes. I didn't understand why everybody couldn't see it. I used to follow you sometimes, just to see the way your face changed when you turned and saw me."

He couldn't have spoken if his life depended on it.

She went on after a moment, her voice tight, forced. "But you went away for so many years. It seemed you were never coming back." She stopped, took a deep breath. "Caleb is a fine man, a good friend, and he loves me in his way. To look at him is . . . very nearly the same."

Around them the insects and night frogs made their pleas for love and immortality. The wet, earthy smell of the woods, the fishy taint of the river, were strong in their lungs. The air was moist and cool after the rain, so that the acrid smoke from the fire lay on it like a drifting shadow, now concealing, now revealing, their faces. Yet between them, in still and perfect clarity, was an understanding that had no need for words.

She knew why he had come from so far across the sea to be with her before she was wed. He knew why she had been able to conquer her fear of deep water enough to endure the storm. They were two parts of a whole, in spite of her promise to Caleb or the pull Conrad felt inside from far distant horizons.

Nothing would come of it. Soon they would be rescued, and the pace of their days, so briefly interrupted, would resume their steady, inevitable course. It was not meant that they should be together. Time and circumstances had prevented it until this moment, and their loyalties demanded that nothing change that now.

Yet for a single, heart-stopping moment they were able to look into each other's eyes in the dancing firelight. And see in bright-hot glory the things that might have been.

She closed her eyes and tossed the small stick she held into the fire. Abruptly the stacked and glowing heart of the fire collapsed on itself. A burning branch tumbled from the heap, skittering, trailing coals and smoke. It spun toward Melly's skirts to lodge in the soft, crumpled folds.

Conrad moved in the same instant, lunging with a swift uncoiling of taut muscles. Stretching, reaching without conscious thought beyond the need to prevent disaster, he snatched the smoking limb from the fragile cloth and flung it back into the fire. Then, using the palm of his hand, he beat out the small flames licking at her spread hems.

Melly cried out, reaching toward him. He raked his gaze over her—her bare feet and arms, her face—in search of injury. Finding none, he demanded, "What is it? Where are you hurt?"

"Nothing. I'm not," she said with a violent shake of her head that set the ends of her hair to dancing. "But you— your hand . . ."

Reaching to catch his wrist, she turned it to the light of the fire. The skin was blackened, stinging, but protected from real harm by a layer of calluses. He had endured far worse many times from rope burns.

"It's nothing," he said, and meant it.

"Not to me." Her voice was quiet. Bending her head, she pressed her lips to the tender center of his palm.

For endless eons of time, he could not move, had no power over the assorted bones, tendons, and sinews of his body. He felt as if the entire surface of his body was man- tled in a hot flush of need. His brain was baking in his skull, on fire with the violent internal conflict between brotherly fidelity and his own need, between honor and fate.

All that was left was instinct. It was that alone which set him in motion finally, only that which guided him as he reached to draw Melly to him. Some part of him looked on with remorse but lacked the power to stop what was hap- pening. Only one thing could now.

"I want you," he whispered.

"I—know."

The catch in her voice shook his heart. "Tell me to stop."

"I would," she said, her gaze fastened on his in fearful honesty, "if I could."

"Please. I don't want to hurt you."

Her smile was at once tremulous and pitying. "You couldn't."

He could, he knew, and so easily, though it would be against his will. Still, he could not resist the lure of her trust. "If I do," he said in low entreaty, "will you tell me?"

"Yes. If." The soft words were both a promise and unspoken permission. They were proof that she knew him from his twin, wanted him for himself.

Her skin gleamed with the soft luster of the pearls of the Far East. It was smooth and firm and warmly resilient under his hands. Her kiss as he took it tasted of the sweetness of the Spice Islands, and was as layered with wonders. He marveled, yet restrained the wild urge to plunge in and take everything at once. He wanted her to know every delicate sensation of which the flesh was capable. That would be his gift, one directed by the force of his deep, abiding love. She would, he vowed to himself, have no regrets.

He knew full well that his own would come soon enough. But he would save them for the time when they were all he had left.

The ground near the fire had been cleared of sticks and debris but was still muddy and wet. He cushioned it with his trousers and shirt, hastily removed, before he laid her back upon it. Then he eased down beside her and drew her against his aching body.

Melly closed her eyes tightly, losing herself in the mindless pleasure of the moment. She would not think, only feel. She touched her fingers to his flame-gilded shoulders, enjoying their warm, hard shaping, sensing the strength he held so carefully in check. No, he would not hurt her.

Under her hand, she felt his muscles shift as he began to open the buttons of her bodice. One by one, they gave under his fingers, allowing the cloth to fall away. He skimmed over her rib cage to cup a breast. She ceased to breathe for long seconds as his gentle kneading sent magic sensations tumbling through her. Only as he drew her camisole aside to take the nipple into his mouth did she let the air in her lungs escape on a soft, strangled sigh.

He knew exactly what he was doing. More than that, he meant to enjoy all the small, encroaching preliminaries. Secure in that knowledge, she felt the release of the stiffness in her muscles.

She wanted to learn his body as he explored hers. She yearned to thread her fingertips through the whorls of golden-brown hair on his chest, touch the small nubs of his paps so they knotted as her own were doing under his ministrations. Her fingers trembled as she brushed them across his chest.

Sensing her need, he gave her access, guided her hand to him, then left her free to do as she pleased. She accepted the invitation, timidly at first, then more boldly.

As he nuzzled the small hollow beneath her ear, she sighed and arched her body toward him, nestling her breasts more securely in his hand. Accepting that mute gesture of need, he cupped their fullness, suckled them, draped them in long, cool strands of hair and licked the pouting rose-red nipples that peeked through. Then, he surveyed his handiwork. And he smiled.

If this was loving, she knew why everyone tried so hard

to keep it from young women. They could grow too easily to crave it, following mindlessly after the man who could make them feel such splendor. There was no embarrassment in it, only voluptuous, spreading wonder.

Entranced by Conrad's deftness and her tingling reactions to it, she barely noticed as he drew off more layers of clothing as if he were shucking an ear of corn to reach the tender kernels inside. He tasted her as he might a freshly roasted ear also, nibbling as he went, gathering her flavor with his tongue.

Amazement rasped in her throat. She cried out, pleading, reaching convulsively for him. Her fingers pressed into his shoulder until her nails bit the skin.

He answered her need, enclosing her in the protection of his arms even as he slid between her thighs. For an instant her tight, desperate constriction prevented entry. He did not force it, but aided her with gentle stretching until she could accept him. Even then, he eased inside by heart-melting degrees, filling her so slowly that her veins pounded with the maddening escalation of glory.

She wanted, needed, all of him, could not bear to be denied an instant longer. Sliding her hands down the powerful curve of his back, she pressed the palms of her hands to his hips as she arched against him.

The pain stung. It was so unexpected that she tightened around him and fell back, taking him with her to impossible depths. He made a short, winded sound in his chest and then was still. He hovered above her and she heard him grit his teeth, felt the slow bunching of his muscles as he fought for control. A moment later he put his hand under her and lifted her, tilted her hips a little while he eased from her, then lowered himself into her again with shuddering slowness.

The abrupt beatitude was so overwhelming that a soft sob rasped in her throat and tears streamed from her eyes into her hair. And suddenly nothing was too deep or too hard or too much. She wanted all of him, needed him with desperate yearning. It was not mere lust but something deeper and more elemental, a passion for love and the life that he could give her by kindling that love inside her.

She moved with its ancient rhythm, hesitant and awkward. He felt the tentative accommodation, accepted it, molded it to his own efforts. As he drew back to carry her higher, she opened her eyes and looked into his face.

The firelight in his eyes was echoed in her heart. She loved him, and spoke the words though her lips did not move and she made no sound. Never would she forget this moment. Never, not even when she was old and bent and had dismissed all else from memory. In this eternal instant he was hers and she was his, and nothing would ever take that from her.

Then he sank into her, banishing thought with his surging power. Together they moved, rising, falling, while their skins glowed with the fiery heat of their blood and their hearts beat in thudding syncopation. Her very being rose to meet him, rushing toward him, pouring out to him like the river that coursed past where they lay. Higher it flooded, deeper, wider. She took his strength and gave him hers until their two beings were merged, so tightly and deeply mixed that there was no way to tell where one ended and the other began. No way, ever, to wrest them apart again.

And abruptly she was caught in the surging tide, racing with it, flowing with it in a run for the sea. She reached its depths and spread, voluptuous, serene. He pressed deep as he met her, welcoming her with hard, enclosing arms.

Afterward, they held each other, staring wide-eyed, glorified yet desolate into the encroaching darkness as they stroked, touched, soothed, sought answers that could not be found. They did not move until the fire died.

Later, when it was no more than a bed of orange-red coals, they rose and struggled into their clothes, tried as best they might to make themselves presentable. Then Conrad searched out more wood to build up the flames again.

They were leaping high, burning in hot tongues far up into the dark heavens, when Caleb found them.


"FIGHT! FIGHT!"

Melly heard the cries from the street as she emerged from the semidetached kitchen at the back of the boarding-house. She had been heating water, getting ready to launder the dress and petticoats that had been so mistreated the day before. She abandoned the task as the yelling broke out, then hurried toward the front porch.

Sarah was standing outside the mercantile with a shopping basket on her arm, shading her eyes against the morning sun as she stared toward the river landing.

Glimpsing Melly as she moved out onto the porch steps, the other girl swung toward her. "It's Caleb and Conrad!" she called, her face as green and pale as a pattypan squash. "They're killing each other!"

Melly had suspected as much, but the anguish of it nonetheless washed over her in a wave. She had to stop them, or at least try.

Picking up her skirts, she began to run. Sarah hesitated only a second before she pounded after her.

There was no way they could miss the confrontation. The shouts and whistles, the cries of encouragement, and the barking of excited dogs, carried plainly down the street. Some idiot was even ringing a bell as if the fight were a spectacle for all to come and see. Graybeards, farmers, drummers in flat-crowned hats, and gentlemen wearing tailored frock coats gathered around the combatants in a wide circle. Some were laying bets, while others spat tobacco juice and showed their companions how they had dealt with past opponents themselves. Several boys crowded between them, though one enterprising towhead stood on a hitching post for a better view over the shoulders of his elders.

Melly did not pause, but waded into the men, with Sarah behind her. There were some scowls and mutters, but they made way for her. Every single one of them knew she was embroiled in this dispute between brothers.

Yet to call what was taking place a fight was totally wrong; the contest was far too one-sided. It was, instead, a punishment. One brother was dealing it out, the other taking it.

Caleb, his face a mask of rage, was pummeling Conrad with his fists. Conrad weaved and ducked, blocking the blows when he could, rolling with them when he couldn't. It was apparent that more than a few had connected, for there was a spreading bruise on his cheekbone and a cut at his brow that streamed blood into his right eye.

"Stop it!" Melly cried out above the noise. "Conrad! Caleb! Stop it this instant!"

If either of the two heard her or noticed her presence, they gave no sign. They circled, one advancing, the other retreating, each identical gaze intent on the other's face. It was disorienting and even macabre to see them, like watching a man battle his mirror image.

"Stand and fight like a man!" Caleb growled, his expression twisting in frustration as he stalked his twin.

Conrad kept moving, his eyes watchful as he spoke. "What I did was wrong, and I've admitted the fault. If you want blood for it, fine. But I won't make a brawl out of it."

"It never stopped you before." Caleb's scorn was plain.

"I don't have anything to prove."

"I think you do. I think that's why you took Melly out on the river, to spite me."

Conrad shifted from his brother's path in a glide of well-oiled muscles. "Taking Melly on the river was a stupid trick that went wrong, nothing else."

The words were laced with pain and self-blame. Melly thought they were for her, that at least Conrad was aware she was witnessing their dispute.

"Oh, I don't think that was it at all," Caleb growled, swinging a hard right as he moved in on his brother. "You're a man of the sea, with a trained eye for weather. You saw the storm signs and took advantage. You know water, read landmarks, remember things like the island because your life may depend on it. You knew exactly where you were going yesterday."

Clasping her hands tightly at her waist, Melly frowned. Could Conrad have known there would be a storm? Had he planned from the first to land on the island, arranged for the loss of the raft?

Caleb was right in one thing at least: Conrad was a sea-man, and a good one. Surely he should have known better than to lash the raft to so flimsy a support? Did it follow, then, that her seduction had been planned?

Conrad, watching Melly's face, took a hard punch squarely over the heart. He gasped, reeling with the blow, but the worst of the pain was in his mind. He could not allow Melly to think that what they had shared had meant so little to him.

Lashing out at his brother with words in place of blows, he said in breathless derision, "It's not really Melly you're concerned about, is it? If it was, you wouldn't be making such a noise about what happened."

"What I'm doing is teaching you a lesson!"

"Are you, now? What kind? To watch out for bad luck? Or would it be about brotherly love?"

"To leave what's mine alone!"

Though his ribs hurt where Caleb had pounded them, Conrad laughed. "Here I was thinking it might be respect for the lady."

"Melly will be my wife in a few days. That's all the respect she needs."

The arrogance of that riled Conrad's temper. "You think so? How generous, giving her your precious name after such a terrible disgrace as being caught in the rain with another man. But I'd say something more is needed if she's to be happy."

"What do you know about it? Nothing, and you never will! I'll give her everything she needs; home, children, a good, solid life at my side all the days of our lives—and nights."

Caleb meant the last as a death blow. Against the pain of it, Conrad said, "She might prefer just to be loved."

"By you, a shiftless sea rover?" Caleb grunted his disbelief as he jabbed at his brother.

"By a man who might trade all the oceans of the world for the right woman."

Rage flashed in Caleb's bright blue eyes, so like his brother's. "She'd be a fool to take you. Unless you proved, out there on that island, that she's really no better than you are."

Conrad hit him then, a hard right with every ounce of his power and anger behind it. And he kept on hitting Caleb until they pulled him off. But it could not erase what had been said, or ease the torment he felt for bringing this final insult down on Melly. Or eliminate his fear that she might believe it.

# Ten

Within twenty-four hours, Conrad had made his decision to leave and packed his trunk to go. It was time: he had outstayed his welcome. Remaining could only make matters worse.

Anyway, his ship would be out of dry dock, outfitted, and ready in Baltimore. The steamer *J. B. Cates* was scheduled to put in at the landing again tomorrow at sundown on its run up to Ohio, with connections from there to the Maryland shore. When it left again, he would be on it.

He would miss the wedding that would take place the next day, on Saturday. That was definitely by design. He didn't think he could bear to serve as his brother's best man, even if Caleb still wanted him, which was doubtful.

The event was still going to take place. At least there had been no announcement to the contrary.

Caleb had apparently made his peace with Melly. He had paid a formal call on her the evening after the fight and stayed some time. What they had said to each other was anybody's guess; what Conrad did know was that Caleb had been whistling on his return. Conrad would have liked to damn him to hell for it, had he not understood the elation too well.

All that was left, then, was saying good-bye to Melly.

He put it off as long as possible. It was forced upon him, finally, on the afternoon of his departure.

Melly, being the lady she was, made it easier for him. She saw him coming up the walk, all rigged out in his gray broadcloth with his hair freshly barbered and his hat in his hand. Rising from her chair, where she had been putting tiny stitches into the hem of a handkerchief, she stood waiting, grave expectation on her lovely face.

"So you're going," she said in clear, musical tones. "Caleb said you would."

Conrad didn't care for the sound of that, but could hardly argue. As he came to a halt on the step below her, he said simply, "It seems best."

"Yes." She swallowed, a visible movement in the graceful line of her throat.

"Melly—"

"No, please, I understand. There's nothing to keep you here."

"There's everything—" he began in fierce contradiction. Then he stopped. Taking a deep breath, he began again without quite meeting the shadowed darkness of her eyes.

"Caleb had a perfect right to be upset over what happened the other day, and I hope you won't blame him. I served him a shabby trick and wound up hurting everybody. Whatever he said was . . . in the heat of the moment and because, well, because he had so much to lose. He didn't mean any of it."

"I know," she said quietly.

He cleared his throat of a troublesome obstruction. "About the way I shanghaied you . . ."

"You forget that I also know you." Her smile was only a flicker across her lips. "I'll admit that I thought for an instant you might have meant to be caught by the storm. But then I remembered what you said on the island and I knew you would never set out to hurt me."

His pent-up breath left him. He pushed his hand into his pants pocket to hide its shaking. Against the ache in his throat, and in his heart, he said, "I did it anyway, in spite of everything. For that I'm desperately sorry."

"Don't be. You didn't—that is . . ." She stopped, began again. "I think we hurt each other, whether we meant to or not. And Caleb most of all."

She met his eyes then, and her own were clouded with regret. Seeing it, he gave a slow nod.

"Caleb will make you a good husband; it would be wrong to think anything else. He's decent and honorable and will do his best to make you happy. More than that, he's my brother. Though you will never be far from my thoughts or my heart, I can't take my own happiness at his expense."

"I understand," she said, the words barely above a whisper. "At least—I know that Caleb is not the only decent and honorable man in this."

His resolve and his voice almost failed him. Straining for control, he said, "Then maybe you can understand why this is good-bye. I can't stay and watch—"

"No." She looked down at her hands, still clutching her

piece of sewing, then up again to meet his gaze. "For me it's easier. I will see Caleb, and it will be nearly like seeing you. I'll always know what you look like wherever you are, no matter how much you change. And sometimes when I shut my eyes at night I can imagine—"

"Don't!" he exclaimed, a sound of stark agony.

She stopped, closed her lips, pressed them tightly together. When she looked up again, her lashes were rimmed with wetness. "That was unfair, wasn't it? Forget it, please."

How could he, ever? "Melly, I—"

"No!" she said again. "I'm bound, too, don't you see? I made my promise, and Caleb has built so much on it. I can't take that away from him any more than you can. In any case, you're better off alone. You always were."

Once he would have agreed. No more. Here, right this minute, was the time to tell her so. Now was the time to say how much he adored her, how much he needed her beside him. It was the perfect moment to beg her to come with him.

But he couldn't; he had no right. He would never know what answer she might have given him—a more fitting punishment, it seemed to Conrad, than anything Caleb had managed.

"I expect you're right." The breath he drew hurt deep in his chest, which had nothing to do with the drubbing he had taken from his brother.

She made no reply, but unshed tears glistened in her eyes. He looked into them long seconds, memorizing their color, their shape, their forthright honesty. Remembering the way they had once darkened with desire, for him.

Then he took her hand and removed the piece of sewing from it before raising her fingers to his lips. He closed his eyes as he felt their coolness, the faint tremors that shook them. Then he released her, turned, and walked away.

He was halfway down the street before he realized he was still holding the handkerchief she had been stitching. He spread its folds, staring down at it as he walked. She had just set the last stitches of an embroidered motif: Caleb's initials—or his own—done in gold thread and enclosed in a blood-red heart.

A wedding gift for the groom, no doubt. He should return it, he told himself, hand it back to her.

Conrad snapped the needle off from the thread, leaving enough length for a finishing knot. He dropped the small, sharp length of steel into the street. Folding the fine linen into a careful square, he put it in his pocket, over his heart. And kept on walking.

"Aunt Dora? Do you ever wish you had married Mr. Prine, after all?"

Melly spoke into a lull in the animated gathering of bridesmaids that took place on the front porch later that evening. She had been subdued yet jumpy, starting at the blast of the whistle from the *J. B. Cates* as it came into the landing, paying more attention to the sun sliding down the slope of the sky toward the featherbed of lavender and gold on the horizon than to the final details of her wedding being discussed around her. Her gaze was pensive now, far away, as she waited for her aunt's answer.

"You asking if I've got regrets, child?" Aunt Dora sent

her a shrewd glance as she looked up from the peas she had brought out onto the porch to shell for supper.

Melly gave a slow nod. "Something like that."

"Now and again. Wouldn't be human if I didn't."

"But you never thought of doing anything about it?"

The older woman grimaced. "Not a lot. There was so much against it. Then you came to me."

Melly looked around at her friends, who were watching her with obvious concern in their faces, when they were not exchanging uneasy glances. "Yes, and now I'm going," she said. "You'll be alone."

Down at the river, the three-note steam whistle of the *J. B. Cates* assaulted the air in token of its departure within the half hour. Melly's aunt waited for the sound to die away before she said, "Sounds as if you're trying to arrange my life for me, honey."

"Not really, but I was just thinking—"

"Don't," the older woman recommended. "Don't trouble your brain about me. You got enough to worry about just taking care of your own problems."

"Too true," Melly said with a smile.

Her aunt looked past her as a buggy came down the street, then drew up at the hitching post outside the front yard gate. "Here comes the main one now."

It was Caleb. He was due for supper, the last time she would see him before the wedding. Though she had bathed and changed her dress earlier, she had not expected him to arrive for at least an hour.

Caleb declined Aunt Dora's offer of cherry cordial, spoke politely to the other young women, then took a chair next to Melly. His unease was plain, however, and he seemed to have something on his mind.

The older woman heaved herself to her feet. "Time I was getting these peas on to cook if we're to have them for supper. Sarah, you and Biddy can set the table if you don't mind. Esther and Lydia can peel a few potatoes for a nice salad. Come along now, girls. It's getting late."

As the sound of the women's voices died away in the direction of the kitchen, Melly sat looking at her hands and searching her mind for some comfortable subject for conversation. So many things were unacceptable: the storm and the cooler weather it had brought; the steamer down at the landing; the lack of a best man for the wedding ceremony. Conrad.

Almost as if he could read her mind, Caleb said abruptly, "I guess you know Conrad is leaving this evening."

"Yes." She was hardly in need of a reminder, with the steamboat whistle signaling every few minutes.

"You said your good-byes?"

She nodded, looking away from him.

"And you're content to see him go?"

How was she to answer that? Perhaps a half-truth would do. "Since he could not stay."

"He might have, if you had asked."

The words, so quietly spoken, had such a sound of Conrad that she turned her head to stare. How unfair it was that even their voices should be so near the same. Could she stand it? Could she?

His smile was wry as he met her gaze, as if he understood what she had been looking for all her life, what she was thinking now. "You do love him, don't you? I didn't want to see it or believe it, but it's so plain since the picnic. I can't help wondering if it was him all along."

"Don't," she said on a quickly drawn breath. "*Please.* Just—don't."

"Why? Because I might say something I'll regret? Or because you might?"

"This isn't necessary, Caleb. I'm going to marry you to-morrow. I promise I will try to make you a good wife."

"I expect so, but I don't know if I want that if it's going to be so hard for you. Anyway, I've fooled myself long enough. Conrad was right: I've been too sure the things I could give you were everything you could possibly need."

"It would be," she said miserably, "if I were different."

"But you're not." He shook his head. "I don't know if I would love you quite so much if you were."

"Oh, Caleb." She shook her head, at a loss as she wondered what it was he wanted her to say.

A crooked smile tugged his mouth. "Never mind," he said abruptly. "If you hurry, you can still make the steamboat."

She returned her gaze to his face. "How—what do you mean? I can't do that!"

"Can't you, for Conrad? He's waiting for you."

"What did he tell you? I don't—don't understand."

"He hasn't said anything. We haven't spoken about it at all. Still, I know how he feels—he's my twin, remember? He's dying inside. He needs you."

"But the wedding—I told you I wanted to marry you."

"You did, and I honor you for it." His smile was weary. "I'm just not fool enough anymore to be certain you mean it. You still have time—just—to change your mind, though you have to make it up once and for all. Stay, and you marry me tomorrow. Go, and Conrad will take you with him to Baltimore and the *Queen of the Sea.*"

"Yes, but what if—"

"He'll do right by you; I know that much, because he's my brother and—but never mind. You can be married at the first town you come to tomorrow. After that, who knows? Foreign places, strange climes, then maybe the life of a riverboat captain's wife when the babies come." Caleb's smile was grim. "Conrad thinks he can plan his family, but I've seen the way he looks at you and expect he's more fool than I am about that part."

"He said nothing when he came by a little while ago." She rose to her feet even as she voiced the protest. Her voice held an edge of doubt amounting to near panic. Yet the light in her eyes glowed like the sunset.

He stood also. "I figured that out, which is why I'm here. Make up your mind, Melly. Do it now, or I swear I'll take back everything and hold you to your word."

Distress invaded her features. "Oh, Caleb! How can I leave you to face this alone? What will everyone say?"

He shook his head with a wry twist of his mouth. "It isn't as if they haven't guessed."

"Yes," she whispered. Still she hesitated, searching his face. What she saw there gave her courage, and a slow smile bloomed across her features.

Whirling abruptly, she ran into the house.

What must she take with her? she asked herself.

So much had been packed and removed to Caleb's house already. Aunt Dora could send it after her. Still, there was her wedding dress; she must have that. It would go in the top of her small valise, which stood ready, her underclothing and nightgown neatly folded inside. What else? Her hairbrush and comb from her dressing table, her toothbrush.

The steam whistle was blowing again. She must hurry, hurry.

Her quilt! She could not leave that behind. It would be a reminder of home and friends when she needed it. The initials set into her bridal square were the same, and the date, pray God, would be right. She had thought so often of Conrad, sailing the seas, buying the silk for her in faroff Cathay, as she was sewing the quilt, and had stitched such dreams and idle fancies into it. Perhaps that was why they were coming true.

Yes, she must take it. She snatched it up in her arms.

What else? She turned this way and that in distraction. Then she stopped.

Nothing. She needed nothing, so long as she had her love.

Aunt Dora was waiting for her on the porch. Caleb, Melly realized, must have told her already; her eyes were suspiciously red, and she had her hands wrapped in her apron. Yet she was smiling bravely. Melly set down her valise and quilt for a quick, fierce hug.

"You write now, you hear?" the older woman said, the words thick. "And take care, honey. You—take care."

"Oh, yes, I will, I will. . . ."

Then Sarah and Lydia, Esther and Biddy crowded around, laughing, crying, all trying to hug her at once. Good-bye, good-bye, so many good-byes. She didn't want the tears to fall, but she was leaving so much behind. So much. Yet there was so much ahead.

Caleb was still there also, waiting behind the others, coming forward as they drew back. Melly turned to him.

"Here," he said, taking her hand and thrusting something into it.

It was a gold wedding ring. Inscribed inside were their initials, just as they were written on her quilt. "Oh, Caleb."

"You can use it until he buys you another, or keep it to remember me. I won't need it."

She loved him then as she never had before. And because of it, she knew, she would indeed keep his ring. There was a loose stitch in the center square of the quilt next to the wedding date; she had noticed it at the picnic. She would slip the ring in there, as a remembrance, and sew it up safe and tight, for surely Caleb was as much her friend as any of the others.

Abruptly she stepped close, flung her arms around his neck, and kissed him full on the mouth. He raised his hands, but did not quite touch her before he dropped them again. She moved back, her lips curving in a tremulous smile. Then she picked up her things and was gone, leaving him staring, white-faced, behind her.

The *J. B. Cates* blew a last long blast as she ran headlong down the street. She saw it ahead of her, a great wedding cake–like pile of lumber lying nose-in toward the dock. Its white paint gleamed pink with the light of the setting sun. A black cloud of smoke was flying from its stacks to smudge the lavender sky. Men on the dock were loosening its lines, flinging them into the water as deckhands on board the boat began to coil them.

"Wait!"

Her voice broke as she called. They couldn't hear her for the beat of the paddle wheel and the cascading of water. The pilot in the small house above the texas deck was watching the river instead of the dock. The boat was drifting away with the river current as it built up steam.

Her side ached as she ran pell-mell with the valise beating against her leg and the long quilt in her arms threatening to trip her with every step. Her lungs were bursting, her heart shuddering in her chest.

"Wait for me!"

Now the passengers on deck were calling, pointing at her. Her hair was coming down as she lost her pins. Her arms ached with the weight of the valise. Tears rose to blur her vision. She ran harder.

But on the upper deck, a man was whirling to stare, sprinting to the railing. Conrad!

He saw her, waved, then spun around and disappeared. Seconds later, he appeared on the main deck at the gangplank. He did not wait for it to be lowered again, but climbed to the end of the raised planking, using its rope guard rails. While passengers shouted encouragement or yelled up to the pilot to stop, the deckhands leaped to crank the gangplank to a level position. Conrad rode it down, weighting it, holding it steady.

But the boat was pulling farther away, getting ready to back into the river's current before swinging to head upstream.

Then Mr. Prine was beside her, come from the saloon nearby. "Give me your stuff, Miss Melly! I'll chunk it on board for ye!"

She pushed the small bag at him, and he swung around at once to give it a hard heave. It landed on the deck and skidded against the bulkhead. An instant later, the quilt followed the same way, rippling, shining, as it sailed over the water to catch on the railing. Eager hands grabbed it and drew it to safety.

Now Conrad was holding to the gangplank railing, grinning with joy, gladness brilliant in his eyes as he leaned out to her. "Jump, Melly! Jump! Now!"

But the gap was widening between boat and land. The water was swift-running, murky yellow-brown. And deep, so deep. A shiver ran over her, tracking down her back with the chill of old terror.

She couldn't do it. She couldn't.

"Jump, Melly, love. Come on, I'll catch you," he called again, his voice deep and true as he held out his hand. *"Jump if you love me. . . ."*

She squeezed her eyes shut, turned away. She took a step back down the dusty street. Then another. Another.

"Melly!"

*It's only water. . . . Life, just life.*

Whirling, she picked up her full skirts and began to run. She did not look at the water, but fastened her gaze on Conrad's face and the aching love in his eyes. Harder, faster. At the edge of the landing, she gathered her courage and her strength and leaped as hard and far as she could go.

The water, the deep flowing river, was under her, its widening stretch between bank and boat dancing in the last glow of the sun. She glimpsed it for a blinding instant before she fastened her gaze on the man who reached for her.

Then Conrad's strong arm whipped around her waist like

a steel hawser. He staggered with the force of her momentum before swinging her onto the gangplank and dragging her roughly into his hard arms. Holding her so tight she could feel the hard thud of his heart against her ribs, he pressed his cheek to her temple. Overhead, the passengers on the decks cheered and shouted in congratulation and approbation.

"Dear God, Melly," he whispered. "I was so afraid."

He did not say of what, but she knew he meant many things. She tilted her chin as she said, "Not me."

He smiled down at her with aching tenderness. "I adore you, sweet Melly Bennington, and will my whole life long. Come away with me and I'll give you the world tied up in a ribbon. I'll show you sunsets and storms, white sails in moonlight and dark nights on a black sea. I'll sing you a chanty and let the waves rock you to sleep in my arms. And always, wherever you may be, there will I be also, and I will be home."

"I love you, my captain," she whispered. Then smiling, she put her arms around his neck, holding on as if she meant never to let go.

The *J. B. Cates* blew a deafening blast on its whistle and eased backward into the river. Conrad and Melly paid no attention.

It was miles before they noticed that the voyage had begun.

# Liar's Moon

## Kristin Hannah

Dear Reader,

As I sit at my computer, putting the finishing touches on "Liar's Moon," evidence of the harvest season is all around me. Outside my window the world is awash in reddish gold, bright yellow, and burgundy. Crinkly brown leaves litter the dying grass. On my kitchen counter, amid a pile of old newspapers and dried ornamental corn, a pumpkin awaits. My son, who has diligently designed the jack-o'-lantern's face, is looking forward to tonight when he and his daddy will sit on the deck and carve it.

Yesterday was my son's first preschool Halloween party. Four Batmans (or is it Batmen?), a cowboy, a witch, a Ninja Turtle, and a fairy princess bobbed for apples, decorated pumpkins, and sang "ghosty" songs. It was like every Halloween party everywhere, and it brought back a rush of unexpected memories. Haunted houses in the high-school gymnasium, homecoming games in the pouring rain, and Halloween parties at my parents' house. It's a great time of year no matter how old you are.

"Liar's Moon" grew out of my memories of small-town life of the small, Pacific Northwest farming community in which I grew up. There, the harvest season was a special time. After a long, hot season of field and crop work, autumn was a time for laughter, relaxation, and camaraderie. A time of parades, parties, and princesses.

In my story I created a town much like the one I remember. It's a quirky, quiet, humble little place where dreams are possible. And where magic exists beneath a harvest moon. I hope you enjoy it.

Best wishes,
Kristin Hannah

# One

Julianna Sparks nudged the wobbly spectacles higher on her nose and stared at the letter in her lap. The envelope was a stark, pristine white against the graying cotton of her ragged, patched apron.

She ran her finger along the expensive, textured paper and felt a rush of anticipation. Sweet anticipation. Her hands trembled with it, but she didn't give in. Not yet. A letter from Nicholas was something to be savored. Each one transported her to a magical place; a world unlike her own, where poverty didn't exist and dreams were always possible.

She couldn't stand the suspense any longer. She eased the envelope open and gently pulled out the letter. With bated breath, she began to read.

*Miss Sparks:*

*It is with great pleasure that I inform you of my upcoming trip to Russetville . . .*

Juli paled. Her fingers tightened on the paper. She hadn't read it right, surely she'd only imagined the words . . .

She glanced down at the paper again, but the words were still there, bold and black and undeniable: *my upcoming trip to Russetville.*

She clutched the settee's threadbare arm. "Oh my God . . ."

Her grandmother Gladys looked up from her sewing and grinned expectantly. "That fella finally propose marriage?"

Juli opened her mouth to speak, but nothing came out except a tiny squeak of dismay.

The bright smile on her grandmother's face slowly faded. She set her sewing aside and called for Juli's mother. "Mildred, get out here."

Mildred pushed open the kitchen door and peeked out. "What's the—" She took one look at Juli and shoved the door fully aside. Wiping her floury hands on her apron, she hurried to the settee and sat down beside her daughter. "Honey, what's the matter?"

The letter slipped from Juli's numb fingers and fluttered to the floor. "He's coming to see me, Mama."

"*He?* Nicholas?"

Juli bit her lower lip to keep it from trembling. Even the word *yes* was beyond her.

"What is it, Julianna?" her mother asked softly. "You've been writing to this man for years. I thought—we all thought—you were waiting for this day."

Juli thought back on all the letters she'd written and received throughout the years. Her stomach twisted into a sick knot. All the lies she'd told. She plopped her elbows on her knees and buried her face in her hands.

Mildred stroked Juli's hair. "What is it, honey?"

Gladys scooted her chair closer.

Juli brought her head up slowly. Her mother was perched birdlike on the edge of the sofa, her faded, flour-sack gown drawn tightly across her bent knees.

Juli felt a rush of guilt. Unable to meet her mother's steady gaze, she looked away. "You remember when I first met Nicholas?"

Mildred smiled. "How could we forget? It was when you went to that society thing in San Francisco."

"That was the best damn newspaper column you ever wrote," Gladys said. "Even better'n the time I put a sack on your grandad's head at the festival dance, and you called it a masquerade ball. I still got it in my scrap book."

Juli swallowed thickly. "Well, things didn't go quite as smoothly as I said."

Mildred frowned. "What do you mean?"

Juli squeezed her eyes shut, fighting a sudden tide of painful memories. The night in San Francisco had been so horrifying and humiliating. All her life she'd known she was poor, but until that night she'd never been ashamed.

God, she wished she didn't have to tell her mother and grandmother the truth, wished there was nothing *to* tell.

But there was. She inhaled deeply and looked at the two women who loved her most in the world.

"It was an awful night," she said quietly. "Everyone was in silk and satin and diamonds. I looked like exactly what I am—a dirt-poor potato farmer's daughter. I . . . I had to lie to you. You were all so proud that I went . . ." Her voice faded away as the memories came back.

The Seattle newspaper had been heralding the charity auction for months, promising the most glittering array of society's stars ever assembled in one place. From the first mention of it, Juli had ached to go. All of her dreams of traveling, of seeing the world, seemed destined to come true on that one night in San Francisco.

For months she'd scrimped and saved for the train fare, and when it was obvious she wouldn't have enough, the whole town had kicked in the difference. There'd been no money left over to buy gowns or shoes or those fancy silver-trimmed handbags all the other women had, but she hadn't worried about that. She was going to San Francisco; nothing else had seemed important.

On the night of the big ball, she had dressed in her best muslin gown and proudly signed in as society columnist for the Russetville Gazette.

She walked slowly across the marble-floored foyer, her mouth agape at the grandeur of the mansion. For a split second, it was magical, her dream come true. Then reality came crashing in.

Veiled glances assaulted her, hushed snickering nipped at her heels. She was studiously ignored by the radiant, well-dressed people clustered throughout the rooms.

She'd tried to ignore them. She'd held her head high and sipped the exorbitantly expensive champagne, but the magic of the night had gone for her. Instead of wonder, all she felt was alone and lonely. And ashamed.

Then she saw him, standing amidst a crowd of people, a head taller and twice as handsome as any of the men around him. She almost forgot her misery. She'd wanted desperately to push through the crowd and meet him, to know—just for a moment—what it would feel like to be the center of his attention.

She hadn't moved, of course, and he'd never even looked her way.

After the pageantry of the ball, the charity auction the next morning had been a subdued, quiet affair. Each participant, chosen for impeccable family name and inestimable wealth, had brought one item to be sold. That's when Juli had seen him again and learned his name. *Nicholas Sinclair.* And that's when she'd seen his paintings.

His work had touched her deeply, revealing a vulnerability that seemed wholly inconsistent with the Adonis-like man standing on the stage at the charity auction, surrounded by people who were everything Juli wasn't. In his art, she'd seen the same restless longing that marked her own life, the same emptiness that caused a thousand tiny, nameless aches in the middle of a cold dark night

She forced her thoughts back to the present, to her mother's sympathetic eyes.

"Oh, baby . . ." Tears welled in the older woman's eyes, "I'm sorry . . ."

Juli sighed. "I didn't meet Nicholas in San Francisco. I never had the courage to actually walk up to him, but after I wrote my column that month, I sent him a copy. I couldn't believe it when he wrote back." She smiled, remembering the exhilaration she'd felt when that first letter had arrived. "He said my comments on his paintings had gratified and, well . . . touched him. One letter led to another, then another. Before I knew it, we were corresponding regularly."

Mildred covered Juli's hand with her own. "Obviously he likes you, honey. So, what's the problem? Are you afraid he won't find you attractive?"

"I wish it were that simple, Mama. I . . . lied to him."

"About what?"

Juli bit down on her lower lip to keep it from trembling. "I was . . . ashamed of my life. Of myself. Oh, Mama, I'm sorry. It's just that when I got that first letter I looked around this house; at the shabby, ripped furniture, and the dirt beneath my fingernails, and . . . I just wanted to make it all go away. I wanted to be the kind of woman who would have *belonged* at that party. I wanted Nicholas to respect me." Her voice fell to a throaty whisper. "Who would respect someone like me?"

"What did you tell him?"

"I wanted my opinions to mean something to him; so I created a woman he could admire and respect. A wealthy, educated, adventurous journalist." Juli saw the pain in her mother's eyes, and it hit her like a physical blow. "I didn't think anyone would be hurt, Mama. I never believed we'd meet."

"Oh," her mother said in a quiet, saddened voice.

"I'm sorry, Mama. I *never* meant to hurt you."

"Oh, for God's sake, you two, quit yer snifflin'," Gladys interrupted loudly. "It ain't like she shot the President. She lied to a fella. Who hasn't?"

Mildred looked at Gladys. "Mom, she—"

"She's just a girl, Millie. Barely past twenty." She shot Juli a wink. "Now, I got an idea 'bout how to fix this mess. You know the Hanafords are out of town on family business? They're usually gone for at least a month." She turned to Juli. "How long is Nicholas plannin' to stay?"

Juli scanned the rest of the letter quickly. "He's arriving late Saturday afternoon and leaving first thing Monday morning. Why?"

"Perfect!" Gladys beamed. "He'll be here for the Ota-top festival."

Juli shook her head. "I can't see him, Grandma. He'll know I've been lying all this time. I've got to make an excuse for being out of town."

"Not necessarily. I'm sure the Hanafords wouldn't mind if we . . . borrowed their house. If we get the whole town together, we can show Nick exactly the Julianna Sparks you created."

Juli felt the beginning of a smile. "You mean *pretend* to be rich and educated?"

"Why not?"

Juli's heart was thumping so loudly it was hard to think. Her dreams tumbled back to her, one after another. *Time with Nicholas.* It had been her every wish, her every prayer.

She'd give anything to make it come true.

Still, it wasn't right . . .

"I don't know, Grandma. It means more lying."

"Lying-shmying," Gladys said with an airy wave of her plump hand. "It's magic. One measly little weekend with the man of your dreams. What could it hurt?" She leaned close, pressed a warm palm to Juli's face. "You deserve this tiny bit o' happiness, honey. Take it."

"I want to," Juli whispered.

"Think about it carefully," her mother warned. "Things

ain't usually so simple—especially not when it comes to lying."

Juli turned to her mother. She understood her mama's concerns, and if there were any other way, she wouldn't pretend or lie. But there was no other way; this was her one and only chance to meet Nicholas. "I just want what every girl wants, Mama: a chance to be Cinderella. Even if it's only for a few days. It can't hurt anyone, and I'll remember it all my life. When it's over, Nick and I can go back to our letters, and I'll have the memory of our time together. It's more than I ever expected."

"I only want you to be happy."

"I know that, Mama, and I love you for it."

"Okay, you two," Gladys cut in. "Before you get all weepy again, we got plans to make. Work to do."

"Work?" Juli and Mildred said at once.

Gladys gave them a crooked grin. "Course. It's Cinderella, ain't it? We got to turn a few potato farmers into footmen."

NICHOLAS SINCLAIR SETTLED DEEPER INTO the plush velvet of his seat and stretched his long legs out in front of him. The sideways swaying of the Pullman car and the hushed clackety-clack of the train's wheels grated irritatingly on his already taut nerves.

He stared down at the Waterford glass in his hand, noting with almost scientist-like detachment the length of his fingers and the perfection of his manicure. Disgust thinned his lips.

There was no paint on his hands, no dirt beneath his

nails, no darkening of his flesh by the sun. His were hands that did little more than lift a fork or pour a drink. Useless hands.

In an angry gesture, he tossed back the last of the drink and slammed the glass down on the table beside him.

"Are you all right, sir?"

Nick didn't spare a glance at the aging, snobby valet whose very presence was a reminder of Nick's "station."

"You can tell my father I'm fine." Turning, he glanced out the window. Dust caked the outside of the glass, obscuring all but the image of his own face. Narrowed, resentful blue eyes stared back at him. They were the eyes of a man who'd let himself be caged by other people's expectations and dulled by too much money.

But no more. He was taking his life back. It didn't matter what his father or grandfather thought, or what anybody thought. Nick was sick and tired of being unhappy.

In the past few months, the boring, useless pattern of his days had blurred into the senseless, alcohol-drenched cycle of his nights. He'd evolved into the one thing he'd always despised above all else: a playboy. A wastrel. He lived fast, talked a lot, drank too much. He no longer had any respect for himself.

Strangely enough, that's why he was on this train, hurtling through the countryside toward a town whose name he couldn't remember and a middle-aged woman he'd never met. In the past years, Julianna Sparks had come to mean something to him, something settling and lasting. With her, he could be himself. He could talk about his art, his dreams, his restless longings. Through the impersonal medium of their correspondence, he had found a kindred spirit, someone who expected more of him than good grooming and a thick wallet. And right now, Nick needed someone who expected something from him. It had been too long since he'd expected anything from himself.

He hoped that maybe some of her goodness, her honesty and integrity, would rub off on him. She was a woman who stood up to the world and did as she pleased. Julianna Sparks would never find herself trapped by someone else's expectations. She was a reporter, a woman who lived on the edge and made her own rules, and lived the truth. God, how he envied her.

# Two

Juli stood at the bedroom window, staring down at the sleepy little town that had been her home for twenty years. It lay shrouded in darkness, with only the barest hint of red-gold along the horizon to mark the coming dawn. Soon, the last remnants of nighttime would be shattered by the rising sun, and the new day would truly begin.

The new day.

Anticipation shivered through her. Today was the day she would meet Nicholas.

She shifted her weight from one foot to the other, too excited to stand still. Thoughts and hopes and expectations cascaded through her mind. She was pretty sure she was ready to meet him. She'd spent the last few days reading from sunup to sundown—everything from the stock market averages to etiquette rules were crammed in her brain.

She'd prepared something witty to say on any of a hundred topics.

She was ready.

Turning away from the window, she looked around, awed once again by the bedroom's opulence. A huge canopied bed, swathed in emerald green moire silk, dominated the center of the room. On either side stood intricately carved mahogany tables, their mirror-polished surfaces cluttered with all manner of gold and silver knickknacks. A beautiful painting of a woman on a thoroughbred horse graced the far wall, its vibrant colors a sharp contrast to the muted, elegant peach and ivory striped wallpaper behind it.

Even now, after hours spent in this room, she couldn't believe she was really here. It was the most breathtakingly beautiful place she'd ever seen. Standing here, she could almost make herself believe she belonged . . .

The secret she'd withheld from Mildred and Gladys surged to the forefront of her mind, bringing with it a bittersweet smile. She loved Nick; she had from the first moment she'd seen him, and every letter over the last few years had solidified her feelings until they were as strong and secure as a rock. As much a part of her as breathing.

She knew he didn't love her and she accepted that fact. She might be poor, uneducated, unsophisticated, but she wasn't stupid and she wasn't crazy. She and Nick could never be together. Besides, whatever his feelings might be, they weren't really for her. She was practical enough to know that.

He was a perfectly cut diamond that deserved—and demanded—a setting of only the finest quality gold. A dirt poor farmer's daughter would never do.

That's why his upcoming visit was so very precious. For the next few days, Juli could dress up in satin and jewels and make believe the world was different. That *she* was different.

For one bright, shining moment, she could pretend she belonged to the man she loved.

THE TRAIN PULLED, CLATTERING AND WHEEZ-ing, into Russetville. As the locomotive came to a complete stop, Nick glanced back at his valet, who was fast asleep in his window seat.

*Perfect.* He picked up his expensive leather portmanteau and the large wooden box that held his gift to Juli. Juggling the heavy items, he tiptoed down the aisle of his private car. At the door, he paused and hazarded a glance backward. His valet was still sound asleep, his pinched, pasty-white face smashed against the glass, his thin-lipped mouth hanging open.

Nick set his black fur fedora at a jaunty angle and disembarked from the train. He stepped down onto the platform just as the whistle blew. Turning to face the window, he rapped sharply on the thick, clouded glass.

His valet came awake with a start. Blinking rapidly, the old man looked around. As he spied his employer standing outside on the platform, the color washed from his cheeks.

"Mr. Sinclair—!" he mouthed, shaking his head in denial.

Nick waved as the train pulled away from the depot.

He sucked in a deep, cleansing breath of country air. For the first time in years, he felt free. There would be no narrowed eyes watching his every move, no tales being told behind his back. He could do whatever he wanted here, *be* whatever he wanted. He could paint.

Grinning broadly, he turned around and saw Russetville for the first time.

His smile faded. The station, a low, rickety wooden building badly in need of new paint, sat huddled alongside the platform. Two dirty windows parenthesized a cracked, half-open door.

The heavy wooden box slid from Nick's grip and landed on the platform with a *thunk*. Frowning, he glanced at the "town." Two-story brick buildings lined a muddy, pockmarked street. No people walked along the makeshift boardwalk, no horses stood at the hitching posts. It looked like a ghost town.

The sign told him he hadn't gotten off at the wrong stop. Yet, certainly, a well respected journalist like Julianna Sparks didn't live in this tumbledown town . . .

With a disappointed sigh, he bent to retrieve his box. As he straightened, he heard the creaking clip-clop of a horse and buggy coming toward him.

"Whoa, Gladiola," said a scratchy male voice.

Nick looked up and saw an unkempt man seated on a dilapidated wooden wagon. The dark-haired, thin-faced man was middle-aged, with skin that bespoke years of hard work beneath a hot sun. He leaned over the side of the wagon and spat a brown stream onto the road, then glanced at Nick. "You Sinclair?"

Nick nodded.

"I figgered so." He tilted his battered felt hat back and gave Nicholas a tobaccoey grin. "I'm George. Juli sent me to fetch you." A frown furrowed the sun-darkened flesh of his brow. "No, that ain't right. What I mean to say is, Miss Julianna Sparks sent me round to . . . convey you to your hotel."

"I'd . . . be much obliged."

"I figgered so."

Nick waited patiently for the driver to get down. When he didn't move, Nick glanced pointedly at his bag and box.

"Best get a move on." George tilted back his hat and spat another thick stream onto the street. It landed with a resounding *thwack* in a mud puddle. "And don't forget that bag. Looks expensive."

Nick glanced into the back end of the wagon. Mud, straw and fallen grain littered the slatted bed. A low layer of steam clung to a pile of fresh manure in one corner.

He winced. Hardly the ideal location for a $37.00 custom-made portmanteau. Holding his luggage firmly in hand, he eased the box over the edge of the platform and let it plunk to the street below, then he jumped down after it. The minute he hit the ground, he sank up to his ankles in oozing mud.

"Watch that mud there, it'll suck up a small goat."

Nick slogged through the mud to the wagon and climbed aboard. He'd barely gotten his things situated in the back when George snapped the reins hard.

The plow horse bolted forward.

Nick flew backward and slammed into the wooden-planked seat. His portmanteau slid into the pile of manure and stuck fast.

They were off.

GEORGE CAST A SIDEWAYS GLANCE AT NICK, but didn't say a word.

Nick shifted in his seat, discomfited by the man's scrutiny. He tried to think of something to say that would break the awkward silence. "Gladiola's an . . . odd name for a horse," he said for lack of anything better.

George drew back on the reins. The big gray plow horse came to a grudging halt in front of a two-story brick building. "Named her after my mother-in-law, Gladys. The two sorta have the same butt. Here we are," he said with a grin. "Spud House. They're waitin' for you."

Nick nodded. "Don't bother moving, George. I'll help myself down."

George gave him a sharp look. "Was I s'posed to help you before? Nobody told me."

Nick sighed and shook his head. "No, you did a fine job, George. Perfect."

His tanned face broke in a bright smile. "Thanks. I'll see you tomorrow tonight at the Otatop festival."

Nick tried to figure out what the hell an otatop was and why it would warrant a festival. "I can hardly wait."

"Yep, it's a humdinger, that's for sure."

Nick got down from the wagon and retrieved his belongings. Bag and box in hand, he went to the hotel's front door. As he reached for the knob, he thought he heard a rustle of activity and a harshly whispered "He's comin'."

Frowning, he turned the handle and went inside. The lobby was unusually dark.

"Goshdarnit! We forgot the lights." There was a flurry of footsteps from somewhere in front of Nick, and then a candle sputtered to life in the darkness. In the trembling halo of light, Nick made out half of a pudgy, smiling face.

"You Sinclair?"

Nick nodded, squinting for a better look. "I am. Do you have a reservation for me?"

The man laughed. "Yeah. Sure." He lit the other candles on his candelabra and then waddled to the center of the room to light a large brass lamp. Gradually the room became visible. It was a large, plank-floored place with a single settee that faced a dirty picture window. Two ragged chairs flanked the threadbare settee and a low-slung, crudely carved table stretched between them.

The man turned quickly and shoved a damp, fleshy hand at Nick. "Welcome to the Spud House. I'm Jemmy Wilson, the owner."

Nick shook the man's hand. "Call me Nick."

Jemmy bobbed his head and grinned.

The two men stared at each other in the half light. Nick waited for Jemmy to call for a man to take the bags. Who knew what Jemmy waited for.

Somewhere, someone cleared his throat.

At the sound, Jemmy perked up. "Oh, right. I'll show you to your room."

Nick grinned. "Good plan, Jemmy." He held his bag out to the man.

"Nice bag," he said. "Looks expensive." Then he turned and headed for the stairs, talking over his shoulder. "Miss

Julianna Sparks has invited you for a late supper. Her da— her *driver* will pick you up in about an hour."

Nick barely heard Jemmy's words. Slowly, he drew the portmanteau back and resettled the unwieldy box beneath his arm. He had obviously spent too much time in hotels like the St. Francis and restaurants like Delmonico's. He'd lost touch with how real people treated each other.

This was good, he told himself. So what if it wasn't what he expected. He'd wanted to break out of his staid, luxury-steeped life.

He just wished the box wasn't so damn heavy.

NICK FELT CONSIDERABLY BETTER AFTER A bath and a shave. The town wasn't as odd as he'd first thought—it couldn't be. The people weren't exactly . . . pictures of big-city comportment, but they didn't expect anything of him, either. And that was a relief.

There was a knock at the door. "Mr. Sinclair? Your carriage is here."

Nick stifled a smile at the characterization of George's wagon. "Thanks. I'll be right down."

"Good," There was a long pause, then Jemmy added as an obvious afterthought, "Sir."

Nick grabbed his hat and coat and headed for the door. Yanking it open, he strode out.

Jemmy was standing in the hallway, grinning. "Hi."

Nick skidded to a stop just in time. "Oh. Hello, Jemmy."

"I figured on leading you down."

Nick glanced sideways quickly, noticing there was no

third floor. The stairs led only one way—down. "Th-thanks."

"You bet." He nodded again, still grinning. "I just want to be the perfect host on this special day."

"An admirable goal," Nick said.

Jeremy lumbered down the stairs, crossed the empty lobby, and opened the door for Nick. "You'll like Miss Juli. Everybody does. She's pretty as a picture."

Nick paused. "Pretty?"

Jemmy nodded. "Prettiest gal in town."

Nick eyed the big man suspiciously. "You aren't related to her by any chance?"

"Nope, can't say as I am."

"Oh. Well, thanks, Jemmy. I'll be back after supper."

"No hurry. I won't wait up. Martha and me'll be decorating the wagon for the festival tomorrow night." Jemmy leaned close, giving Nick a proud smile. "The Princess rides in my wagon."

"Really?" Nick banked a smile. "That's . . . outstanding. Goodnight, Jemmy."

" 'Night, Mr. Sinclair."

Turning, Nick walked across the boardwalk and climbed onto George's rickety old wagon. Bracing himself this time, he sat steadily as Gladiola bolted forward.

As the horse settled into a slow, plodding gait, Nick's death grip on the wooden side eased. He leaned against the loose seat back and closed his eyes, listening to the sounds of the country: the slurping smack of the horse's shod hooves on the muddy road, the whining turn of rusted wheels, the creak of the wooden seat. In the distance, he heard the lowing of hungry cows and the whooshing current of a river. The sounds relaxed him, reminded him with every turn of the wagon wheels that he was here, in Russetville, and he was finally going to meet his best friend.

*Pretty.*

It was strange, but in all the times he'd pictured—or tried to picture—Miss Sparks, he'd never once thought of her as anything other than a thirty-five-year-old spinster with prematurely graying hair and spectacles.

*Pretty.*

He smiled. Somehow that single word changed everything.

JULI GAZED AT HERSELF IN THE MIRROR, UN-able to believe the transformation. Her ordinary brown hair was a down of curls and ringlets interwoven with tiny sapphire-hued bows. Beneath the dark mass, her skin looked almost translucent.

A soft, wistful smile shaped her mouth. Her grandmother had done it. She'd waved her magic wand and sprinkled fairy dust across Russetville and Juli. Tonight, for the whole town—but especially for herself—she was going to be Cinderella. And she was going to meet her prince.

*Tonight.*

She threw a nervous glance at the mantel clock. It was 6:49. He'd be here any minute.

She fought the urge to wring her hands together. (She was pretty sure it wasn't something a lady would do.) So, what did *ladies* do with enough nervous energy to heat a small room?

In a quick movement, Juli spun away from the mirror. Pacing back and forth across the plush carpet, she said a prayer over and over again. It was, like all her prayers, short and sweet and to-the-point.

*Please God, don't let me screw up.*

NICK RAPPED ON THE DOOR. AGAIN.

From behind the door came the sound of shuffling feet, and then a curious stillness.

Nick tried again.

This time the door was wrenched open so hard it banged against the wall. Inside, stood a stoop-shouldered old man in an ill-fitting servant's uniform. The man's eyes narrowed, sweeping Nick from head to foot in a single, judgmental glance. "You Sinclair?"

It was obviously the only greeting he was going to receive in Russetville. Sort of the country version of "Hello, how are you?"

"I am." Stepping forward, Nick pulled the hat from his head and handed it to the doorman.

The servant looked at the hat as if it were a live snake. "Sorta . . . furry, don't ya think?"

"Psst!" said a feminine voice from somewhere inside the house. "Take the damn hat."

The man yanked the expensive fur hat from Nick's hands. "I'll take that."

Nick stared at his hat, smashed against the man's concave chest, and wondered if it would ever fit his head again. "Is Miss Sparks home?"

"I hope to hell she is after all this trouble."

There was a loud gasp from the hallway. "Je-sus Christ, Jonas." Suddenly a stocky, gray-haired woman in a danger-ously tight black and white uniform barreled out of the kitchen and hurried toward them, her utilitarian heels click-ing matter-of-factly on the marble floor. The moment she saw Nick, her fleshy face broke into a bright, yellow-toothed grin. "Holy mother o' God, you're good lookin'."

Nick felt an unfamiliar heat crawl up his throat. He cleared his throat and wished fervently that Miss Sparks wouldn't keep him waiting long. This was the oddest set of servants he'd ever met.

The heavyset woman walked over to the doorman and elbowed him. Hard. "Idiot," she hissed, before turning a charming smile on Nick. "Can . . . I mean, *may* I take your coat?"

Nick shrugged out of his elegant caged black Mackintosh and handed it to the woman. She gazed down at the thick black wool, running her work-roughened fingers over it as if she'd never seen anything so fine.

Then she looked up. "I'm Gladys." She cocked her head at the man beside her. "This here's my husband, Jonas. We're the—"

"Poor slobs who—"

Gladys nudged her elbow in his gut. Jonas's breath ex-pelled in a tobacco-scented rush. She didn't miss a beat. "Servants."

Jonas glared at Nick. "No good comes from puttin' on airs. That's what I always say."

"The only thing you *always* say, you crotchety old man, is 'where's supper?' "

Nick was having a hell of a time not smiling.

Gladys turned her attention away from Jonas and focused her gray eyes on Nick. "You're even better'n we expected."

This time he couldn't help smiling. It was such a damn *odd* thing for a servant to say. Before he could say "thank you," Gladys threw his coat toward the upholstered settee against the wall. It hit with a hushed *thwack* and slithered to the floor.

"What were you aimin' for? The potted plant? Even *I* know you're supposed to hang it up, dear," Jonas said.

Gladys shrugged easily and looped her arm through Nick's, offering him a charming smile. "Come on."

She headed toward the foyer in a stride that would have made Stonewall Jackson proud. Nick bit back a grin and kept up.

At the edge of the sitting room, she stopped dead and turned so quickly, Nick felt light-headed.

"There she is."

Nick followed her gaze. At the top of the stairs stood a vision in jewel-toned blue. His breath caught, a tingling heat crawled through his blood.

Jemmy had been wrong. Dead wrong.

Julianna Sparks was a long way from pretty. She was stop-in-your-tracks gorgeous.

# Three

"He's looking at you," Mildred whispered.

Juli clung to her mother's arm for support. She wished desperately that she'd mentioned her poor eyesight in the letters to Nick. But *no*, she'd had to write that she was a sharpshooter on top of everything else. So, now her spectacles were tucked in the nightstand and she was as blind as a bat.

Suddenly Juli was afraid. She thought of all the mistakes she could make, the possible pitfalls. She was no lady. She turned to her mother. "Oh, Mama—"

"Ssh now. It's your Cinderella night. Have fun."

Juli forced herself to turn away from the safety of her mother's arm. Carefully she lifted her skirt—just the right amount to show an elegant shoe and no stocking—and took her first step toward the man of her dreams.

Unfortunately, without her spectacles, she misjudged the distance. Her tiny French heel came down on the edge of the step. In one split second, she realized she was going to fall. She flung her hands out for balance, but found none. With a shriek, she tumbled down the carpeted steps and landed with a *thunk* on the expensive oriental rug at the bottom of the stairs.

Nick surged toward her and kneeled. "Are you all right?"

His face swam in and out of focus. She caught sight of piercing blue eyes and a smear of jet black hair, and the colors sparked a dozen treasured memories. She'd had her spectacles on at the ball in San Francisco, and his every feature was seared into her brain. She didn't need her spectacles now to see his face. It was firmly set in her heart.

"Nicholas," she whispered, aching to reach up and touch his face, to feel the warmth of his skin against hers. She fisted her hand and bolted it to her side, afraid she'd embarrass herself even further by pawing him.

"That's our Juli," Gladys said. "She knows how to make an entrance."

Juli smiled up at Nick. "I've been practicing that fall for weeks. It's for a . . . circus act I've been writing a book about. Mr. Ringling has asked me to join. What do you think?"

Nick laughed. It was a rich, rumbling sound that seemed to wrap Juli in layers of warmth. "I must admit, I thought it was real. Here, may I help you up?"

"Yes, thank you." Juli wiggled to a sitting position and offered him her hand. When his fingers curled around hers, squeezing ever so slightly, she momentarily lost the ability to breathe. She wished fervently that she wasn't wearing gloves, that she could actually feel the warmth of his touch.

But, of course, gloves were the one necessity in the little charade.

A society columnist wouldn't have a potato picker's hands.

But that was something she didn't want to think about now. She got awkwardly to her feet and smoothed the thick blue satin of her gown.

"Juli?"

The rich timbre of his voice sent tingles down her back. Slowly she looked up. Their faces were close, inches apart. She felt the whisper-soft movement of his breath against her parted lips.

"It's good to finally meet you," he said.

Juli swallowed a lump of emotion and nodded. "It's nice to meet you, too, Nicholas. I've . . . waited a long time."

"I must admit, you're not how I pictured a wealthy, intrepid journalist."

"I'm not?"

He stepped even closer. Juli felt the brush of his sleeve against her bare arm. "You're so young and beautiful."

"Beautiful?" Juli bit her lower lip to keep it from trembling. No one but her mother or grandmother had ever called her beautiful before. Even her daddy just said she was pixie-cute. She felt a blush seeping across her cheeks and she looked away. "I don't know what to say . . ."

He leaned close—so close she could feel the warmth of his breath along her cheek. "How about thank you?"

She met his gaze. "Y-yes, that's it. Thank you."

Nick grinned and offered her his arm. "Shall we sit down?"

She looped her arm through his. "Certainly. The parlor is just through those doors."

Juli squinted hard, trying to see as she moved along beside Nick. She hoped she'd pointed at the right doors, but she couldn't be absolutely sure. The house was a blur of dark brown wood and clear glass and sparkling light. She gave a sigh of relief as they came to a stop in the sitting room.

Nick stood there, apparently staring at her as he withdrew the comforting support of his arm. He appeared to be waiting for something. For what? she wondered. What was she supposed to do?

*Sit down, you ninny.*

That was it. The lady sat down first. Smiling, Juli plucked up her skirts and started to sit.

"Aah!" Nick grabbed her hand and yanked her back to a stand.

Juli winced. *Damnation.* What in the world had she been about to sit down on—the fireplace tools? *Probably the poker.*

"H-here," he said. "Why don't you sit here?"

Mortified, Juli stumbled along beside him and sat down on the tufted burgundy velvet settee. He sat in the chair to the right of her. She brought her hands into her lap and twisted them into a nervous ball. *Sit straight. Don't fidget— a lady never fidgets. Smile politely and speak when spoken to.*

The rules turned through her head until she was half dizzy. The hardest one was not fidgeting. It was something that came quite naturally when she was nervous. And right now, she was as nervous as she'd ever been.

"I don't even know where to begin," Nick said. He propped his elbows on his bent knees and leaned toward her. "We're both nervous and unsure of how to act, but we shouldn't be. We've been friends for years."

"You're nervous, too?"

He laughed. "As a schoolboy."

The anxiety coiled in Juli's stomach released itself. She took a deep breath and smiled. "Thank you."

"For what?"

"You said that to calm me down."

"And did it?"

She laughed easily. "Yes."

"I'm glad. But the truth is, Juli, I *am* nervous. I came out here because you meant something to me. I came to find a wise, independent, honest older woman who would help me set my life back in order. And what do I find?"

Juli swallowed hard. "What?"

"A beautiful young woman who could have my heart with the snap of her fingers."

Juli let out her breath in a dreamy sigh. She leaned forward. He did the same. Their gazes locked.

Suddenly the door banged open. Jonas stood in the doorway. Juli couldn't see her grandad's face, but she was pretty sure he was frowning.

"Supper's ready," he growled.

Juli popped back into her seat, settling a respectable distance away from Nick. "No, it's not, Gran—Jonas."

"It ain't? Your cook said it was."

Juli realized her error instantly. "It's only just seven o'clock, Jonas."

"You said supper was at seven."

"Seven means around eight or eight-thirty," she explained.

"Well that's the dog-damndest thing I ever heard." He leaned against the doorjamb, and even through her blurry vision, Juli could see that he had no intention of going anywhere.

Nick saved the situation. "Perhaps you could get us some tea and biscuits to sustain us until supper?"

"Sustain you?" Jonas snorted. "Well, if that don't beat all. Supper's ready right now—all hot and good-smellin'—and you two wanna wait 'til eight-thirty to eat it, but you want a snack to *sustain* you. Missy, your *cook* ain't gonna be happy about this."

Nick got to his feet and offered a hand to Juli. "Maybe we should eat now?"

Juli gave him a relieved smile. "Perhaps that would be best."

Jonas nodded. "Well, I hope to shout it is. Damn rich-folks rules." He turned and headed toward the dining room.

As they followed Jonas, Nick leaned down to Juli and whispered, "They've been in your family a while, haven't they?"

Juli laughed. "You could say that."

NICK SETTLED DEEPER INTO THE PLUSH CHAIR at the head of the long table and stared down the polished wooden surface at Juli. She was staring at him intently. At least, he *thought* she was staring at him. All he could see was the top of her head and her blue, blue eyes focusing on him from above the ridiculously huge floral centerpiece.

Silence stretched the length of the table. Juli leaned sideways and peered past the flowers. She smiled, then frowned and squinted at him.

"Nick?" Her tone of voice was odd. Almost hesitant. As if she thought perhaps he'd left the table.

"I'm right here," he answered. *Just west of New Jersey.*

"It's certainly a long table," she offered.

"It certainly is. Do you think—"

Jonas barged into the room. The elegant windowed doors cracked against the wall and rattled ominously. "You want some wine?" he asked.

Nick stared at the old man, wondering what he had against guests. "That would be fine."

Jonas cocked his graying head toward Juli. "*She* don't get none."

Juli gasped. "Jonas!"

He spun on her with amazing speed for one so old. "Remember your allergy, miss. How just a whiff o' spirits makes you puke?"

Juli's face turned flamingly red. "*Puke?*"

Jonas tugged at his white collar, as if it were suddenly overtight. He shot a nervous glance at Nick. "Er . . . throw up?"

Juli forced a smile. "Fine. I'd forgotten about my . . . allergy. I appreciate your reminding me. I'll not have a glass of wine, thank you, Jonas."

A satisfied smile stretched through the old man's wrinkled cheeks. "I din't think so, miss. Very good." Turning, he hurried from the room and returned a few moments later with a dusty green bottle.

He stopped directly beside Nick. "This 'ere one looked

the oldest, and that's what Juli tole me to get." He lifted the bottle and blew hard on the label.

Dust flew at Nick's face in a cloudy puff.

Jonas seemed unaware that he'd blinded his guest. "It's somethin' called port. Is that good enough fer the likes o' you?"

Nick tried to open his eyes and couldn't. He nodded instead. "That'll be fine, Jonas."

"Good." Jonas poured a ridiculous amount of the after-dinner drink in Nick's glass, then set the bottle down with a resounding clunk. "I'll be back."

Nick watched him leave through a painful blur.

Juli peered around the flowers again. "Is something wrong?"

Nick blinked hard, feeling gritty tears pool in the corners of his eyes. Pulling out his handkerchief, he wiped his eyes and shook his head. "Everything's fine."

She immediately smiled. "Good."

They lapsed into another long silence. Finally Nick couldn't stand it anymore. "Do you think we could get rid of the flowers?"

She looked momentarily confused. "Flowers?"

He pointed toward the centerpiece.

"Oh! The flowers. Certainly." She got to her feet and felt her way along the table. Taking the crystal vase in her hands, she very carefully—inordinately carefully, Nick thought—moved the arrangement onto the sideboard. Then, with an almost triumphant smile, she returned to her seat. He got the odd, but rather distinct impression that she'd been afraid of missing the sideboard.

"Did you know that this year the United States is producing more pig iron than Great Britain?" she said suddenly.

Nick was so surprised by her choice of topic, he could only stare at her. "Really?"

She blushed. "I remembered you telling me once that your family had an interest in iron, so I knew you'd be interested. Why, just the other day I was reading about . . ."

Nick couldn't believe it. She'd done research to find a topic of conversation that would interest him. At the realization, a thread of warmth curled around his insides. Of course, she couldn't know that the family "interest" in iron extended to stock ownership alone, and that Nick himself cared nothing whatsoever about any metal—including gold.

But that was unimportant. What mattered was the fact that for the first time in his life, Nick felt special. This young woman, whom he'd never even met before, had given him the one thing his parents had never even attempted: attention. For whatever period of time she'd spent reading about pig iron, Nicholas Sinclair had been important to her.

He felt a slow smile start. Her words rambled together in his mind, becoming a swirling, confusing mass. But it didn't matter because he wasn't listening to her. He was memorizing her. Everything about her; the way her blue eyes sparkled with happiness over his feigned interest, the way her perfect, rose-colored lips moved as she spoke, the almost absentminded way she tossed a wayward lock of hair from her eyes.

"You're beautiful," he whispered, surprised to realize he'd spoken aloud.

Juli sputtered something about the care required in handling molten metal and looked up at him. Their gazes locked

across the table and for an instant—a split second, really—
it was as if they were alone in the world.

The spell was broken by Gladys as she pushed a heavily
laden, clanking tea cart into the room.

Disappointment flashed through Nick. He eased back into
his chair.

"It smells delicious, Gladys," Juli said.

Gladys's wrinkled brow crinkled even more. "Yeah. I
hope so. The damn—er, darn glass is sorta small. I don't
know . . ."

Nick glanced down at the cart and almost burst out laughing. He covered his near-miss with an extended bout of
coughing.

Gladys slapped him on the back. Hard. "You okay,
sonny?"

He swallowed the last of his laughter and nodded.

The maid looked at him, then at her two plates of food.
"Somethin's wrong, ain't it?"

Nick chewed on his lower lip. "Pheasant under glass?"
he guessed.

"Chicken, actually. We couldn't find no pheasants."

Nick eyed the food. "What are those things on top of
the birds—pickle bowls?"

"Yep. They're glass, sure as sugar beets, but they don't
quite fit, do they?"

Nick's lips twitched traitorously. "Not quite."

She turned to him. "It doesn't matter, does it?"

The uncertainty in her voice touched Nick, reminded him
that she was offering her best. And that was more important
than perfect preparation of pheasant under glass. "No,

Gladys, it doesn't matter a bit. But, you know what does matter?"

"What?"

He crooked his finger. "Come closer."

She shuffled sideways and bent toward him. "What?"

"There's a beautiful woman at the other end of the table, but she's so damn far away I can barely see her."

Gladys grinned. "Yep, I can see where that's a bit of a problem."

"What are you two whispering about down there?" Juli demanded.

"Come on down here, girl," Gladys said with a wave of her hand, "this here gentleman wants to see you better."

"Oh." Juli got to her feet and made her slow, hesitant way down the length of the table. Near the chair, Gladys grabbed her by the arm and maneuvered her into her seat.

"That's much better," Nick said.

Juli blinked owlishly at him. "It certainly is."

Without another word, Gladys served the meal of chicken-under-glass-pickle-bowls, fresh green peas swimming in butter, mashed potatoes, piping hot biscuits, and applesauce. Then she turned to leave.

Nick got a clear picture of her . . . healthy backside. He bit back a smile at the sight. "Gladys, you aren't by any chance George's mother-in-law, are you?"

Gladys spun around and drilled Nick with her eyes. "You comparin' my butt to that damn horse's?"

Nick almost spit up his port. "Uh . . . no."

Gladys burst out laughing. "I'll take you to task for that someday, sonny."

Nick grinned up at her, relieved by her easy laughter. "I don't doubt that in the least, Gladys."

Chuckling, she left the room. Nick and Juli stared at each other for a long, awkward moment, then both began to eat.

"So," Nick said between bites, "tell me about Rome."

"Ed Roam? The butcher? How do you—"

Nick laughed. "Rome, Italy. You just got back from there. How did you like it?"

Her smile seemed to freeze in place. "Of course, I don't know what I was thinking. Rome was . . . fabulous. That statue of David—"

"Florence."

"No, David. Michelangelo's statue."

Nick frowned at her. "That's in Florence."

Juli dropped her fork. A blush crawled across her cheeks. "Oh, right. Well, the trip was such a dizzying blur, the cities sort of blend. You know how it is." She glanced at him sharply. "Don't you?"

"Of course." He took a sip of the port.

She pushed her plate aside. Propping an elbow on the table, she rested her cheek in her gloved hand and gazed up at him. "Tell me about your painting."

Nick's response to the innocently uttered question was lightning fast. Pleasure seeped through his body like the port had, leaving in his blood a swirling, heated wake. God, he'd waited so long for someone to ask about his painting, for someone to *care* about what he cared about.

For years, he'd told himself it didn't matter what other people thought, but now, in this darkened dining room with Juli at his side, he saw the truth. It did matter; it mattered a lot.

"That article you wrote about my paintings," he said softly, finding his voice embarrassingly husky, "it meant . . . a lot to me."

*More than a lot.* Even now, years later, the memory of that simple article had the power to warm the dark, lonely spots in Nick's soul.

"You're so talented, Nick. Every time I read about an art exhibit, I expect you to be listed as a participating artist, but you never are. Why is that?"

Nick picked up a fork and pushed the food around on his plate. "You're the only person who thinks I'm any good, Juli."

"What about you, Nick? Don't you think you're good?"

Nick sighed. It was a question he asked himself all the time—every time his father ranted and raved and called him a "no-talent."

"I don't know . . ."

Juli leaned toward him. Their eyes met. "Yes, you do."

Her blue eyes beseeched him silently to be honest, with her and with himself. He thought about her life, her integrity and her honesty. Julianna Sparks wouldn't run from the truth. He'd traveled a thousand miles to draw upon her strength, and by God, he wouldn't walk away now.

Her presence, her quiet assurance and acceptance, gave Nick a courage he'd never found before. He looked deep within himself, deeper than ever before, and there, buried beneath a lifetime's worth of doubt, was a grain of certainty. "I could be good," he said quietly, half afraid she'd laugh. When she didn't, he added, "All I need is training. A year or two in Paris, and who knows?"

"Paris." The word slipped from her mouth in a wistful sigh. "It must be so beautiful there."

"Have you ever been there?"

She drew in a sharp breath. "Have I?"

He frowned. "I just meant, you've never written to me about Paris . . ."

She smiled suddenly. "Of course, I haven't. I've never been there. But I've read everything there is to read about it." Her eyes lit up. "Can you imagine the Louvre? Seeing the Venus de Milo and Winged Victory and the Mona Lisa . . ." She blushed again and looked away. "I'm sorry, I must be boring you."

Impulsively he touched her cheek in a featherstroke-soft caress. "Never."

Nervously she wet her lower lip. But she didn't look away. "You're being polite. Ladies don't go on about museums. We're supposed to talk about needlework and charity balls."

"I've never cared much about ladies, and less about needlework. I care about people, about how they think and feel about life, about art. I care . . . about you."

Her gaze dropped to her plate. "You don't even know me."

"Are you joking? We've been writing to each other for years. I know you as well as I know myself. There's been many a time in my life when I found myself asking *what would Julianna Sparks do in this instance?* Truly, your honesty and integrity and fearlessness have been my light in a dark world."

"My . . . honesty." Juli squeezed her eyes shut for a moment, surprised by the swift stab of pain his words brought. Beneath the concealing ledge of the table, her gloved hands curled into fists.

*Don't think about it. If you do, you'll go mad.*

She took a deep breath and forced herself to look at him. "It means a lot to me that you like my letters." Her voice was soft, with only the barest hint of a tremble in it.

"I can't imagine life without them."

Juli tried to smile. "Neither can I."

Indeed, it was her biggest fear that someday Nick would marry and their special correspondence would end. He was *her* light in a cold, dark, poverty-stricken world, and she couldn't imagine the emptiness of her life without his letters.

Nick put down his fork and took another sip of port. "Tell me something about you, Juli. Something special."

"I want to go to cooking school in Paris. I know it sounds silly, but cooking is something I do well. I love it."

"So, we both have dreams of going to Paris," he said softly, smiling enigmatically above the rim of his wineglass.

The observation jolted Juli. It seemed so . . . intimate. A thread of warmth slid through her, bringing a smile to her lips.

Their conversation spun out from there, gliding from topic to topic with the ease of long-time friends. They sat at the table for hours. Nick drinking port and Juli sipping tea. They talked of many things, important and unimportant, deadly serious and hilariously funny.

The evening was everything Juli hoped it would be. Oh, deep inside her, there was still an ache—a longing for that which she could never have—but it spoke to her in a small, weak childish voice that was easily ignored. Especially on so magical a night.

# Four

Nicholas was wakened by the sound of someone pounding on his door. Bleary-eyed, he pushed to his elbows amid the mass of pillows. The battered Bee Nickel clock beside his bed came slowly into focus. Seven o'clock. A.M.

He swore softly. No wonder people moved into cities. The hours were better.

"Who is it?"

"It's me, Juli. I've brought you breakfast."

Nick's heart did a strange little flip at the sound of her voice. "I'll be right out."

"Dress warmly."

He tossed back the thick eiderdown coverlet and got out of bed. After quickly brushing his teeth at the crockery washbasin and running a comb through his unruly black hair, he donned a charcoal-colored wool cutaway suit and hurried to the door.

Juli was standing on the landing, waiting for him. The sight of her was like a breath of fresh air. He smiled.

She backed up, her hands twisting together at the movement. "I-I hope I'm not unfashionably early . . ."

Her shyness sparked a surge of protectiveness in Nick. For all her strength and grit, she looked incredibly vulnerable right now, almost afraid.

*She needs me.* The thought surprised him. It went against everything he'd ever believed of Julianna Elizabeth Sparks, and yet, somehow he knew it was true, knew that deep down, she was as lost and lonely as he.

*And you need her.* The second the words sped through his mind, he expected to combat them with cold, rational arguments about how little he needed anyone.

But none came to mind.

Nick smiled at her. "I couldn't wait to see you, either."

A hesitant hope filled her eyes. For a moment he felt as if he were tumbling head-first into those fathomless blue pools. He gave himself a mental shake and moved toward her, his arm outstretched. "Where are we going, mademoiselle?"

Looping her arm through his, she smiled up at him. "Paris, monsignor."

He laughed with an ease that was completely foreign. "I think you mean *monsieur*."

She missed a step, then paused, looking up at him with a worried frown. "Really?"

He laughed again, and damn, it felt good. "Really."

She gave a small shrug and took a hesitant step downward, her gaze pinned on the dark wood beneath her feet.

When they reached the bottom, she let out a sigh of relief. "We're here."

"You sound as if it's unexpected. Did you expect to get lost?"

She laughed. "It would not have surprised me. Now," she said, pulling a length of fabric from her pocket. "I'm going to blindfold you."

"What?"

She pressed up on her tiptoes and tied a soft flannel strip across his eyes. The sudden darkness made his other senses come alive. He felt the feather-softness of her breath against his lips, sensed the warm outline of her body pressed so closely to his. The jasmine-scent of her hair filled his nostrils.

"There. How's that?"

"Fine. But what—"

She pressed a warm finger against his parted lips. Then, slipping her hand around his waist, she called out. "We're ready."

The hotel door creaked open. Footsteps shuffled across the woolen floor.

Nick smiled. "You need help to lead me to the door, Juli?"

"Only if I want to find it," was her enigmatic reply.

Nick allowed Juli and the mystery man to lead him across the hotel lobby and outside onto the boardwalk. It was surprising how much he enjoyed the game. He couldn't remember the last time he'd done something so wistful and childish. It was fun.

Suddenly Juli stepped. "We're in front of a wagon, Nick. I'll help you up."

She guided him into the wagon's manure-pungent bed. They sat side-by-side on a rough woolen blanket, their backs tilted against two rickety wooden slats.

There was a harsh *whkk* sound, then a splatter.

Nick grinned. "Hi, George."

A man's throaty chuckle floated in the air. "Hiya, Mr. Sinclair. You ain't no dunderhead, are you?"

"Darn it, George, I asked you not to spit," Juli said.

"I know, missy, and I'm sorry. But sometimes a man jest has to. Ain't that right, Mr. Sinclair?"

Nick kept a straight face by sheer force of will. "Either that or bust, George."

Juli gave a delicate snort. "Well, if either one of you feels the busting urge to spit, I hope you'll point your mouth downwind."

George laughed quietly. Nick heard the creaking sounds of the older man turning forward in his seat, then the snapping crack of the reins. There was a momentary lull before the wagon lurched forward.

They bumped along deeply rutted country roads for about an hour. All the while Juli and Nick spoke quietly, their heads bent together.

Finally, George reined Gladiola to a halt.

Nick breathed deeply of the clean, fresh air. He heard the telltale creak of George turning around in his seat.

"Here we are, pumpkin. Paree."

"George," Juli answered with a laugh, "a good *driver* doesn't call his employer 'pumpkin.' "

"Course he don't," George answered.

Nick reached up to remove his blindfold. "May I take this off now?"

Juli stayed his hand. "Not yet. George, help Nick down, would you? I've got a few things to do." She rustled around for a few moments, then got to her feet and made her creaking, thumping way from the wagon.

"What's she carrying?" Nick asked, hearing the wheezing sound of her breath and the occasional *thud* of something heavy hitting the wooden boards. "A cannon?"

George's spit hit the ground with an unmistakable *thwack*. "Ain't none o' my bizness. Come on, young fella. Let me help you down."

Nick allowed George to guide him down from the wagon. The older man led the way across a rolling field, toward the sound of rushing water.

"By the way, George, I met your mother-in-law."

"Course you did. Was I right about the butt?"

"I think I'd best decline to answer that."

George laughed. "No wonder you're a millionaire. Yeah, she has a butt on her, that Gladys, but her heart's pure gold." He came to a stop. "Here he is, Julianna."

Nick heard footsteps coming toward him, and his heart picked up its pace. A foolish grin spread across his face. He was acting like a callow youth on his first date, and he couldn't have cared less. It felt good to care about something again. To be happy.

"Thanks, George," Juli said. "You'll be back in . . . an hour?"

There was a sputtering sound of disbelief from the old man. "I ain't goin' nowhere, missy. It wunt be proper."

"George, we all agreed—"

"I din't agree to leave my baby gi—"

"*George*—"

He cleared his throat. "I mean, I din't agree to leave my *young* employer stranded up here with a fella I don't know nothin' about. Oh, no, missy. I did *not* agree to that."

Nick struggled with a smile. It was really touching the way everyone in town watched out for Juli. "George is right, Juli. It wouldn't be proper for us to be un-chaperoned."

Juli let out an irritated sigh. "Fine. George, you go sit in the wagon." She waited a beat, then added firmly, "Quietly. And no spitting."

"Good nuf."

Nick listened to George's footsteps as he made his way back to the wagon.

Juli came up beside Nick. She was muttering something quietly, but he couldn't make out the words. She reached up behind him and untied the blindfold.

The flannel slipped away from his eyes. He blinked hard at the unexpected brightness. It took him a minute to focus on his surroundings, but when he did finally get a good glimpse of the world around him, his breath caught. "Good God . . ."

"It's beautiful, isn't it?"

He looked around. The field was a rich, lush green dotted with red-gold maple leaves. A frothy white waterfall spewed past a barricade of granite blocks and tumbled downward, melting into a swirling, pewter-hued pool. Behind it all was a craggy, snowcapped peak that obliterated all but the hardiest rays of the sun. Cool gray clouds scudded overhead, leaving a series of dancing shadow-like shapes on the surface of the water.

Slowly, he turned to look down at her. She was looking

up at him through eyes that held nothing back. In the clear blue depths, he saw a longing that mirrored his own.

She smiled and pointed over to his right. "Look."

He turned. There, in the center of the field was a wooden easel with a large academy board on it. An inexpensive box of oil paints and brushes lay in the grass beside it.

"It's from my grandparents," she said quietly.

A warming sense of wonder crept through Nick. He looked down at Juli and felt a surge of longing so sharp and strong his knees almost buckled from the force of it. Emotion filled his throat and kept words at bay.

She was offering him so much more than she knew. It wasn't just a piece of paper and a few paints. It was acceptance, an unconditional belief in him and his talent.

Such a little thing, he thought. And so damn big. For the first time in his life, he felt as if he mattered to someone. Self-confidence surged through his blood, and its sudden presence was like a bright light, reminding him how long he had lived in the darkness, alone and lonely. Now, with her standing beside him, he felt as if he could do anything.

"What will you paint?" she asked. "The waterfall, the sky . . . what?"

He shook his head. "I'll paint the most beautiful thing here."

"What's that?"

He touched her face. "You."

"THERE'S A BUG ON MY LIP."

"Don't move." Nick frowned. The arch of her eyebrow wasn't quite right.

"I think it's a bee."

He added a dab of brown paint. Much better. "Is it buzzing?"

"No. I think it's getting ready to sting."

Nick laughed and looked up from his painting. Juli was sitting on a bright red blanket atop the grass. Fallen leaves in a dozen autumn hues lay scattered around her. She was frozen in the position in which he'd placed her. And there was a horsefly on her lower lip.

"Don't move," he commanded. Setting down his paintbrush, he walked across the pasture and kneeled beside her. Moisture from the dewy grass seeped through his pantleg and chilled his skin. He barely noticed.

At the movement, the horsefly disappeared.

She flashed him a bright smile. "Can I see it yet?"

"The horsefly?"

She laughed. The sound filled the clearing and knocked at Nick's tired heart. "No, silly. The painting."

As he stared at her, a painful sense of longing seeped through him. Never in his life had he wanted to kiss a woman more. She looked incredibly lovely right now, with her hair let down and her lips curved in a smile. And her eyes, sweet God, her eyes . . .

It wasn't just that they were big and blue and fringed by thick black lashes. Beautiful women were commonplace in San Francisco society. It was what he saw *in* her eyes that made her so extraordinarily attractive. Caring, compassion, humor. All the things he'd searched for in his own life and so rarely found.

He'd never felt as free as he did with her.

"Nick?" she said. "Can . . . I mean, *may* I see the paint-ing yet?"

He pushed to his feet and offered her a hand. "Of course. But don't expect much."

She brushed the leaves from her skirt and placed her gloved hand in his. Together they walked toward the easel.

With each step, Nick felt his gut knot up tighter. Nerves twisted his stomach and dampened his palms.

At the last moment, he stopped. He couldn't do it, couldn't reveal himself so completely. Not even to her.

Juli looked up at him. "What is it, Nick? Don't you want me to see it?"

*I want you to like it.* The ridiculous thought made him feel weak and stupid. "Yes," he said quietly. The small word eased the burden from his shoulders. Once he'd said it he felt stronger, more in control.

"Are you sure?"

He looked down at her, and knew he'd never been more sure of anything in his life. "I'm sure."

Juli stepped around Nick and looked at the painting. A small gasp escaped her. She clasped a pale, shaking hand to her throat. "Oh, my Lord."

"What?" he asked sharply.

She looked up at him through huge, earnest eyes. "It's magnificent."

Nick was so relieved he laughed out loud. "Thanks."

"Is . . . is that how you see me?"

He looked at the painting, then at Juli, wondering what error she found in his work. "Isn't it how you see yourself?"

She laughed, but it was a small, self-deprecating sound that inexplicably tugged at his heart. "Only in my dreams."

Nick frowned. There it was again: that unexpected vulnerability. He moved toward her. Taking her face in his bands, he forced her to meet his steady gaze. "You're much more beautiful than my painting."

"What if I weren't in this expensive gown?"

With the question came an instant image. Nick almost said *I wish*, but then he noticed the earnestness in her eyes and he paused. For some strange reason, this absurd question was important to her. "What do you mean?"

"I mean, what if I were wearing a worn, patched flour-sack skirt and had dirt under my fingernails?"

Nick smiled, relieved that it was nothing serious. "After all my letters, surely you know the answer to that question."

She seemed to deflate before his eyes. Her shoulders sagged. "Yes, Nick. I do know the answer."

He slipped an arm around her waist and drew her close. "Good. Now, what do you say we delve into that picnic basket I see?"

She nodded, but didn't look up at him. "Certainly, Nick. That sounds wonderful."

SUNSET DRIZZLED ACROSS THE PASTURE IN hazy streaks of red and gold as the wagon headed for home.

Juli sat beside Nick, her legs drawn casually up to her chin, her arms wrapped around her ankles. There was a wistful, faraway look in her eyes that roused his curiosity.

"I want to know everything about you, Julianna Sparks," he whispered.

She flinched and cast him a guilty look. "Y-you do."

Nick laughed quietly. "I was joking. I know a lady has to have her secrets."

He sidled closer to Juli, feeling the heat of her body against his. He turned his head, slightly, slowly, trying to see her better in the quickly fading light. She was close; close enough to kiss. Her perfect profile was like an ivory cameo against the darkening sky beyond.

God, how he wanted to kiss her right now, *ached* to kiss her. And yet, for the first time in his life, he was nervous.

This wasn't like the other times; Juli wasn't like the other women. She was different. As fresh and important as the first day of spring is to the last cold night of winter. He didn't want to frighten her away.

She turned to him. Their eyes met, and in the sapphire depths he saw a restless longing that mirrored his own.

"Nicholas . . ." His name was but a whisper of promise, a question unasked. Her breath grazed his cheek, left a trail of warmth. "Kiss me."

He couldn't believe it. A groan slipped up his throat. He moved closer. His lips brushed hers in a hesitant sweep, lingering barely long enough to savor her sweetness. "Come with me to Paris," he whispered against her lips.

She pulled away. "Don't say that, Nick." There was an odd, desperate tone to her voice.

Nick worked to calm the erratic racing of his heart. The taste of her lips, like wildflowers and light, remained on his mouth, the jasmine scent of her filled his nostrils. He thought fleetingly of all the women he'd kissed, all the women he'd courted and sat beside in a gilded scrolled carriage, all the women he'd slept with. And now, just like with all the others, he felt a heady sense of sexual attraction, a building heat in his groin.

And yet, he felt something more. Something so tentative and frightening it filled him with awe. Never in his life had he felt this compelling sense of well-being, of peace and relaxation. Of coming home.

Smiling, he curled an arm around Juli and drew her close. She melted against him. Together they leaned back against the wagon and stared at the falling darkness.

The memory of the kiss was so consuming, it took Nick a few minutes to remember what he'd asked of her. What she'd denied him.

"Why can't I ask you to come to Paris with me?"

She laughed, but it sounded forced, almost bitter. "I'm not that kind of woman."

Nick frowned. It was a pat answer. Not really an answer at all.

An evasion, he realized. Not at all the sort of thing he would have expected from Julianna Sparks.

# Five

Juli stood at the Hanaford's bedroom window, staring down at Front Street. The town was abuzz with activity. Floats were being decorated for the upcoming parade, people were running around for last-minute costume adjustments.

Normally the scene would have made her smile. But tonight was a long way from normal.

She hugged herself tightly, fighting a sudden chill from within. Today with Nick had almost broken her heart. It was beginning to hurt just to look at him.

*Come with me to Paris.*

She never thought she'd hear those words from him. They should have filled her with happiness; instead they brought an almost crushing sense of regret and pain.

She'd been wrong to lie. Terribly, desperately wrong. She saw that now. The lies were an invisible wall between her and Nick, every deception a brick that kept them apart.

When she'd started this charade, all she'd wanted was a

few nights of make-believe, a chance to be Cinderella. She'd thought there was no risk. She and Nick would spend a couple of fun-filled, bittersweet days and then go their separate ways—it had made such perfect, exciting sense to her.

Now, however, she saw that she'd been wrong. Everything was at risk. If Nick found out about her lies, it would all come crashing down around her, burying her in the rubble of her own deceit.

The letters—the friendship—would stop.

The thought filled her with horror. Nick and his letters were all she had. All she cared about . . .

"Oh, God," she whispered. Her breath clouded the pane, obscured the outside world.

She couldn't tell him the truth now, not even if she wanted to. If she did, she'd lose it all.

She had to keep her head up, keep smiling. Keep pretending.

"It's only another day," she said aloud. "You can do it."

But even as she said the words, she wondered if they were true.


TODAY HAD BEEN ABSOLUTELY PERFECT. NICK couldn't remember when he'd had a better time.

He smiled, thinking about the day, about Juli's carefree laughter, her beauty, her caring. After the picnic, he'd returned to his painting, and when he finished, they sat beside the pool, talking and laughing. They hadn't talked about anything earth-shattering or world-altering; just things.

They'd been together for hours, and yet now, as he sat

in the sitting room of Spud House, waiting for George to pick him up he couldn't wait to see her again.

"Hi, Mr. Sinclair." Jemmy Wilson's voice broke into Nick's thoughts.

Nick looked up. Surprise rendered him momentarily speechless. There was a tall, fat green thing looking down at him through ragged eye holes.

Nick tried unsuccessfully not to smile. "Jemmy?"

The green woolen sack with a thorny crown nodded. "Do I look like a zucchini?" he asked in a worried tone. "Last year's costume was too tight, so I had to make another one. I think it looks a bit too . . . pepper-like."

"A zucchini was my first impression."

"Phew. Well, I gotta go. The vegetables are first."

Nick nodded solemnly. "They would be."

"Yeah, but sometimes the fruits get tricky—and the tomatoes always try to lead." He tried to wave. The movement was a ripple of the green sack. "See yah at the festival."

"I'll certainly be able to find you," Nick said, watching Jemmy waddle away.

As the door closed behind Jemmy, Nick finally let himself grin. He shook his head. What the hell kind of man appeared in a zucchini costume with no stammering excuses?

The answer came easily: A man happy to be a zucchini.

Nick's grin flattened. Suddenly it wasn't funny. It was . . . humbling. He crossed to the big window and stared outside at the slow-moving Snohomish River and the endless green and yellow fields beyond. This was such a quiet little town: a place where people lived as they wanted and dressed as they cared to.

Jemmy didn't care what Nick—or anyone—thought. He wanted to be a vegetable in the legendary Otatop festival, and damn it, he wore the ridiculous suit with pride.

It was exactly that kind of ease and self-confidence Nick had sought all his life. And Jemmy Wilson, innkeeper-cum-zucchini, had Nick beat to hell on that one.

No, Nick thought. There was nothing to grin about.

Behind him, the door creaked open. An early evening breeze wafted into the room, bringing with it the rustling flutter of autumn leaves and the fecund scent of moist earth.

Nick grabbed his coat and turned around. George was standing in the door in a dull orange sack with slitted eye holes.

"Hiya, Mr. Sinclair. You ready?"

"I am." Nick grinned suddenly. "Get it? I *yam*."

George laughed. "Let's go. The vegetables are first."


JULI STARED AT THE EXQUISITE GOWN DRAPED across the bed. The rich moirè fabric shone like a sheet of polished copper against the bed's deep green coverlet.

She should start getting dressed. Nick would be here any moment.

But she couldn't move. She could only stand there, her hands twisted together, her gaze pinned to the expensive walking suit. Anxiety was a freezing cold knot in her stomach.

She couldn't pull off the charade tonight. If Nick touched her, or kissed her, or asked her to come with him to Paris again, she'd burst out crying and ruin everything.

She'd never felt so miserable in her life. Now she truly

understood why lying was a sin. In the past, her little fabrications had never seemed like lying. The whole town loved it; Juli took the ordinary facts of their dull, hard-working existence and transformed them into a fictionalized fantasy.

SOCIETY MAVEN GLADYS FIPPERPOT HOSTS
 Tea for Town Officials
 Elegant Masquerade Ball Held by George and Mildred
  Sparks
Postmaster Jim Butterman Overwhelmingly Re-elected to
 Third Term

HEADLINES LIKE THESE HAD FUELED THE town's imagination for more than four years. Juli loved the challenge of taking the mundane and making it seem extraordinary. And her readers cherished her every word.

But now, looking back, it didn't seem like fiction as much as it seemed like lying. She'd been lying to herself, and everyone, for as long as she could remember.

Now that she realized that, realized the cost of lying, she didn't have the strength to continue. She couldn't see Nick tonight . . .

There was a knock at the door.

She sighed tiredly. "Come in."

Her mother came into the room and carefully picked up the heavy gown. "You'd best get dressed, honey. Your young man will be here any minute."

Juli groaned. "He's not my young man. That's the problem." Her voice cracked a little. She turned to her mother, seeing her through a blur of hot tears. "I love him so much . . ."

"I know you do, sweetie."

She ran a shaking hand through her unbound hair. "Oh, Mama . . . it's such a mess. I don't want Nicholas for one Cinderella night. I want him for my whole life. I want to wake up with him beside me, and hold our babies in my arms. I want to sit for hours and watch him paint. I want—" She spun away. "Oh, damnation, who cares what I want? I'm not going to get it. Not now."

"Why not?"

"I've lied to him about everything. He'll never respect me."

"Does he respect you now?"

"I . . . I think so."

"Does he love you?"

Hot tears stung Juli's eyes again. She bit her lower lip and nodded slowly. "I think he might."

Mildred pressed a warm hand to Juli's cheek. "Then everything's fine. You've lied about *things*. That's not what's important to two people who love each other. So, you told him you were a journalist instead of a farmer's daughter. So what? Have you lied about what's in your heart?"

Her answer was a quiet "No."

"Then you still have a chance with him. Don't let it slip away. Love doesn't come along that often."

*A chance.* Juli clasped her cold hands together and bit down on her trembling lower lip. That's all she wanted—just one measly chance.

Maybe her mother was right. *Please God, let her be right.*

"I . . . I never lied about what I believed in, or how I felt about something."

Her mother smiled. "You see? Your words showed him the real Juli Sparks and that's who he fell in love with. A few trimmin's like gowns and houses don't matter a whole lot when you know what's inside a person's heart."

Hope spilled through Juli at her mother's simple words. Then came a wave of doubt. "But if I tell Nick the truth, he'll hate me for lying to him." She turned to her mother. "He could stop writing to me."

Mildred nodded sadly. "That's the risk, Julianna. I never said it would be easy. You'll have to decide: Do you want to keep your love a secret and pretend to be someone you're not? Or do you want to put yourself on the line and risk your heart for love?"

Juli let out her breath in a tired sigh. Put that way, there was only one thing she *could* do. "I don't want to spend my whole life wondering 'what if.' I love Nick. I'll just have to risk . . . everything and tell him the truth."

"When will you do it?"

Juli shrugged. "Tonight, I guess. After the festival." Apprehension scudded through her at the thought. *Please God,* she thought, *don't let him turn away in disgust. Please . . .*

"It'll be all right," Mildred said. "You'll see."

Juli turned and looked at her mother. "Will it, Mama? Will it really?"

A sad, nervous frown plucked at her mother's lips. "I don't know, honey. I hope so."

Juli bit down on her lower lip to keep it from quivering. "Yeah, Mama. Me, too."

But deep inside, in that tiny place reserved for intuition, Juli knew the truth. It wouldn't be all right. It would be the end of everything.

NICK AND JULI STROLLED ARM-IN-ARM ALONG the river. On either side of them was magic. The wide, slow-moving river was a swath of pewter liquid edged in ever-darkening green. At even intervals along the banks were lanterns set atop metal poles. Light cascaded onto the water, creating shifting, dancing circlets of gold.

To their left was a huge cow pasture that, tonight, had been transformed by light and laughter into another world. Children streaked back and forth from the food to the "potato-tivities" like sack races, pie-eating contests, and pumpkin carving. At one end of the field was a makeshift dance floor ringed by bales of hay and strung with candlelight. The whiny, high-pitched squeal of a fiddle filled the cool night air.

"I-it probably seems pretty . . . providential to you," Juli said quietly.

Nick smiled softly. "You mean provincial. And no, it doesn't. It seems magical." He turned and looked down at her. "Like you."

Guilt washed through her. "Nick . . ."

He stopped, turned her toward him. "Last week, I would have seen this place as a desperate attempt to make poor lives seem rich for a single night. But now . . ."

"Now what?"

"I see it differently. These people"—he indicated the laughing, loving, gesturing people milling through the pasture, running three-legged sack races, and chasing after greased pigs—"are so much richer than I've ever been." He leaned down to Juli, until their lips were almost touching but not quite. "Thank you."

"F-for what?"

"You've changed how I see the world."

Juli tried to smile, but couldn't. Her heart felt heavy and aching inside her chest. The lies stood between them like a living, breathing presence, keeping them ..part. It wasn't fair, not to either one of them. Her mother was right. Juli had to risk it all for love, and pray that everything would work out.

She pointed to a small wooden bench up ahead. "Let's sit down, shall we? This dress is incredibly heavy."

Nick laughed. Tightening his hold on her hand, he led her to the bench. They sat side by side, silent, staring down at the river.

The silence between them stretched out, thickened.

Juli searched her soul for the right words—just the right words. They eluded her. A tiny, cajoling voice whispered in her ear: *Let it go. Be happy with what you have. The letters are enough. Don't risk it all . . .*

She gave herself a mental shake and glanced heavenward. A huge, red-gold harvest moon hung suspended in the charcoal-hued sky, its color muted by a nearly transparent pewter-gray cloud.

"Liar's Moon." The words slipped from her mouth.

"What?" Nick asked.

Juli pointed at the sky. "My grandad calls that a Liar's Moon."

"It's beautiful."

Juli took a deep breath and turned to him. "What do you think of lying?"

He grinned. "I'm against it."

Juli forced a smile. "I . . . I mean, what if you found out someone had lied to you about something important? Could you forgive them?"

A cold implacability came to Nick's eyes. "That's a question I've thought a lot about."

Juli frowned. "Why?"

He tried to give a casual shrug, but the movement appeared stiff and forced. "My father is a liar."

"Have you . . . forgiven him?"

"No. I never will."

Juli's pent-up breath released in a sharp gust. If he wouldn't forgive his father for lying, he certainly wouldn't forgive a woman he barely knew.

Sadness was a wrenching pain in Juli's heart. What little hope her mother's words had given her evaporated. Tears flooded her eyes and she looked away.

Hope had always been something she could rely on, the bedrock of her personality. Even in her poverty, she had always had hope in the future. Now, without it, she felt cold and lonely and more than a little afraid.

He would leave her.

A tiny, miserable moan escaped her.

"Juli!" someone shouted her name.

Juli brought her head up and saw Jonas running toward them. Her grandfather came to a wheezing stop directly in front of them. "It's time fer the parade. Juli, you best run along to Chester's store." He cocked a head toward Nick. "I'll stay with the nabob."

"All right." She gave Nick a last, trembling smile and got to her feet. "See you in a few minutes."

He stood. "But—"

Turning, she hiked up her skirts and ran into the darkness.

NICK AND JONAS EXCHANGED SLY SIDEWAYS glances. Neither said a word. The noises of the night seemed to fade away, leaving only the old man's harsh, labored breathing and the gentle lapping of the river against its grassy bank. Far away a child laughed, but the sound was transient, lost almost immediately in the quiet stirring of the breeze.

Nick frowned. A strange sense of apprehension scurried down his neck.

"Let's go," Jonas said suddenly.

Nick followed Jonas across the rolling green field, past the makeshift dance floor, to a rutted dirt road on the edge of the field. There they stopped.

People buzzed like excited bees all along the road. Carefully placed lanterns cast the field in pockets of shimmering light, their glowing centers dollops of concentrated gold amidst the darkening night. Old folks whispered, young ones laughed. Anticipation was a throbbing, tangible presence in the air.

Somewhere in the distance a bell tinkled, then another and another. The sound swelled and grew and rode the breeze. A fiddle joined in.

"Look!" someone yelled.

Almost as one, the crowd turned. Far down the road,

where the light ended and the charcoal-hued shadows began, there was a subtle shifting of movement.

Nick found himself caught up in the excitement of the moment. He leaned forward, craning his neck to see.

Gladiola the plow horse surged into the light. The whining creak of rusted wagon wheels accompanied her every step.

As the wagon came more fully into the light, Nick grinned. The bed of the wagon had been transformed by huge bent willow circlets into a pretend platter. On the huge oval sat a profusion of harvest foods.

The vegetables were first.

After the wagonload of harvest vegetables came a carefully constructed "basket" full of summertime fruits, then a wagon filled with children dressed as Pilgrims sharing the first Thanksgiving.

Wagon after wagon rumbled past, each one filled with a different part of Russetville's past, present, or future. Mothers along the parade route smiled and waved, shouting encouraging remarks to their vegetable-husbands and Pilgrim-children.

At the last wagon, a rousing cheer swept the crowd.

Nick turned to leave, but Jonas grabbed his sleeve. "It ain't over yet."

Nick glanced down the road. "There's nothing coming."

"Wait."

"For what?"

"The Otatop princess."

"I keep hearing that word, Otatop. What is it, Indian?"

Jonas laughed. "No, we ain't too big on fer'n languages."

"What then?"

"College boy like you shoulda figgered it out. It's potato spelled backward. It's our biggest crop, don't ya know."

Nick could help himself. He chuckled. "You actually have a potato princess?"

"Here she comes!" someone yelled.

"Ssh," Jonas whispered harshly.

Grinning, Nick turned his attention back to the dusty road.

A pure white horse stepped out of the darkness. Behind it, a wagon had been magically transformed into a huge orange pumpkin that seemed to sparkle with fallen gold dust. On top of the pumpkin sat a woman, waving.

Nick's grin faded as he looked at the princess. It was Juli, and she was so beautiful she took his breath away. A longing ache settled around his heart and squeezed.

He watched, spellbound, as she came closer.

As she passed him, their eyes met and held across the crowd. In that moment, time seemed to stand still for Nick. He felt as if they were the only two people in the world. The crowd melted away, became a distant blur of color and sound.

She smiled down at him. Long brown hair haloed her face and fell down her back like a velvet curtain. A crown of wildflowers circled her head. Her gown had been transformed into an almost magical thing of beauty by invisible netting and colorful maple leaves. Her eyes glittered so brightly they seemed filled with tears.

The wagon moved on.

Nick snapped out of his reverie. All around him the crowd was cheering and clapping and laughing. Slowly, the people disbursed, and Nick and Jonas were finally left standing alone.

"You really care about her, don't you?" Jonas said softly.

Strangely, Nick wasn't surprised by the question. "Yes, I do."

Jonas turned to him. "Remember that."

Nick frowned. "Why would I forget?"

The old man's gaze moved pointedly to the moon. "Just don't." And with that odd statement, he walked away.

Nick was about to follow him, when he heard Juli calling his name.

"Nick!" She waved at him and started to run.

Nick saw where she was headed and his heart stopped dead. "Juli, stop!"

She ran right into a tree.

He raced to her side and kneeled beside her. Obviously dazed, she blinked up at him. "Nick?"

"Are you all right?"

She gave him a wobbly smile. "I'm fine."

Nick's heart was thudding so hard it took him a moment to catch his breath. "You scared me."

She touched his face, gazed steadily into his eyes. "Nick, I . . ." Her voice trailed off. The edges of her mouth quavered and turned down, but she didn't look away. "I love you, Nick. I want you to know that. No matter what happens later, or what you think of me, I want you to know I love you."

The simple declaration breathed new life into Nick's lonely heart. "Juli." He said her name quietly, almost reverently. She was so unlike any other woman he'd ever known. So straightforward and direct. She cared and she told him so. No games, no coy eyelash fluttering, no trembling fan. Just a plain, simple "I love you."

"And I love—"

She pressed a finger to his lips, silencing him. "Not yet, Nick," she said in a throaty voice. "*Please*, not yet. First we have to talk."

He helped her to her feet. Together they stood beneath the huge willow tree. The night-black branches formed a shadowy bower around them. A strand of moonlight slithered through the leaves and cast Juli's upturned face in blue-white light. He gazed down into her face and saw the sadness in her eyes. She looked young suddenly: young and afraid and vulnerable.

He brushed a finger along the velvet-softness of her cheek. "What is it?"

She shook her head. "Not here. Let's go back to the . . . house."

Nick was confused. This ought to be the greatest moment in his life. For the first time ever, he'd been ready to say "I love you."

But Juli had stopped him. Why?

He looked down at her, standing so quietly beside him. Something was wrong. Desperately wrong. And he couldn't figure out what the hell it could be. She appeared to be on the verge of tears.

"Let's go," she said quietly.

He nodded. Silently, together and yet somehow achingly separate, they started the long walk back to town.

# Six

He'd been about to say "I love you."

Juli clung to his arm and stared straight ahead, battling a tidal wave of regret. Her heart felt as if it were being torn in half.

*It's what you deserve.*

*But it's not what he deserves . . .*

It was that thought, more than any other, that almost brought Juli to her knees. Her pain was one thing; she'd brought it on herself with her lies and her exaggerations. But not Nick. He was the innocent in all of this.

Now it would end. They would make their slow, silent way back to the house, and then Juli would force herself to look in his eyes and tell him the horrible truth. The tiny thread of hope she'd had only moments before was now completely gone. The Liar's Moon had shown her the naive folly of her girlish dreams.

If only she'd been strong enough—proud enough—to

stand up at the beginning and say "I lied." If she'd said that last night before supper, even after supper, they might have had that chance she wanted so desperately. Or if she'd met him at the depot in her own clothing. If she'd done anything but add lie to lie to lie.

Juli squeezed her eyes shut and stumbled along beside Nick. Pain and regret and shame merged into a huge, throbbing knot in her throat.

That was the cruelest irony of all. She'd misjudged Nick. If she'd bitten the bullet and told Nick the truth then, he probably would have accepted her. Maybe even fallen in love with her anyway.

But not now. He might have forgiven her letters' unimportant fabrications. What he wouldn't forgive was the past two days. She hadn't trusted either him or herself, and that he wouldn't be able to forgive. The lies stood between them like a thick brick wall. Insurmountable and unbreakable.

God knew she didn't want to crack that wall. She wanted to simply pretend for another day, then wave good-bye to the man she loved and go back to the way things were.

She could do that if she didn't love him so much. She thought she'd loved him before they'd even met, but that emotion was a pale shadow of the way she felt about him now. He was part of her, twined through her soul so deeply she couldn't imagine living without him.

She loved him enough to do the right thing. She had to tell him the truth. Because he deserved it.

"Hey, Juli!" yelled a familiar voice.

Juli caught her breath. *Don't stop us, Daddy*, she thought desperately. *I've got to tell the truth. If you stop me now, I might never find the courage again to try . . . .*

George came running up beside them. Panting loudly, he unbuttoned his yam costume and yanked it from his face. "It's time fer the games, Julianna. You don't want to miss that."

She shook her head. "George, I don't—"

"No, you don't, missy. We have you all set up for blind man's bluff." He winked knowingly at her. "Get it? You're *all set up.*"

Juli's stomach sank. She'd forgotten that this night wasn't hers alone. It belonged to the whole town, and they were waiting with bated breath to see her and Nick together. They'd worked so hard, all of them, to give her this incredible, magical night. How could they know that magic and deception were incompatible?

She cast her gaze downward and nodded dully. "Certainly, George."

Her father led them to the makeshift dance floor, where Gladys was standing with a blindfold.

At their entrance, a crowd appeared as if by magic. Within a matter of seconds, the area filled with laughing, talking people. Her mother and father stood together in the corner.

"Let Juli go first," someone yelled.

"Yeah, she don't need the blindfold," answered another.

Gladys bustled up to Nick and Juli. "I'm glad you two could make it." Without a word to Juli, she commandeered Nick and led him to a bale of hay. "Sit here."

Smiling, Nick did as he was told.

Gladys hurried back to Juli and dragged her to the center of the dance floor. Loudly enough for all to hear, she said, "I'm gonna blindfold Juli here, twirl her around, and set her to find . . ." She brought a pudgy finger to her lips and appeared to think a minute. "That package over there."

Every head turned to the large, gaily wrapped and beribboned package beside Nick.

Gladys slipped the blindfold over Juli's eyes and tied it tightly. "All right, honey," she whispered. "Here goes." She spun Juli around and around, then stopped her dead and gave her a hard shove.

Juli stumbled forward. She knew exactly where she was headed, whom her grandmother had pushed her toward. Fighting tears, she played along.

All around her, people were laughing and talking and calling out directions.

She moved cautiously forward, step by step.

Something warm and solid touched her leg, kept her from moving to the right. She leaned down and touched it. Soft, expensive wool brushed her skin, told her immediately whose leg it was.

She started to move to the left, but another leg came up and boxed her in.

The crowd gasped and twittered.

Juli's heartbeat increased. She drew in a shaky breath. The proper thing to do would be to back away. A *lady* would never be so bold as to stand between a man's legs in public.

*But you're no lady, Juli Sparks. God knows there's proof enough of that.*

She should back away and remove her blindfold. But she couldn't move. Her breath came in shallow, almost painful spurts.

This was her last chance. After she told him the truth she'd never be this close to him again.

She took a deep, trembling breath and boldly leaned toward him. Her hands searched for and found his shoulders, moving along the hard ledge, and up the fine column of his neck to his face.

The crowd whooped and hollered with approval.

Juli barely heard them. She breezed a fingertip across his lip. He shuddered, exhaled heavily.

Desire coursed through Juli at his response. For the first time in her life, she felt sexy. Her own breathing quickened. Swallowing hard, she leaned forward. Close. Closer.

She felt his every breath against her face, and still she inched forward until their lips were almost touching. Her costume crinkled with every breath.

"Juli . . ." Her name slipped past his lips. It was a quiet plea, a promise of magic.

Juli froze. *Back away now, while you still own a piece of your heart.*

The sound advice shot through Juli's mind, and she knew it was the smart thing to do. She knew, too, that it was too late to be smart with Nick. Far too late. And thus might be her last opportunity to kiss him.

If she pulled back now, she'd be left with nothing. Not even the most wonderful of memories.

She touched her lips to his. The kiss was soft and short and filled with all the yearning in her soul. A gasp rippled through the crowd, the sound underscored the erratic beating of Juli's pulse.

The beauty of the kiss, its very perfection cut through Juli's heart like a jagged blade. She didn't deserve this moment. It was as wrong as anything she'd ever done—and after this weekend, that was a sizeable list.

With a pain-filled gasp, she stumbled backwards. Distance, she thought. *Dear God, I need some distance between us.* Her heart was beating so hard she felt dizzy. Self-loathing and regret was a tangible, acrid lump in her throat.

"Juli?" Gladys came up beside her.

Juli forced a laugh. "I guess I'm not so good at this," she said, removing the strip of cloth from her eyes.

Disappointment moved through the crowd in a buzzing mumble. The people got to their feet and stared at Juli. No one moved.

Her mother pushed her way to the center of the room, dragging her father behind her. "All right, everyone, the show's over. It's time for the pumpkin carving contest." Then she turned to Julie and lowered her voice. "What do you want us to do?"

Juli glanced at Nick. At the sight of him, so handsome and out of place in the musty, makeshift dance floor, she felt an almost sickening wave of shame. Regret tugged at the corners of her mouth. "Bring the wagon around, Daddy."

Mildred gave her a worried frown. "Are you going to tell him?"

"Yeah, Mama," she answered tonelessly.

"He loves *you*," Mildred said. "Not some rich hoity-toity writer."

Before Juli could answer, Nick walked up beside them. He looked pale and more than a little shaken.

Juli blushed. "I'm sorry about that. I didn't mean to—"

"I could tell," he said quietly. "I wish you had."

Juli turned away before he could see the tears glazing her eyes. He reached for her arm, but she lurched sideways and hurried over to the box by the bale of hay. "Here," she said, forcing a lightness in her voice that wasn't in her heart. "This present is for you."

A smile softened his face. "You didn't have to do that."

"I . . . wanted to."

"I've got a surprise for you in George's wagon. What do you say we open them at your house?"

It took every scrap of Juli's courage to keep her gaze on his. "All right, Nick. Let's go."


FOR THE FIRST TIME IN HIS LIFE, NICK WAS excited about the future, about the possibilities spread out before him. The world was his now. With Juli beside him, he could be anything, *do* anything. The burden of his name and the strictures of his society-conscious parents meant nothing, less than nothing. He was an artist, by God, and whether he made a living at it or not, he wasn't going to deny his heart any longer. He was going to go after what he wanted. From this day forward he lived his life the way he wanted to. As long as he made Juli happy, he'd answer to no other.

*Juli.*

Her name filled him with the most intoxicating sense of peace he'd ever known. He understood finally, with a longing that was almost an ache in his soul, what it meant to be in love.

He glanced at Juli. She was sitting beside him, staring straight ahead. She had that vulnerable look again, as if she were battling with some weighty inner question. There was

the barest downturn to her full mouth, and an almost unde-
tectable trembling in her hands.

He scooted closer to her and slipped an arm around her
shoulders. "Cold?"

She stiffened, swallowed hard. He thought he saw a glittering of moisture in her eyes. "No." There was a wistful,
almost frightened edge to her voice.

A cold breeze seemed to curl around Nick's heart. There
was something wrong. He wanted to touch her chin and
force her to look at him. To ask her what was on her mind.
But he couldn't do it here, with George less than three feet
away and the night as silent as a tomb.

Finally, they came to a stop in front of the house. Nick
grabbed both wrapped boxes and jumped down from the
wagon. Carefully placing the gifts on the porch, he returned
for Juli.

When she slipped her small, gloved hand in his, he felt
the shaking of her fingers. He curled his hand more tightly
around hers, a silent offer of support and warmth.

She stepped down from the wagon and followed Nick up
the front steps. Together they waved good-bye to George.

Then they were alone. The darkness of the porch enfolded
them. Wind crept up the steps, tugging at Juli's hair. Behind
them, a rocker creaked. Crickets chirped somewhere in the
night.

Nick had to shake off an eerie sense of impending doom.

Juli leaned down and dragged the wrapped box toward
Nick. "Here," she said. "Why don't you open it?"

"Let's take them inside."

Juli's eyes widened. "I don't want to go inside."

She looked . . . frightened. Nick breezed a finger along her cheek, felt the coldness of her skin. "You're freezing." He cocked his head toward the door. "Come on. I'll make a fire."

She looked away. "All right."

Nick picked up both boxes and carried them in the house. He set them down in the parlor, then turned around and waited for Juli.

She seemed to have difficulty crossing the threshold. Her hands were curled into a tight wad at her midsection, her gaze was pinned to the floor. There was a tremble in her lower lip.

He was beside her in a few steps. "Juli? Is something the matter?"

She looked up at him through wide, sad eyes. "No, Nick, nothing's wrong." Her voice was as insubstantial as a whisper.

Nick was at a loss. He could tell that something *was* wrong, but he had no idea how to get her to talk about it. He was a loner; he had been all his life. His experience in talking with women consisted largely of bedroom banter and dance floor flirting.

Maybe opening her gift would cheer her up. He slipped a hand around her waist and led her to the parlor. Side by side, they sat down.

He moved the present closer to her. "Here," he whispered, leaning near her, "open it."

She brought shaking hands to the big red bow. She hesitated for a heartbeat, then eased the ribbon away. Setting it on the table beside her, she carefully unwrapped the gift and pulled the painting from its box.

"Oh, Nick . . ." Her voice cracked with emotion. She

moved her fingers across the canvas, feeling the paint as if she were blind. "It's beautiful."

Warmth spilled through him at her simple words. "It's Paris, in the springtime. At least, that's how I imagine it would look."

She turned to him, her eyes filled with tears. "I've never had anything as magnificent. Thank you."

Smiling, Nick opened his gift from Juli. As he pulled it from the narrow wooden crate, his smile fell. It was the most beautiful picture frame he'd ever seen. His fingertips grazed the intricately carved mahogany. The wood was as smooth as silk. "Juli, this is . . . incredible."

"My father made it for you."

"Your father?" Nick turned to her. "Does he live here in town? I'd like to meet him. I have an important question to ask him."

Juli let go of the painting and lurched to her feet. Whirling away from the settee, she began to pace.

Nick frowned. Her movements were jerky, nervous. She marched from the room, her gaze pinned to her feet. She missed hitting the doorway by the barest of margins.

Nick followed her out to the foyer. "Juli?"

She turned toward his voice.

He walked up to her and took her hands in his. They stood closely, holding hands, their gazes locked, in the middle of the huge, marble-floored room. Above their heads, a gaslight chandelier sparkled and hissed, sending a dozen dancing, multi-hued lights across them.

"Juli," he said her name softly, on a sigh of wonder. He still couldn't believe he'd found her. Couldn't believe how much he loved her. "Marry me, Juli."

She paled. "Oh, God . . ."

"I hope you're crying because you're happy."

She took a deep, quavering breath and shook her head. "I'm not happy, Nick. I . . . I have something to tell you."

Cold fear slid through Nick. He pulled her into his arms, hugged her with sudden desperation, as if by holding her close he could keep her close. Before she could say a word, he leaned down and kissed her.

The kiss was nothing like the others; it was hard and hungry and filled with longing.

"Nick . . ." she whispered, drawing back.

He brought his hands to her face, his fingers burrowed in her hair. He covered her face with dark, desperate kisses. "Don't leave me, Juli," he murmured.

She made a soft, whimpering sound. "Oh, Nick. I'd never leave you. I love you."

Nick pulled back and looked down at her. Relief spiraled through him. "Marry me," he said again.

Before Juli could answer, there was a sound from the front door. A key turned in the lock; the metallic twisting sound seemed obscenely loud in the silent foyer. The crystal knob turned slowly and the door opened.

A well-dressed older couple stood in the door.

Juli gasped and started to shake.

The woman, a gray-haired, grandmotherly-type frowned. "Julianna Sparks, is that you, dear?"

Juli made a strangled sound of assent.

"Whatever are you doing in our house?" She brought a monocle up to her eye. "And in my daughter's dress?"

Nick looked at Juli. "What does she mean?"

Juli looked up at him through wide, frightened eyes. "I was trying to tell you, Nick . . ."

"Tell me what?"

She lowered her voice. "Let's go outside to talk—"

"No, damn it. Let's talk here. What the hell's going on?"

She swallowed hard. "Nick, have you ever been so desperate for something, you'd have done anything to have it close to you. Even for a minute—"

He sighed impatiently. "Juli, what are you talking about?"

"I love you so much, Nick. So much." Tears filled her eyes. "I couldn't believe you'd ever love me."

Her vulnerability touched his heart. "Oh, Juli . . ."

She took a deep breath. "This isn't my home, Nick. I'm not who you think I am."

Fear settled in Nick's gut as a cold, hard knot. He frowned, pulled away from her. "What do you mean?"

"I . . . I live about ten miles out of town in a cabin with newspaper on the walls and hard-packed dirt for a floor. My family is dirt poor and I never made it past the sixth grade. I'm no journalist."

Disbelief swept through Nick. "You lied to me?"

She nodded dismally.

He tried to make sense of it. "All of it . . . all these years . . . lies?"

"I'm sorry, Nick."

"*Sorry?*" For a moment Nick couldn't breathe. A stinging, red-hot sense of betrayal suffocated him. Then he got mad. "You give me the woman of my dreams, make me fall head-over-heels in love with her, then tell me it's all a lie, and you're *sorry?*"

She reached for him. "Nick—"

He wrenched away. "Don't touch me."

She bit down hard on her lower lip and fisted her hands at her sides. "I didn't mean to hurt you."

He laughed. It was a short, bitter sound as brittle as broken glass. "I loved you, Juli."

Juli heard the ache in his words and felt as if she were being slowly drawn into a cold, dark hole. She wanted to say something—anything—but there was nothing to say. Her lies had said it all.

Finally he brought his gaze back to her face. His eyes were narrowed, angry. "Poverty?" he spat the word as if it were offensive. "How could you think it would matter?"

She shook her head. Tears slipped past her lashes and streaked down her cheeks, but she didn't bother wiping them away. "You can't know what it's like, Nick. I just wanted . . ." She squeezed her eyes shut in shame. "I just wanted you to respect me."

"I *respect* people who tell the truth."

Pain almost brought Juli to her knees. She took a deep breath and banished it. She deserved this pain, this and more.

Nick pivoted suddenly and strode into the parlor. Wrenching up his overcoat, he started to leave. Then, slowly, he turned back around and touched the frame. "Did your father really make this?" he said in a husky voice.

"Yes." Juli pushed the word up her too-tight throat.

He wedged the frame beneath his arm and headed for the door. The Hanafords, wide-eyed and gape-mouthed, stared at him. He nodded curtly and reached for the doorknob.

"Nick, wait. Please—"

He tried to ignore her, but couldn't. Cursing his own weakness, he turned. Juli was standing in the center of the room, barely breathing, her skin as pale as moonlight. She looked young and vulnerable and afraid. Her cheeks were slick with tears.

Sweet Christ, how he wanted to take her in his arms and kiss her right now.

He had to get out of here. *Now.* He was about ten seconds away from crumbling like old clay. His insides felt dry and lifeless and gone.

She swallowed hard. "I . . . I never lied about anything important, Nick. Not about my feelings. I love you."

Her words drove through his heart like a stake. He bit back a groan of anguish. "Good-bye, Juli." He opened the door and paused. Without turning back around, he added, "Or whoever you are. And don't write to me again."

Trembling, breathing hard, he walked away from her and shut the door behind him.

# Seven

The train rolled out of Russetville and hurtled through the stark, autumn-draped landscape. Field after field sped past the window in a golden blur. Nick settled deeper in his chair and stretched his legs out.

He closed his eyes, tried to force himself to relax.

It was impossible. The scene last night kept churning through his mind. Juli's words matched the whirring clackety-clack of the train wheels and thundered through his brain.

*I didn't lie about the important things, Nick. I love you, love you, love you, love—*

"Enough!" Nick sat upright in his chair.

He had to let go of this obsession, had to forget about Juli. Last night he'd tossed and turned in his lonely hotel bed. Aching for the respite of sleep, oblivion, he'd found that slumber was irritatingly beyond his grasp. Every time he closed his eyes, he thought about her. About the smile that came so easily to her mouth, the softness of her lips, the gentleness of her touch. About the way her eyes lit up when she saw his painting.

A lie, he thought for the thousandth time. It was all a lie.

He rubbed the bridge of his nose and sighed raggedly. He felt drained, as if the life had been sucked from his veins and left him stranded in a dead, useless shell of a body.

How could she think so little of him? That was the question that haunted him most. He'd offered her everything that he was and everything he could be. His past, present, and future. He'd never allowed himself to be so vulnerable with a woman—with anyone. He'd bared his very soul.

She'd taken it, curled her little fingers around it, and offered him nothing but meaningless words and gilt-tongued lies in return.

Sweet Jesus, it hurt . . .

He felt so damned empty inside.

"Get used to it, Sinclair," he said bitterly. "You're going back to your old life."

JULI NUDGED THE WOBBLY, WIRE-RIMMED spectacles higher on her nose and re-read the words she'd just written. A small frown tugged at her mouth. Her heart just wasn't in it any longer.

"You settled on a story?" her grandmother asked quietly.

Juli shook her head. "I can't seem to do it anymore."

Mildred set down her cup of coffee and moved over to the settee. She sat down beside Juli. "Last time we all got together in the middle of the day your headline was: *Society Maven Gladys Fipperpot Hosts Elegant Tea for Town Officials.* How about something like that?"

"I don't think so, Mama."

Mildred cast a worried glance at Gladys, who only shrugged.

"I saw that," Juli said. "I'm depressed, not blind."

Gladys put down her knitting. "I shoulda wired Kate Hanaford about our plan. She was sick to death about ruinin' your special time."

"It wasn't Mrs. Hanaford who caused the problems, Grandma," Juli said softly.

Gladys frowned. "I didn't figure on him leavin' like that."

"Me neither," Mildred agreed. "I thought he'd at least stick around long enough for an explanation."

Juli appreciated the effort her mother and grandmother were making, but it didn't matter anymore. Nick was gone. He'd left on the early train, and he wasn't coming back. Tears scalded her eyes; she held them back by sheer force of will. She was sick to death of crying. She'd done nothing else all night.

"What explanation was there?" she said. "I lied."

Gladys snorted. "Hell's bells, so what? If he really loved you, he'd have stuck around."

Juli's head snapped up. The tears she'd been holding back squeezed past her lashes and streaked down her cheeks. She threw down her pen and raced for the quiet sanctity of her bedroom, slamming her door shut behind her.

"Good job, Mom," Mildred said.

Gladys sighed. "Aw, hell."

NICK GLANCED OUT THE WINDOW, SEARCHING for something—anything, damn it—to take his mind off the pain of her betrayal.

The countryside was a golden-green blur with a steel gray edge of clouds and sky. As he stared, unseeing, into the fields, the train began to slow. It huffed and clanged into a tiny, ramshackle town that could have been Russetville.

A dirty, pockmarked road unfurled along a silver-bright stream. Whitewashed wooden buildings squatted along the street like mismatched building blocks.

Nick's gaze cut across the river, where a farmhouse lay shrouded in early morning mist. A small, unkempt clap-board house sat naked amidst a rutted, brown-earthed field. There were no shutters on the windows, and the door hung at a cockeyed angle from a single hinge.

Nick sat up straighter. A small frown worked its way across his brow. The horse—there was only one—stood huddled alongside a thin-trunked maple tree, his big black hindquarters backed against the wind. Gaping holes mottled the barn, providing little or no shelter from the elements.

But it was the house that held Nick's attention. It was small, smaller than Nick's bedroom at home. Moss furred the slanted wooden roof.

He didn't need to go inside to know that newspaper lined the walls and dirt made up the floor. What must it be like to live in such a place?

He began slowly to understand, and it made him feel sick inside. It wasn't that Juli underestimated him. It was more simple than that, more basic. She was ashamed.

*I couldn't believe you'd ever love someone like me, Nick . . .*

Her words came back to him, wrenching in their shame and anguish.

He banged his head against the window and closed his

eyes, feeling ashamed of himself. What an idiot he'd been.
What a goddamn, thick-headed, egocentric idiot. All he'd
thought about was *his* pain, *his* anger.

He glanced at the letter lying in the seat beside him.
George had given it to him this morning, when he'd driven
Nick to the train station. But Nick hadn't bothered to read
it. He'd been too steeped, too mired, in his own self righteous pain.

He picked it up, running his fingertips atop the bumpy,
porous paper. Then he took a quick breath, broke the seal,
and began to read.

*My dear Nicholas:*

*I can only say again how sorry I am for hurting you. It
is yet another shame I must bear. You are, even now, the
most precious part of my life, and I would rather die than
hurt you. But, of course, words are cheap, and mine most
of all. I won't bother you with my remorse and regret.*

*The purpose of this last letter is to tell you to keep paint-
ing. You said once that you came to Julianna Sparks for
advice. Allow me to give this final bit to you: You have a
great talent, a rare gift. Do not squander it.*

*With the love in my heart,*
*Julianna Elizabeth Sparks*

Nick squeezed his eyes shut. Even now, in the midst of
her own obvious pain and shame, she was worried about
Nick.

He slowly opened his eyes. And saw the frame she'd
given him.

It was still flawlessly beautiful. But now it was something else, something that twisted Nick's heart. *Empty.* Without a painting to lend it color and vitality, it was a lifeless, useless piece of carved wood.

Like Nick without Juli in his life.

OUTSIDE, A STORM RAGED. WIND POUNDED AT the thin-paned glass and howled through the rafters overhead, but inside the Sparks' home, it was warm and cozy.

Mildred bustled from the hot kitchen, carrying a platter of squash. The sweet, brown-sugary scent filled the small, dark room. She set it down on the dining table alongside a perfectly cooked turkey. "Light a few lamps, will you, George?"

George lit the hanging brass lantern in the living room and the one suspended above the dinner table. Then he lit a couple of candles and set them on the cracked piecrust table by the settee.

"You gonna cut the damn bird, or set the house on fire?" Jonas grumbled.

Gladys elbowed her husband. "Shut up, you mean-spirited old man. We're tryin' to make the place festive for Juli."

Jonas sighed and propped a wrinkled cheek in his palm. An unfamiliar sadness settled on his wizened face. "How is she?"

Gladys shook her head. "Not good. She's been holed up in that room o' hers all day."

All four of them cast worried glances at Juli's bedroom door.

"Go get her," Mildred mouthed to her husband, taking her seat across from Jonas.

George gave his wife a hesitant look and glanced at the closed door. Then, slowly, he crossed the room and knocked. "It's time for supper, honey."

"I'm not hungry, Daddy."

He leaned closer to the door. "Your mother and grandmother worked really hard on this meal. Please, come out."

After a seemingly endless moment, the doorknob turned.

At the dinner table, Gladys, Jonas, and Mildred drew in a collective breath.

Juli opened the door and came out. "Hi, Daddy."

George smiled, though his heart felt as if it were breaking. "Hi, pumpkin."

She glanced over at the rest of her family at the table. "Sure smells good." It was a feeble attempt at normalcy, but no one cared.

Gladys touched the chair beside her. "Come on, honey."

Juli went to the table and sat down. Her back was to the front door, with Gladys and Jonas on one side of the table, and Daddy and Mama on the other. The family joined hands for prayer time, then George stood to carve the bird.

Before his knife even touched the turkey, there was a rattling burst of thunder. Wind whipped the front door open and extinguished the lanterns and candles. Darkness swallowed the room.

Gladys lurched to her feet and re-lit the lantern above the table. A movement caught her eye and she turned toward the now open door.

"Oh, my God!" she screeched. Her fork clattered to the table.

Jonas followed her gaze and got slowly to his feet. "Well, I'll be damned."

George grinned. "I told them to cook extra."

Mildred started to cry.

Juli glanced at the faces around her. "What in the world is going on?"

"Turn around, Juli."

Juli froze. The soft, rich voice wrapped her in warmth and longing. "Nick?" His name slipped from her lips, alone, with nothing to follow it.

Slowly, shaking, she got to her feet and turned around. He was standing in the doorway, hat in hand.

Juli was too stunned to move. She just stood there, gape-mouthed, afraid to believe it was really him.

He grinned at her. "Being poor was the secret, right? I mean, you aren't hiding something else, are you?"

She shook her head and self-consciously removed her spectacles.

"Put them back on," he said.

"But, I look—"

"Beautiful. Now put them on. I want you to see my face when I say I love you."

Juli gasped.

His features softened. "I love you, Juli. Marry me."

Juli's spell snapped. With a strangled cry of joy, she ran to Nick and threw herself in his arms. He held her tightly and there, in the midst of a dark, shabby room with the scent of turkey and trimmings thick in the air and her family looking on, he kissed her.

It was a kiss that lasted all the way to Paris.

# A MIDSUMMER
# DAY'S DREAM

## Linda Lael Miller

# One

GRIMSLEY, ENGLAND, 1993

Frankie ran one fingertip over the raised letters on her American Express Card—*Francesca Whittier*, it read—while she waited for the clerk to emerge from the back of the small, dusty costume shop at the end of Ainsley Lane.

If she ended up with nothing to wear to the Medieval Fair, an occasion she'd been looking forward to through a long and unusually gray Seattle winter, she would have no one to blame but herself. She might have phoned from the United States weeks ago and reserved something, or had a gown and headdress made by a local seamstress. Instead, she'd been so caught up in running her own small shop that she'd let some important vacation details slide.

For one, she'd counted on her cousin Brian to look after Cinderella's Closet, her store, while she was away, but at the last minute he'd landed a job waiting tables on a cruise ship.

When, she wondered, had a promise stopped being a promise?

Frankie flipped the credit card end over end on the countertop, listening hopefully to the sounds of bustling enterprise coming from the rear of the shop.

"Have you found anything?" she called out, unable to contain her eagerness any longer. There was no discernible reply, just more industrious noises.

Frankie sighed. She had seriously considered canceling her long-awaited trip to England, but in the end she'd taken a deep breath and dialed an employment agency specializing in temporary workers. They'd sent over Mrs. Cullywater, a retired schoolteacher who had once managed her nephew's hamburger franchise.

Mrs. Cullywater was no Lee Iacocca, obviously, but she seemed competent enough, and she was likable. She would hold things together until Frankie returned.

While Frankie was mulling that over, the clerk, a stout man with a monk's halo of graying brown hair and overlapping front teeth, burst into the main part of the shop again. He was carrying a plain muslin dress over one arm, and his expression conveyed both hope and chagrin.

"I'm afraid there's nothing, Miss Whittier, except for this. More seventeenth-century, really, with the lacing up the front of the bodice and all, but it could pass as medieval, I suppose . . . ."

Frankie surveyed the butternut gown in polite dismay, but she had few choices. She could return to London and spend her precious week sightseeing. She could hide out in her room just down the lane and feel sorry for herself because for the last eighteen months or so, everything had gone wrong for her.

Or, she reflected, she could do what her late-great dad would have recommended—rent the muslin dress, hie herself off to the fair, an event she'd been anticipating ever since she'd read about it in a travel magazine months before, and have the best possible time.

"Will it fit?" she asked, taking the gown from the clerk's hands and holding it up in front of her. She turned toward the full-length mirrors at one side of the shop, but her gaze stopped at the front window.

A man dressed in a wizard's flowing robes and high, pointed hat was hovering there, peering in at her. The shiny threads in the rich purple fabric of his clothing seemed to be spun from moonbeams, and his beard curled grandly down his chest, white laced through with silver.

For a moment, all of time seemed to stop.

*Just a guy in a costume*, the logical left side of her brain said. *There's a fair going on, remember?*

Frankie blinked, the magician was gone, and the sidewalk was filled with people who were purely ordinary, even in their costumes.

"That must have been the grandest outfit you had in stock," she said, feeling peculiarly off-balance.

The good-natured clerk squinted toward the window. "What? Oh, that knight who just passed? We have lots of those—"

"No," Frankie broke in. "It was Merlin. You must have seen him—he seemed to fill the whole windowpane—"

The clerk frowned. "Didn't see him. Say, are you feeling

quite well, miss? You look a mite on the peaky side, if you ask me. It's a cuppa you need."

Frankie yearned for tea, strong, rich, English stuff, of the sort rarely found in the United States, with plenty of milk and sugar. Still, she would wait until she'd returned to her room at the inn, where she could sit down, catch her breath, and sort through her thoughts as she sipped.

"No, thanks," she said in bright tones that sounded brittle even to her.

Nothing unusual had happened, really, and yet Frankie had been moved on some deep level by the sight of the splendid wizard. He was probably just a solicitor from London or a vacationing dentist from Albuquerque, but dressed up in that costume he had seemed the personification of some private myth.

Frankie felt a twinge of the same mysterious enchantment she'd known as a child, when Christmas Eve came around.

She drew a deep breath, pushing her loosely curled blond hair back from her forehead with a slightly damp palm, and indicated the dress. "Will it fit?" she asked again.

The clerk still looked worried, but he smiled. "One size suits all," he said.

Frankie pushed her American Express card toward him. "Fine. Then I'll take it for the whole week of the fair, please," she said.

Approximately five minutes later she left the shop, carrying the muslin dress in a plastic garment bag. The narrow cobbled streets of Grimsley were brimming with happy tourists, most of whom wore medieval clothing.

Miraculously she'd been successful, selling antique jewelry and vintage clothing in her shop, and later recycled designer stuff on consignment as well. She'd even dated a few harmless types.

Still, Frankie had truly loved Geoffrey, and she'd been fragile for a long time, concentrating mainly on survival.

Fate had never seemed crueler than it did the day a year after the divorce, though, when Frankie's dad, her only living relative besides the capricious Brian, had died suddenly in an accident on the freeway.

After that she'd sunk into a sort of functional depression, eating, sleeping, working, doing those things and only those things, in endless succession.

Then she'd read about the yearly week-long medieval fair at Grimsley, just a short bus ride from London, and the idea of going had rolled into her mind and clattered to a stop, like a runaway hubcap. It was just what she needed to jolt herself back on track, she decided, a complete change of scene—even the *illusion* of a different century. Talk about getting away from it all!

Inspired, Frankie had made the decision to stop grieving, to stop hiding, to venture out into the big world again and do something spectacular. Right away she'd been up to her eyeballs in preparations to fly to England and enjoy the fair.

Frankie brought her thoughts sharply back to the here and now and was surprised to find herself giving a little sniffle. Her eyes were filled with tears, and she angrily wiped them away with the heel of her palm.

She shook off the bittersweet reflections that had been quivering on the clear surface of her mind and tidied up the tea tray.

It was time to put the past out of her mind and follow through on a dream.

Frankie set the tray in the hallway, then took off her white shorts and coral tank top to put on the muslin dress. Her gray eyes widened as she looked at herself in the antique cheval mirror that stood in the corner of the room. Although she saw her own face, her own curly, chin-length blond hair, she also saw a hitherto unrecognized facet of Frankie Whittier. A saucy medieval wench gazed back at her, full of joy, adventure, and mischief.

For a moment the sun-washed dust speckles floating in the room seemed to sparkle, even to make a very faint sound, rather like the tinkle of wind chimes.

Then Geoffrey's influence struck again.

Get a grip, Frankie. You're always living in a fantasy world. That's your trouble.

Frankie smiled and held the muslin skirts wide, as if they were French silk instead, but it was the wench who replied aloud, "Go to hell—and take your opinions with you!"

Frankie laughed, tightened the ribbon laces on the bodice of the dress so that her modest cleavage looked more impressive, then tucked a packet of traveler's checks into her pocket, along with her room key. Her thin platinum watch, a life-goes-on gift from her father after the divorce, was Frankie's only other concession to modern times. She slipped it onto her wrist, where it was hidden by the cuff of her dress, and set out barefoot for the fair.

The sunshine seemed especially bright that day, and the sky was a memorable blue. It seemed to Frankie, as she stopped to purchase a wreath of tiny delicate flowers and trailing ribbons for her hair, that there was magic abroad; sweet, dangerous magic.

She watched the puppeteers for a time and cheered the jousting knights. She laughed and clapped as the mummers put on an impromptu play, then bought a small "dove" pie—which was really made with pheasant—and found a place on the banks of the stream that flowed through the center of the village. There she was, eating her lunch and soaking her bare, dusty feet in the cool water, congratulating herself on what a bold and modern woman she was, when the air around her began to hum.

That excited feeling pooled in her stomach, that Christmas-Eve sensation of old. But this was something much, much bigger.

Frankie leaned back against the trunk of an ancient oak tree and closed her eyes. Not a migraine, she thought, for she hadn't had one of her headaches since before Geoffrey left her. Too young for a stroke. And why do I feel so happy?

The humming sound grew to a roar, and Frankie waited. Maybe she was having a nervous breakdown or some kind of manic episode. That would explain her exhilaration— wouldn't it?

When she opened her eyes again, she was stunned to see that the world had altered itself during those tumultuous seconds just past.

The stream was wider and deeper, and there was a wooden bridge where the stone one had stood before. The grass she sat upon was fragrantly verdant and quite untrampled. The village itself stood at a distance, and the brick buildings had been replaced by cottages and huts of wattle and daub, with thatched roofs. Though there were people about as before, they weren't the *same* people. Their clothing was rustic, rougher looking than before, and most of them had bad skin and even worse teeth.

But what drew Frankie's attention was the spectacle of Sunderlin Keep.

The castle loomed whole and sturdy and magnificent against the soft blue of the English sky. The drawbridge looked sturdy, and there was a moat, full of murky water.

Frankie stared in amazement, blinked, and stared again. The scene did not fade.

She climbed unsteadily to her feet, crumbling the pie in a nervous grip, and pressed her back to the oak tree. It too was different, a younger tree, hardly more than a sapling, and flexible.

One of the villagers pointed at her and spoke to a colleague, and some sort of stir began. Frankie was both terrified and intrigued as mummers and jugglers, merchants and minor nobles all stopped to stare.

The way they were acting, *she* might have been the hallucination, and not them. Fleetingly she wondered again if she was experiencing some kind of individual myth, a colorful gift from her subconscious mind, fraught with meaning.

The crowd began to press around her, pointing and gaping. The smell of them, coupled with the wild confusion she was feeling, nearly overwhelmed Frankie. They were babbling, questioning, but their language was like the Chaucer stuff she remembered from high school, and she could comprehend only a word here and there.

Just when Frankie thought her knees were sure to give

out, that she would drop helpless to the ground, someone
came pushing through the crowd, a tall, broad-shouldered
someone with golden-brown hair and eyes of the same in-
triguing color. He wore gray leggings, leather shoes, and a
purple tunic with a complicated image of a lion embroidered
on the front. At his side swung a sword that might have
been a cousin to Excalibur.

Frankie stared up into those sharply intelligent brown
eyes, at the same time reaching behind her to clutch the
supple oak with both hands, in an effort to stay on her feet.

"I don't know how you people managed to make this
all seem so real," she blurted out, her tongue driven by
nervousness rather than wisdom, "but I'm impressed."

The towering vision before her frowned, and his brow
furrowed slightly. The crowd around them began to murmur again, and he stilled them with a gesture of one hand
and a brusque, "Silence!"

One disjointed moment hobbled by before Frankie realized that he'd spoken in modern vernacular. She felt an odd
certainty that her deeper mind was translating his Old English into words she could understand.

She put out one hand. "Hello, there," she said, her voice
shaking only slightly. "I'm Francesca Whittier."

The giant looked at her hand, then gazed into her eyes
for what seemed like a long time before grasping her fingers
in greeting.

Frankie came close to fainting again, this time because
his grip was so tight. "And you are—?" she managed to
squeak.

He bowed slightly. "I am Braden Stuart-Ramsey, Duke
of Sunderlin," he said. He ran his impudent gaze over her

rented muslin dress. "Are your favors for hire? You look suitable for an afternoon's entertainment."

Frankie felt as though she'd been caught between two revolving doors, both turning in opposite directions. She was awestruck on the one hand, not only by the situation but by the Duke's title. On the other hand, she was outraged at his blatant presumption.

Her dignity prevailed. "You're not anything like I imagined you to be from what I read in the guidebooks. Furthermore, you will have to look elsewhere for your afternoon's amusements, I'm afraid, because I don't sing or dance."

The Duke threw back his head and laughed, and the rich, masculine abandon of the sound stirred Frankie on a level of her being she had not been aware of before. "Take her to the keep," he said to someone standing just outside the hazy edges of Frankie's vision.

"But, Your Grace—"

"Now," Sunderlin interrupted.

She felt someone grasp her arm as the Duke turned and walked away, parting the crowd like the waters of the Red Sea as he passed.

"Now, just a moment, you," Frankie protested. She took a step away from the tree. When she did, the sky did a quick spin, her stomach jumped, and then the ground seemed to rush toward her.


BRADEN PAUSED WHEN SHE DARED TO challenge him, turned, and saw the wench crumpled in the summer grass. No one came forward to offer her aid, and from the way all the villagers hung back, staring and pointing, it was plain they were afraid of her. Damn them and their incessant superstitions; their lives were ruled by fearful imaginings of all sorts.

He went back, crouched, and lifted her into his arms. She felt strong and at the same time fragile, and something tugged at Braden's gut, deep down. Reaching his horse, he swung up onto the gelding's back, hauling his captive along with him.

A grin lifted one corner of his mouth as she opened her stone-gray eyes, looked up at him, sighed, and then sank against his chest again.

Braden turned his mount toward Sunderlin Keep and the drawbridge, reflecting as he rode, leaving the midsummer fair behind. She was a spectacular creature, this insensible wench in his arms, unusually fine and strong, clearly a misfit. He empathized with the loneliness of that, having always felt strangely misplaced in the world himself.

The villagers surely thought this woman was an angel, or a splendid witch.

She sighed again, looking up at him in a guileless way, and said, "If you're wondering why I'm not kicking and screaming right now, it's because I know I'm dreaming this. You aren't real—none of this is real—it's probably all part of some weird sexual fantasy."

Braden frowned. What an odd pronouncement. "Sexual fantasy"? Why would anyone indulge in such fancies when the real experience was so easily had?

He thought again of what the villagers were probably saying by now, and shook his head. It could not be denied, however, that this wench was different. She was bigger and stronger than any woman he'd ever seen—God's breath but she felt heavy on his arm, even though she was sleekly made—and her skin and teeth *were* uncommonly good. Still, Braden reasoned, he himself was of rare good health and sturdy construction, and he was certainly neither angel nor warlock.

"What," he began as they crossed the drawbridge, the hooves of his charger making a rhythmic sound on the wood, "are you blathering about?"

She took a deep breath, wiping aside the two bright ribbons that dangled across her face from the halo of flowers, now sitting askew on her head. "Well," she replied, "it's not something I can explain easily. I've always had a thing for knights and castles, and I played Guinevere in our high school production of *Camelot*—"

They passed beneath the points of the iron portcullis and into the lower bailey. "Guinevere?" Braden asked, somewhat shortly. He'd heard the legends of King Arthur as a child, and loved them, but he couldn't see what they had to do with the afternoon's events. "I thought you said you were called Francesca."

She smiled, and the effect was startling; rather like sunlight flashing suddenly upon very clear water. Once again he felt a lurching sensation, much like the time in his boyhood when he'd nearly toppled off a cliff and a companion had caught hold of his tunic just in time to pull him back. "My friends call me Frankie," she said.

Braden couldn't help smiling back, even though he didn't approve of a woman having such a name—even if she was a lightskirt, selling her favors at a country fair. "Frankie" was better suited to a lad; to him, she would always be "Francesca."

*Always?* The word stretched through Braden's mind like a vine gone wild, making him distinctly uncomfortable.

"Are you traveling with the mummers or the puppeteers?" he asked. "I haven't seen you before."

She laughed, and the sound quivered in his heart like a lance, at once painful and sweet. "You know, it's just like me to have a fantasy where the man who is going to ravish me turns out to be a nice guy. You are nice, aren't you?"

He was baffled again, and at no behest from him, his arm tightened slightly around her. "I don't know," he replied thoughtfully. "No one has ever described me that way as far as I know." Braden felt his neck reddening, drew back on the reins, and swung one muscular leg over the saddle horn, at the same time lowering Francesca to the ground. "Furthermore," he said, "I've never *ravished* a woman in my life. They've always come to my bed quite willingly."

Francesca's flawless cheeks turned pink, and the gray eyes sparked. "Fantasy or no fantasy, buddy," she replied, "I'm not going to your bed, period. Willingly or otherwise."

Braden dismounted. "We'll see," he said. He tossed the reins to a stable boy and gripped Francesca's arm with his other hand, propelling her up the slope toward the keep.

# Two

Solicitously the Duke straightened the beribboned floral wreath Frankie had bought earlier, in the real world. Then, with an air of amused ceremony, he squired her under a high archway and into the keep's Great Hall.

There were rushes on the floor, and knights lounged at long trestle tables, playing dice and arm wrestling. There was no hearth or chimney but instead a huge firepit in the center of the hall. Smoke meandered toward a large round hole in the roof, turning the air acrid before disappearing into the sky.

Frankie coughed, blinking because her eyes burned and because she couldn't believe what she was seeing. Surely this was the most elaborate hallucination anyone had ever had, without taking drugs first.

She rubbed her right temple nervously. Maybe the scones she'd had at the inn that morning had been laced with something. Or perhaps someone had slipped her a mickey at the fair.

Both scenarios seemed unlikely, but so did finding herself in a place she'd only read about, a time centuries in the past. Just then, not much of anything was making sense to Frankie—including the staggering and surely ill-advised attraction she felt toward the Duke.

The men-at-arms looked up from their mugs and games to leer at Frankie in earnest, but one quelling glance from the Duke made them all subside again.

"What year is this?" Frankie asked, squinting up at Sunderlin's daunting profile as he double-stepped her over the rushes toward a wide stone stairway lined with unlit torches.

He looked down at her and frowned, but he didn't slacken his pace. "It is the year of our Lord thirteen hundred and sixty-seven," he answered. "Where have you been that you had to ask such a question? Even in nunneries, they mark the passage of time."

Frankie's head was spinning, and she felt a peculiar mix of desire and utter terror. They were taking the stairs at a good clip; evidently, this fantasy was going to reach its dramatic crescendo soon.

"If I told you where I'd been, you'd never believe me," she replied. "Suffice it to say, it wasn't a 'nunnery,' as you put it." She dug in her heels, or tried to, but the Duke just kept walking. "Wait a second! Could we just stop and talk, please? I mean, I know this is all a production of my subconscious mind, starring me, with a guest appearance by you, but I'm not ready to play out the big scene."

Sunderlin finally halted, square in the middle of the upper

hallway, and stared at Frankie as if completely confounded. It was all so real—the dank stone walls of the castle, the burnt-pitch smell of the torches, the remarkable muscular man standing beside her. She marveled at the power of the human imagination; clearly, her yearnings for adventure and romance had run much deeper than she'd ever guessed. Now her mind was producing the whole dream like some elaborate play, though she must remember that it was all taking place inside her head.

"What in the name of God are you talking about?" he demanded. Even in his consternation, the Duke exuded self-confidence and personal strength.

Frankie reached out and pressed one palm to the cold rock wall, to steady herself. She was ready to wake up now, ready to go home to Kansas, so to speak, and yet the idea of never seeing Sunderlin again struck a resonant note of sorrow in her heart. It was a sensation she couldn't have explained, as mystical as the experience in general.

"I don't feel so good," she said.

Sunderlin bent his knees and peered into her face, which was probably quite pale by then. "You don't have the plague, I hope," he replied.

Frankie could only shake her head.

"Here, then, you're probably starving, and it's plain that you've come from some far place." He lifted her into his arms again, just as he had at the fair, when she'd been surrounded by curious villagers. "I'll send for some food and wine, and when you've had a rest, I'll bed you."

Frankie's temper flared, even though she knew she was only dreaming. "That's very generous of you, my lord," she said tartly. Sunderlin carried her into yet another large, drafty chamber and dumped her onto a bed roughly the size of her whole apartment back home. "Now, what on earth does *this* symbolize?" she muttered, distracted for a moment, as she patted the thick feather mattress with both hands.

"Enough of your strange chatter," Sunderlin growled, bending over her and forcing her backward until she was lying flat. His arms were like stone pillars on either side of her as he leaned on the bed. "God's kneecaps, woman, the villagers are sure to think you're either a witch or an angel. There's something very different about you, and to their minds, anyone who is different is dangerous. If they decide you're a sorceress, they might very well stone you or burn you at the stake!"

Frankie was completely undone, but not by the delusion she was having or even by the prospect of being executed for sorcery. No, it was the proximity of Braden Stuart-Ramsey, Duke of Sunderlin, that was making her so wildly nervous.

She reached up, with a trembling hand, to touch his tanned, clean-shaven face. "You seem so real, so solid."

He made an exasperated sound, then leaned closer still and brushed his lips across hers. His mouth felt soft and warm, and a hot shiver rushed through Frankie's system.

"I am definitely 'real,'" Sunderlin said, his voice hoarse. Then, just when Frankie wanted the fantasy to continue, he pushed himself away from her and stood straight beside the bed. Never taking his eyes from hers, he unbuckled his sword belt and laid it aside, weapon and all. "Who are you, Francesca?" he asked. "Where did you come from?"

Frankie knew she should have bounded off that bed immediately—everything she believed as a modern, right-thinking female demanded it—but she was possessed of an odd lethargy. She yawned. "This is not going to compute," she said, "but since you insist, here goes. My name is Francesca Whittier, and I'm from the United States."

Sunderlin pulled his tunic off over the top of his head, revealing a broad, hairy chest and powerful shoulders. His glorious caramel-colored hair was rumpled by the process. "The United States?" he asked, giving a braided bellpull a hard wrench and then reaching for a ewer of water sitting on a nearby table. "I've never heard of that place. Where is it?"

"On the other side of the Atlantic Ocean," Frankie said, watching him. As hallucinations went, the Duke of Sunderlin was downright delicious. "At this point you could only describe it as—underdeveloped."

A servant entered the room, probably in reply to Sunderlin's yank on the bellpull, a bow-legged little man in leggings and a tunic that looked as though it might have been made of especially coarse burlap.

The Duke spoke to him in an undertone, and he disappeared again. Even though the servant had not so much as glanced in Frankie's direction, his curiosity had been palpable.

"Mordag will bring you bread and wine," Sunderlin said. He'd washed his face and upper body and was now drying himself with his discarded tunic. "As I said, you may eat and sleep for a reasonable time. Then you and I will work out an agreement."

Frankie felt her cheeks turn hot again. "I very much appreciate your hospitality," she said in measured tones. "However, there's no need for us to 'work out an agreement.' As I told you before, I am not a prostitute."

Sunderlin's white teeth flashed in a grin so lethal it should have been registered somewhere. He folded his arms, which Frankie now noticed were scarred in places, and tilted his magnificent head to one side. "I see," he teased. "Then you must be a lady—one who's fallen upon unfortunate circumstances." He sketched a deep bow, and Frankie was flushed with fury, knowing he was mocking her.

At last she found the strength to scramble into a sitting position; not an easy task, since the mattress was so deep and soft. "I'd have *been* a lady if I'd gotten to the costume shop on time," she blurted.

"What?" he asked, frowning again.

"Never mind!" Frankie floundered around on the mattress for a while, making no progress. She finally turned over onto her belly and wriggled until she reached the side, where she swung her legs over and stood. "My point is," she went on, while Sunderlin stood grinning at her, "you shouldn't assume that I'm a loose woman just because of my clothes!"

Sunderlin approached, hooked one finger through the laces that held Frankie's bodice together. Underneath, she was wearing only a thin camisole of sand-washed silk. "Witch or angel," he said, his voice low and throaty, "you are fascinating."

Frankie swallowed and retreated a step. "Don't touch me," she said, without conviction.

Sunderlin reached out and pulled her against him. "Fascinating," he repeated.

She stiffened. "Are you planning to force me?" she demanded. "Because if you are, I'm warning you, I'll knee you where it hurts, and I'll scream my head off, too. Your reputation will be completely ruined!"

He threw back his head and laughed, and when he looked into her eyes again, a moment later, she saw kindness in his gaze, along with desire and amusement. "My reputation will be ruined," he corrected, "if the servants do not hear you crying out in passion." Sunderlin paused, sighed philosophically. "Didn't I tell you before, little witch? I have never in my life taken a woman who did not want my attentions." He held her loosely, his arms linked behind the small of her back, and bent to kiss the pulse point at the base of her throat.

Frankie felt faint. "Good," she replied when she could manage to speak. "I'm—I'm glad."

Sunderlin touched her breast, very gently, his thumb passing over one muslin-covered nipple and causing it to blossom. "Of course," he went on, idly entangling a finger in the laces that held her bodice closed, "I have no doubt that I can rouse a fever in you."

His arrogance was like a snowball in the face, and Frankie jerked back out of his arms just as the servant reappeared, carrying a tray. She turned away, embarrassed, and when she looked in Sunderlin's direction again, he had pulled on a clean tunic and the servant was gone.

"Refresh yourself," the Duke commanded, pausing in front of a looking glass to run splayed fingers through his hair. "I will return later." He paused as Frankie inspected the items on the tray. "Just in case you're thinking of escaping," he added, in grave tones, "don't. My men would find you before sunset, and honor would require that I punish you."

Frankie was too confused and scared to think about escape just then, but she meant to entertain the notion later, when she'd had a little time to gather her wits. She sketched a curtsy every bit as mocking as his bow had been earlier. "Your word is my command, O Pompous and Arrogant One," she said. Then she took a piece of dark bread from the trencher and examined it for weevils and other moving violations.

Sunderlin only grinned, strapped on Excalibur again, and walked out of the massive room, leaving Frankie quite alone.

She bit into the bread and reached for a brass bottle, which contained a bitter and very potent red wine. Normally, Frankie didn't drink, but on that day all the other rules of the universe seemed to be suspended—why not that one?

Having eaten, and consumed the wine, Frankie began to feel light-headed and sleepy again. Good, she thought. I'll wake up in my bed at the Grimsley Inn, or even back in Seattle, in my apartment, and all this will be over. A dream and nothing more.

As before, the thought of leaving Sunderlin left her strangely bereft, and close to tears.

She sniffled once as she stretched out on the featherbed.

Hours later she awakened to the same room, the same stone walls, and her shock was exceeded only by her relief. The dream or delusion had not yet ended, and she was glad, though she couldn't have offered a rational explanation for her attitude. Luckily, no one was asking for one.

"Mr. Stuart-Ramsey?" she called tentatively. "My lord?"

There was no response, but in the distance she heard the sounds of raucous male laughter and the music of some sort of pipe, as well as a stringed instrument or two. Frankie rolled to the side of the bed and struggled to her feet, smoothing her hair and her muslin skirts.

By the light of the moon, which came in through narrow windows empty of glass, Frankie found the bellpull, stared at it for a few moments, and then gripped the cord in both hands and gave it a good jerk.

The spindly servant appeared almost instantly, and Frankie wondered if the poor man was compelled to work at night as well as during the day. He carried a flickering candle, which he used to light oil lamps set around the room.

"You may tell the Duke that I will see him now," Frankie announced, with great dignity. Never mind that it was mostly pretense; she *sounded* sure of herself even if she wasn't.

Mordag merely looked at her in bewilderment and something like awe. His Adam's apple traveled the length of his scrawny, unwashed neck as he stood there, apparently at a complete loss to understand her instructions.

She drew a deep breath and very patiently began again. "I said—"

"He won't speak to you," a familiar voice interrupted. "He probably fears you'll either cast a spell over him or strike him dead for some secret sin."

Frankie turned and saw Sunderlin standing in the doorway. He said something unintelligible to Mordag, and the servant rushed from the room, plainly eager to be gone.

"Couldn't you just tell these people that I'm an ordinary woman?" she asked, exasperated.

Sunderlin smiled and ran his gaze over her in a leisurely way. "They wouldn't believe me," he replied after a moment's reflection. "And why should they? It's plain to any man with eyes that you're no 'ordinary woman.'"

Frankie felt dizzying confusion, as well as a terrible attraction to this strange and powerful man. She averted her eyes for a moment, wondering that a mere delusion, a figment of her imagination, could stir her the way Sunderlin did.

"Have you rested?" the Duke asked when she failed to continue the conversation, sitting down at a rough-hewn table near the bed and putting his feet up.

Unconsciously Frankie tightened the laces on her rented dress. "Yes," she said. "If you would just take me to a hotel now, I would appreciate it very much."

"Take you where?"

"An inn," Frankie said in frustration. "A tavern—"

Sunderlin swung his powerful legs down from the table-top and rose to his feet in a graceful surge of rage. "You would prefer such a place to my bed?" he demanded, breathing the words more than speaking them.

Frankie figured since this was a fantasy, she might as well be honest. "No," she said. "I guess not."

He approached her slowly. "You are a beautiful and very complicated creature," he said. "And you will be even lovelier in the throes of pleasure. Let me show you, Francesca." Sunderlin untied the laces at the bodice of her dress, and she did nothing to stop him.

"If—if I want you to stop—then—?"

"Then I shall stop," the Duke said.

Frankie closed her eyes as she felt the dress part, felt the cool night air spread over her breasts, causing the nipples to jut against the thin silk of her camisole.

"Lovely," Sunderlin said. He smoothed the dress down over her shoulders with excruciating gentleness, then removed the camisole, too. "So lovely."

Frankie trembled, afraid to meet his gaze even though his words and his tone held quiet reverence. He made her feel like a fallen goddess, too beautiful to be real.

"Look at me," the Duke commanded as he caressed first one breast and then the other. His touch had the weight of a moonbeam, the fierce heat of a newly spawned star.

She could not resist the order, could not move away or lift a hand to stop his sweet plundering. She met his eyes, entranced.

"What are you?" he asked in a raspy voice. "Tell me now, be you angel or witch?"

Frankie gave a long, quivering sigh as he fondled an eager nipple. "This is some fantasy," she said. "Wow."

Sunderlin bent, took the morsel he'd been caressing into his mouth, and suckled, wringing a cry of startled pleasure from Frankie's lips.

"Answer me," he said when he'd raised his head again.

Frankie wanted to press him back to her bosom, to nourish him, to set his senses ablaze as he had hers. "I'm whatever you want me to be," she replied, and she was rewarded by a low groan and the conquest of her other breast.

God only knew what would have happened if the clanging sound of metal striking stone hadn't sounded from the passage outside Sunderlin's chamber, along with a good-natured and exuberant male voice.

"Braden!" the visitor called as the Duke swore and

Frankie dived for the shadowy end of the chamber, struggling to right her dress. The clang sounded again, louder and closer. "Are you in there wenching, like Mordag says?"

Frankie heard Sunderlin swear and peered out of the gloom, holding the bodice of her dress closed, her breathing still fast and very shallow. A handsome man, younger than the Duke and much darker in coloring, swaggered into the room, sheathing his sword as he entered. Apparently, it had been the blade of that weapon that Frankie had heard striking the stone walls.

Sunderlin shrugged, adjusting his tunic. "Alaric," he greeted the other man, and there was an undercurrent of humor flowing beneath his irritation. "I thought you were in London Town, pandering at court."

Alaric laughed, ignoring the Duke's jibe and looking around with an expression of impudent curiosity. "Come now, Brother, where is she? I must see the creature or perish of wondering. Mordag says she's too beautiful and too perfect to be a human woman."

"Mordag talks too much," Sunderlin answered. He went to a side table, though it couldn't have been plainer that he didn't welcome company, and poured wine into two ornate silver chalices. "Show yourself, Francesca, or my brother will seek you out. He's just brazen enough to do it."

Frankie would have preferred to remain in the shadows, since she'd never found her camisole and, even though she'd pulled up her dress and tied the laces, there was still a lot of skin showing through. She came out of her hiding place anyway, her arms crossed demurely across her chest.

Alaric was definitely a new development, and she wondered where he fit into her fantasy.

He studied her with dark, shrewd eyes. Clearly, Alaric had the same forthright, supremely confident nature as his brother. Frankie was both relieved and puzzled to realize that she understood him clearly, as she did Braden.

"Neither angel nor witch," he said in a speculative tone, the hint of a smile lifting one corner of his mouth. "No, Brother, this is surely a wood nymph, or a mermaid weary of the sea."

What a line, Frankie thought, but she liked Alaric. It would have been impossible not to, for he was charming. She smiled as he took her hand and lightly kissed her knuckles. Out of the corner of her eye, she saw Sunderlin frowning ominously.

"Do not become too enchanted," he warned in a quiet voice. "Nymph or mermaid, angel or witch, Francesca is mine."

Frankie's proud heart pumped hot crimson color into her cheeks. "Unlike your favorite horse and your hunting dogs," she said, "I am not 'yours'! I'm my own."

Sunderlin's jaw tightened, and Alaric chuckled, obviously amused by his brother's annoyance. "Such a quick tongue," he said.

" 'How sharper than a serpent's tooth,' " Frankie quoted, getting into the spirit of things. She might as well enjoy this delusion to the hilt; there was no telling when or if she'd be able to work up another one like it.

"That's very good," said Alaric, waggling an index finger. "Someone should write it down."

"Someone will, someday," Frankie assured him.

Sunderlin narrowed his eyes again. "Witch talk," he said. "Have you no sense at all?"

The words stung. "Yes," Frankie snapped. "I also have a sense of humor—a claim *you* certainly can't make!"

"Sparks!" Alaric cried, spreading his arms in a gesture of expansive delight. "The air is blue with them!"

"Silence!" Sunderlin boomed, but it was Frankie he was glowering at, not his brother.

"In your dreams," Frankie answered, folding her arms and lifting her chin. Okay, so she was having a fantasy. Okay, so it was probably a *sexual* fantasy. That didn't mean she was going to let a man push her around, no matter how attractive she found him.

Alaric laughed again, bracing himself against a table edge with both hands. "At last," he said. "A woman who doesn't tremble before you like a blade of grass in a high wind. Brother, your fate is sealed. You are doomed. Congratulations!"

"Out," Sunderlin said. His gaze rested on the pulse point at the base of Frankie's throat, or so it seemed to her, but there was no doubt that he was addressing Alaric.

The younger brother bowed, but his good spirits were as evident as before. "As you wish," he said graciously. "Never fear, Braden. I will carry the news of your conquering to every part of England."

At last Sunderlin's stare shifted from Frankie to his sibling, and she let out an involuntary sigh of relief. The expression on the Duke's face could only have been called ferocious. "We will speak privately," he said to Alaric. "Now."

Frankie watched, a little nettled that she'd been forgotten so easily, as both men left the chamber.

# Three

It was that night, while she waited in vain in Sunderlin's bedchamber, alternately cursing Braden and praying for his return, that Frankie started to accept the possibility that the experience she was having was not a flight of fancy at all, but some new facet of reality.

A delusion, she reasoned as she lay beneath the covers on Braden's bed, clad only in her silk camisole and tap pants, would surely have faded by this time. Furthermore, while no sensible person would ever have described Frankie as a hardheaded realist, she wasn't given to wild imaginings, either. She wasn't insane, and her surroundings were simply too solid for a hallucination. The only other explanation was that she had slipped through some unseen doorway, into another time.

How could such a thing happen? Frankie had no answers, only questions. What seemed most remarkable to her was her own resilience—nervous breakdowns are made of such stuff as she was experiencing, and yet she had a sense of well-being and belonging now that had eluded her since childhood.

The first pink light of dawn was just creeping across the stone floor when Braden reappeared, looking rumpled and somewhat bleary-eyed.

Frankie sat bolt upright in bed, heedless of her near-naked state, furious jealousy flowing through her. Even with Geoffrey, she had never felt any emotion so intense. "Where have you been?" she demanded.

To her infinite exasperation, Braden grinned. "Not with a wench," he replied, "so calm yourself." He went to a table uncomfortably near the bed and poured water from a ewer into a waiting basin. He made a great production of stripping off his tunic and washing.

That done, he removed his soft leather shoes and woolen leggings as well. He loomed beside the bed, gloriously naked and utterly without self-consciousness.

Frankie's arousal was complete, and unbidden, and she was mortified by it. Blushing, she wriggled down under the bedclothes.

Braden promptly tossed back the thick fur coverings and surveyed her. "Such a strange manner of dress," he said, clearly confounded by her lingerie. "Still, I imagine you're a regular woman underneath."

Frankie's cheeks burned. She was two women, all of a sudden—one sensible and modest, one wanting nothing so much as to thrash beneath this man in noisy abandon. "Why is this happening?" she murmured. "Why me?"

The Duke bent over her, hooked his big thumbs under the waistband of Frankie's tap pants, and slid them deftly down over her thighs. She could only watch, stunned at the depths of her own feminine need, as he frowned, apparently more interested in watching the elastic stretch when he pulled, then snap back into place.

Finally he tossed the tap pants aside and looked at Frankie with a possessiveness and hunger that made her blood heat. With one hand he parted her thighs; with the other he tugged upward on her camisole.

Frankie closed her eyes and groaned softly as Braden's fingers claimed the most private part of her. It did no good, telling herself that this was no fantasy after all, that what was happening was real and would have its consequences. This was more than a mere encounter; Frankie felt as though she and Braden had been drawn together from separate parts of the universe.

She thrilled to his weight and warmth as he stretched out beside her. He bent his head to nibble at her breasts, one and then the other, all the while gently caressing her most feminine place.

He made a low, sighlike sound as Frankie began to twist and writhe under his attentions. Although she had thought she'd known pleasure before, with Geoffrey, the fitful realization came to her that she had instead been entirely innocent until this man, Braden Stuart-Ramsey, Duke of Sunderlin, touched her.

Braden nipped lightly at Frankie's nipple while at the same moment plunging his fingers deep inside her, and she arched her back and gave a strangled, joyous cry of welcome.

"*Braden,*" she pleaded, not precisely sure what she was

begging for, clutching at his bare shoulders with both hands. "Oh, dear God—Braden—"

He raised his head from her breast to look straight into her eyes. "This is what you were made for," he said, "and what I was made for. No, no—don't close your eyes, witch. Let me see your magic."

Frankie was practically out of her mind with need by that point, and Braden showed her no quarter. While his thumb made an endless, tantalizing circle, his fingers alternately teased and conquered.

She began to toss her head from side to side on the pillow while the incomprehensible ecstasy carried her higher and higher. Braden was choreographing her every move, and he would not let her look away, yet she had never known a greater sense of freedom. She was, in those fiery moments, more truly herself than she had ever been.

Frankie arched high off the mattress, a long, high, keening cry spilling from her throat as wild spasms of pleasure seized her. Again and again, her body buckled in fierce release, and Braden held her entranced the whole time, not only physically, but emotionally as well.

When at last she was sated, and she lay breathless and quivering, her flesh moist from her exertions, Braden caressed her, all over, with his big, gentle hands. He spoke soothingly and kissed places that still trembled with the aftershocks of cataclysmic pleasure, and then he held her. The holding, in its way, was as fulfilling as her repeated climaxes had been.

Frankie could not have said how much time had passed by the time Braden mounted her; she was only half-conscious, lost in bliss.

Braden took her wrists in his hands, frowning a little when he felt the band of her watch but not pausing to examine it, and raised her arms high over her head so that his body lay flush with hers.

"As I told you," he said, kissing her jaw as he spoke, "I have never taken a woman against her will. I want to be part of you, Francesca, to make you a part of me. Will you allow that?"

She whimpered softly, sleepily, feeling her nipples harden against his hairy chest and her feminine passage expand to receive him. "Please," she said, opening her legs. She was still intoxicated, and sleep beckoned seductively. "But—you will forgive me, won't you—if I drift off—?"

He chuckled. "You will be wide wake in a moment, witch," he said. "What happened before was only a preparation for this."

Truer words had never been spoken.

Frankie's heavy eyelids flew up as Braden entered her in one strong stroke, arousing her sated body all over again, bringing every nerve ending to frantic awareness.

Braden glided in and out of her a few times, still holding her wrists above her head, though gently, watching her face as though he found every changing expression fascinating. He was a modern lover, ahead of his violent, uncaring time.

When he knew she was wild with need, he withdrew and whispered raspily, "Tell me, beautiful Francesca—are you angel or witch?"

"Witch," she half-sobbed, and Braden lunged deep into her, covering her mouth with his own in the same instant and swallowing her shouts of passion.

It was dizzying, like riding some cosmic roller coaster.

Every moment, every nuance had to be experienced; there was no going back.

Until that morning Frankie had considered herself a knowledgeable woman. Admittedly, her past was unspectacular when it came to romance; she'd been intimate with Geoffrey and before him, a guy she'd dated in high school and college. She'd been aroused and, yes, satisfied, in a sweetly innocuous sort of way.

Now the Duke of Sunderlin, a man who might not even exist, had shown her that there were whole universes yet to be discovered and explored. He'd turned her inside out and outside in, and somehow, in a way she couldn't define, he'd given her a totally new sense of herself.

Braden held her for a long time, like before, then rose whistling from the bed to don a fresh tunic and woolen leggings. "I have things to attend to today," he said, pausing to pat Frankie solicitously on the bottom. "You can explore the keep if you want, and the grounds, too. Just don't wander into the village."

Frankie sat up, her sense of challenge stirred. "Why not?"

Braden shrugged. "Do as you wish, then. Be advised, though, that the villagers are saying you appeared out of nowhere—one moment, nothing, the next, there you were. Half of them want to declare you a saint and worship you accordingly, and the others lean toward roasting you on a spit, like a pig."

Frankie's eyes went wide, and her throat constricted as she imagined a martyr's death. "I'm scared!"

He kissed the tip of her nose. "Wise woman. I don't suppose I have to tell you that from the beginning, saints have fared even worse than witches. People can't bear the contrast, you see, between what they are and what they believe they should be."

"Thanks for trying to reassure me," Frankie snapped as Braden straightened and began strapping on his sword belt.

Braden grinned. "You're most welcome, milady. I'll have Mordag bring you one of my sister's gowns, as well as some breakfast."

Frankie brightened at the prospect of female companionship. "You have a sister, then. I would enjoy meeting her."

Braden's expression had turned stony, all in the space of a few moments. "That is impossible," he said. Then, without further explanation, he turned and walked out of the chamber, leaving Frankie alone.

True to his word, however, Braden sent Mordag with an underskirt and kirtle of the softest blue wool, brown bread and spotted pears for breakfast, and a ewer of clean water for washing.

Within half an hour Frankie had eaten, given herself a bath of sorts, and gotten dressed. The underskirt and kirtle were delightful; just what she'd hoped to find in the costume shop, the morning after her arrival in England.

Frankie stopped on the stone stairway, pressing one hand to the cold wall as if to test its substance. Odd, but her "memories" of a world six centuries in the future seemed to be fading, like a random dream.

It was real, she told herself, as real as this. Seattle, the inn, the costume shop, all of it was real. I mustn't forget.

She proceeded, after a moment, keeping to the rear passageways. She paused and hid in the shadows when she heard voices, not wanting to encounter superstitious servants or men-at-arms who might well consider her fair game.

Alas, Frankie had little or no experience at sneaking out of castles. She had almost gained the kitchen, and was looking back over one shoulder to make sure no one was following her, when she collided hard with Alaric.

He steadied her by gripping her shoulders. "Please, lovely one," he pleaded in a teasing voice, "tell me you've found the strength of soul to spurn my legendary brother."

Frankie was uneasy, even though Alaric's smile was ready and his touch was gentle. She sensed that he harbored some dangerous fury behind those bright, mirthful eyes. She shook her head. "Sorry," she responded, somewhat gravely. "I've never met anyone like Braden, and I rather enjoy his company."

*That* was certainly an understatement, she thought, as memories of just how intensely she'd enjoyed the Duke's company filled her mind. She was grateful for the dim light of the hallway, not wanting Alaric to see her blush.

For a fraction of a moment, a time so brief that Frankie would always wonder if she'd imagined it, Alaric's grasp on her shoulders tightened. His dazzling grin seemed slightly brittle as he released her.

"You shouldn't be wandering through the keep alone, milady," he said with a courtly bow of his head. "I'm surprised Braden allowed such a breach, as a matter of fact." Alaric paused, shrugged. "He leaves me no choice but to uphold the family honor by escorting you myself."

Frankie was still troubled by something in Alaric's manner, but she had to agree that it was safer to have a companion. "I'm happy to know that chivalry is not dead after all," she said.

They crossed the kitchen, a massive room empty except for two great hounds that lay sleeping on the hearth. When Alaric led her into a grassy sideyard, where sunlight played golden, like visible music, Frankie's spirits rose a notch.

Like all natives of Seattle, Frankie was reverently fond of sunshine. She raised her face to the light and spent a moment just soaking up the glorious stuff. When she opened her eyes, Alaric was smiling at her.

"I'm told that you arrived—er—quite suddenly yesterday, at the village fair," he said. "Is that true?"

Frankie lifted the skirts of her cloud-soft woolen dress and set off across the grass, headed for a copse of trees she'd spotted earlier, from Braden's window. She wondered if the branches of the maple were sturdy enough to support her, and if she'd be able to see over the castle wall if she climbed high.

"Of course not," she lied blithely, sensing that it would not be wise to tell Alaric what had really happened. "I arrived with a mummers' troupe and simply took my place in the crowd without being noticed."

Alaric kept up, taking long strides. His build was similar to Braden's, except that he was smaller, and his bone structure seemed fragile by comparison. "Of course I wouldn't think of questioning your word, milady, but it's hard to imagine you passing unnoticed anywhere. You seem to glow, and there's a knowingness in your manner, as if you might be privy to secrets the rest of us could never grasp."

They passed through tall grass, moving between stone

outbuildings that looked deserted, while Frankie considered her reply. She saw the maple trees up ahead, beckoning, offering her solace in their fragrant green leaves.

In the end she decided to respond by countering with a question. "What does it matter where I came from? Surely you don't believe that superstitious rot about my being a witch or an angel."

Frankie thought she saw a muscle tighten in Alaric's jaw, though she couldn't be certain. "Of course I don't believe that. Like my brother, I am an educated man, but I know how dangerous the beliefs of simple people can be."

They had reached the copse, and Frankie inspected a promising tree with a fork in its trunk and a great many sturdy branches. "I've had this lecture already," she said, without looking at her companion. Instead, Frankie was recalling her happy childhood in Seattle, and the big elm that had stood in the backyard. "Don't worry, Alaric. I have no intention of wandering off to the village and getting everyone all worked up again."

With that, Frankie hiked her skirts a little, gripped the trunk of the tree in both hands, and hoisted herself up into the fork.

"Here, now," Alaric protested. "You'll break a limb!"

Frankie proceeded upward, rustling leaves as she went. "Since I know you meant that in only the kindest sense of the word," she called down cheerfully, "I won't take offense." Clinging to the gnarled old tree, she fixed her gaze on the world beyond the orchard, beyond the castle grounds.

The village, made up of tiny daub and wattle structures with thatch roofs, stood in much the same place as it would six hundred years in the future, but the forests to the west looked denser and far more primordial. The remaining three directions were choked with fields, and narrow cow paths served as roads. Far out, beyond the thriving crops, Frankie saw a croft or two, but it was plain enough that Braden was pretty much master of all she surveyed.

"Come down," Alaric wheedled, a thread of irritation vibrating in his voice. "It's not ladylike, climbing about like that!"

"Surely you've guessed by now that I'm not a lady," Frankie replied sunnily, settling herself on a thick branch and smoothing her borrowed skirts. In doing that, she remembered Braden's sudden mood change when he'd mentioned having a sister. "Is it just you and Braden, Alaric, or are there more Stuart-Ramseys running around the countryside?"

"We have a sister," Alaric answered. "Now get yourself down here before I'm forced to climb up after you."

We *have* a sister, he'd said. When Braden had spoken of a female sibling that morning, he'd used the past tense. "Calm down—I'm an expert tree-climber. Tell me about your sister. What is her name? Where does she live?"

Alaric's sigh rose through the maple leaves with a soft summer breeze. "Her name is Rianne, she's seventeen, and Braden sold her off to a distant cousin in Scotland. Furthermore, he'll have me chained to a wall and whipped if he finds out I've been talking about the matter. Now—please come down."

Frankie lingered, swinging her legs and thinking. "You don't mean he forced her to marry someone she didn't love?"

"Love." Alaric practically spat the word. "Now, there's a fatuous notion." He gripped the trunk of the tree and gave it a slight shake. "Love didn't enter into the bargain, Francesca. Braden caught Rianne kissing the chandler's boy, and he was outraged. He gave her a choice between our esteemed cousin and a long stay in a nunnery and—and I can't imagine why I'm telling you all this."

"Did she choose the cousin over the nunnery, then?"

"No. She said she was going to travel all the way to London and then throw herself into the Thames. *Braden* chose the cousin. He believed Rianne would be better off with a man to keep her out of trouble, and he was probably right."

Frankie was horrified to comprehend just how wide the breach of time and custom between herself and Braden really was. "She should have spit in his eye—he had no right to make such a decree!"

When Alaric replied, which wasn't until several moments of vibrant silence had passed, he sounded confused, nervous, and not a little exasperated. "Braden is a duke. Everyone obeys him, except for the King and the Almighty Himself. Rianne was foolish to anger him in the first place."

Just as Frankie opened her mouth to announce that, in her opinion, the Duke was long overdue for some consciousness raising, a very strange thing happened. A loud thrumming sound filled Frankie's ears, and she felt dizzy, as if she might topple out of the tree. Her vision was blurred and her stomach lurched.

Looking down, she barely made out the figure of Alaric. He was standing eerily still and staring up at her with his mouth open, one hand outspread in a conversational gesture.

Frankie wrapped one arm tightly around the tree trunk and held on. "All right," she said aloud, "what's going on here?"

She heard a rustling sound, saw a glimmer of blue silk out of the corner of one eye. When she made herself turn her head and look, she was flabbergasted.

Sitting on a branch in the next tree was the wizard she'd seen the day before, peering through the window of the costume shop in Grimsley. He was a tall man, obviously not at home in the high regions of a maple, and he held on to his splendid, pointed hat with one bejeweled hand. His white beard was filled with twigs and parts of leaves, and ice-blue eyes snapped behind round glass spectacles as he glared at Frankie.

"Who are you?" she demanded.

"My name is Merlin, not that it's important," he replied with a distinct lack of enthusiasm. Plainly, he had not situated himself in the branches of a tree, decked out in full wizard gear, to make small talk. "Kindly listen, Miss Whittier, and listen well. We don't have much time."

Frankie swallowed. Merlin, she thought skeptically. Right. She couldn't think why the sudden appearance of a wizard surprised her so much, given all that had gone before, but she was definitely in shock. "Wh-what did you do to him?" she asked, looking down at Alaric, who was still standing down there with his mouth open.

Merlin made a dismissive gesture with one hand and nearly fell out of the tree. "He'll be perfectly all right, more's the pity. It's his job, in fact, to run the Stuart-Ramsey estates into rack and ruin."

Frankie thought of Braden, and how much his small kingdom probably meant to him, and felt wounded. "What about Bra—the Duke? He's the firstborn son. The title and the estates are his."

The wizard sighed. "Not for long," he replied regretfully. "There's a tournament coming up, about a week hence. Sunderlin will be killed, run through with an opponent's blade when sport turns to deadly combat."

"No," Frankie breathed. In that instant, of all instants, she realized that, as incredible as it seemed, she loved Braden. If he died, she might well perish from the grief, no matter how she fought to stay alive. "No, it can't be—I'll warn him!"

"He won't listen."

Frankie was desperate. "Isn't there some way—?"

"Perhaps," Merlin answered grudgingly, and his expression was grim. "I wasn't in favor of your coming here, but since a mistake had been made in the Beginning—"

"A mistake?" Frankie held on tighter to the tree, and her voice came out in a squeak. "What are you talking about? And why *did* I end up here in Merry Old England?"

"You and Sunderlin were matched, long ago, before the tapestry of time was woven. There was an error, and somehow he was born in the wrong century, to the wrong parents. On some level of your being, you must have known, and come in search of him."

"Impossible," Frankie breathed. It was no comfort that the wizard's remarks rang true, somewhere deep inside her. "I don't know how I made the trip, but I didn't do it on purpose. The whole thing came as a big shock."

"I understand that," Merlin answered, somewhat brusquely. "Well, there's nothing for it. You'll just have to think long and hard of your own time. That should put you back where you belong, though I can't promise you won't find yourself an old woman or a very young child. These matters are not precise, you know. You can only be sure of landing somewhere in your original life span."

Frankie heard the vaguest humming sound, and she sensed that the magician would disappear in a moment, and that Alaric was already beginning to stir from his enchantment. "Never mind all that," she blurted. "Just tell me how to help Braden!"

For the first time Merlin smiled, but the expression in his eyes was regretful. "Love is the answer to every question," he said, and then, between one instant and the next, he was gone. He didn't even take the time to do a fade-out.

Frankie hesitated a few moments, collecting herself, then shinnied quickly down the tree, practically landing on a befuddled Alaric, who had just started to climb up after her. Gaining the ground, she lifted her skirts, without pausing to offer even a word of explanation, and ran toward the castle as if all eternity hinged on haste.

# Four

Frankie found Braden on the other side of the castle, his upper body protected by chain mail, wielding his fancy sword. His opponent was a young knight, obviously eager to prove his prowess on the field of battle.

Thinking only of what Merlin, the magician, had just told her—that Braden would die by the sword in a week's time—Frankie hesitated just briefly. She would have marched right into the center of the large circle of loose dirt if Alaric hadn't crooked an arm around her waist and stopped her.

The small fracas drew Braden's attention, and in that brief moment of distraction, his adversary struck, reckless in his enthusiasm. Bringing his sword downward, from shoulder height, he made a deep gash in the Duke's right thigh.

There were eight or ten men crowded around, watching the morning exercise, and a shout of outrage went up as blood stained Braden's gray leggings to crimson.

For Frankie, all of this took place in a pounding haze, rather like a slow-motion sequence in a movie. In reality, of course, it happened in the space of seconds. She screamed and struggled so violently that Alaric could not hold her.

Braden was still standing when she fought her way through the crowd of men pressed close around him, but she was alarmed by the ghastly paleness of his face. He looked at her as though she were an enemy, as though she herself had wounded him.

There were mutterings in the small assembly, and Frankie heard the word *witch*, but she didn't think of the implications. All that mattered then was Braden, that he be well and whole, and somehow saved from the fate that awaited him.

A rotund bearded man in coarse robes took charge. "Steady him," he ordered, crouching at Braden's feet. Two men immediately came forward to stand close, lest their leader need them. The big man tied a band of cloth around the Duke's upper thigh, just above the deep cut, and pulled it tight.

Braden flinched and swayed slightly, but remained on his feet. His gaze, accusatory and bewildered, had never left Frankie's face. "Continue with your practice," he said to his men, and then he limped toward her.

Only when Braden was standing close did Frankie realize that her cheeks were wet with tears.

"I'm sorry," she said brokenly. "I didn't mean—"

"Come along, Your Lordship," the heavy man interceded. "You'll be in need of some looking after."

Braden raised one hand and, with the rough side of his thumb, wiped Frankie's cheek. Then one corner of his mouth rose in the merest hint of a smile. "What was so important, Francesca, that you would burst into the middle of swordplay like that?"

Frankie shouldered aside the man who'd been hovering close to Braden and slipped under the Duke's arm to help support him. She couldn't very well explain about Merlin, not with so many superstitious ears about. Besides, she was more concerned, for the moment, with the state of Braden's health. Her thoughts had shifted to medieval medical practices.

"Never mind," she said, feeling injured because Braden was. "We can discuss that later. You're not going to let these yokels put leeches on you, I hope—you've lost enough blood as it is, and the possibility of infection—"

The heavy man, who was supporting Braden on the other side, leaned around the Duke's chest to glower at Frankie. "Yokels?"

An exasperated sigh burst from Braden's lips. "Perhaps you two could argue this out later, when I may be spared the pleasure of listening."

Alaric, who had been following the small party, sprinted ahead to walk backward in front of Braden, talking a mile a minute. "I tried to stop her," he said, taking care not to meet Frankie's gaze. "God's knees, Braden, but you look like a walking corpse—"

Frankie tuned him out, concentrating instead on the Duke's needs. She was no doctor, of course, but she'd had intensive instruction in first aid while being trained as a flight attendant. She wasn't about to leave Braden to the mercies of people who might pack his wound with sheep dung or drain away still more of his blood.

They entered the Great Hall, and the smoky atmosphere

made Frankie's eyes burn. Braden stumbled once as they moved toward the stairs, and then his knees buckled.

"No farther," ordered the heavy man, who had taken charge from the first. "You must lie down, milord."

"You make much of little, Gilford," Braden said, and Frankie heard affection in his voice, as well as impatience and no small amount of pain.

Nevertheless, one of the great trestle tables lining the Hall was cleared of salt cellars and wine ewers, and Braden lay down on the surface without further protest.

Gilford looked across the table at Frankie, who stood staunchly on the other side, keeping her stubborn vigil. "You are in the way, wench. Leave us."

"Not on your life," Frankie replied.

Braden chuckled, but he was looking worse with every passing moment, even though the tourniquet had slowed the bleeding from his thigh. "Don't waste your breath arguing with her," he warned his friend. "Francesca's opinions are as immovable as the walls of this castle."

Gilford treated her to a scathing glare. "Then perhaps she can make herself useful in other ways. By fetching wine, and my herbal kit."

Frankie tightened her grip on Braden's hand. "Alaric can do those things, or one of the servants. I'm staying right here."

Alaric needed no urging; he rushed off to get the things Gilford wanted. In the meantime, the castle medicine man took a knife from the folds of his robe and began cutting away Braden's bloody leggings.

Frankie swayed slightly when she saw just how bad the

wound was, but she willed new strength into her knees and somehow stilled the tempest in her stomach. "Shouldn't someone be boiling water?" she asked shakily.

"The water is filthy," Gilford said. "I will clean the area with wine."

His statement jarred Frankie, and she lifted her gaze to his face again. "You know about antisepsis?" she asked.

"You," Gilford replied, "are not the only stranger in these here parts, young woman."

Frankie's mouth fell open. Automatically she stroked Braden's sweat-dampened forehead with one hand, but it was the castle physician who held her attention. "When?" she asked in barely a whisper. There was no one else close by, since Alaric had gone off on his errand and the sword practice had continued outside, per Braden's orders.

"Seventy-two," Gilford said. "I came here to get away from my practice in London for a while—I was suffering from what you Americans call burnout. Went to sleep there, woke up here. For a long time I thought I'd lost my mind."

Frankie nodded her understanding, but could say nothing. Merlin hadn't mentioned that there were other time-travelers abroad, but then, they hadn't talked for very long.

"What in the name of God's Great Aunt are you two talking about?" Braden asked, slurring his words. He was waxen, and although his flesh felt cold, he was sweating.

"Cabbages and kings," Gilford told the Duke. "Just lie there, please, and conserve your strength." Alaric returned with the wine and the doctor's herbal kit, and Gilford used the alcohol to clean the wound. Braden drifted in and out of consciousness, and the physician talked to Frankie in even tones as he worked. "I've never wanted to go back, you know. Strange as it seems, I feel I belong here. What about you? What part of the Rebel Colonies do you hail from?"

Frankie was trying to funnel her own strength into Braden, and she didn't look up from his face when she answered. "It was nineteen-ninety-three when I left," she said. "And I'm from Seattle, in Washington State."

"Hmmmm," said Gilford, packing Braden's wound with an herbal concoction. "He's going to have a nasty scar, here, but I've no catgut to stitch him up with. I was in Seattle once, on a holiday tour. My wife and I flew there by way of New York and Chicago and took a sailing ship up the coast to Alaska. Spectacular experience."

Braden laughed stupidly. "Flying," he said. "There's a picture, Gilford—you, flying. Didn't your arms get tired?"

Despite the fact that her eyes were red and puffy from crying, Frankie laughed, too. "Do you miss your life in the twentieth century?" she asked Gilford when she'd had a few moments to regain her composure. "Your wife must be very worried."

Gilford sighed. "I suppose I'm on some police roster," he said. "One of those pesky people who've just disappeared from the face of the earth without leaving a trace behind. As for my wife's state of mind, well, Zenobia is the resilient type. By now, she's probably sold my practice and remarried."

"You've been here a long time, then?"

"Roughly twenty years, now," Gilford answered, binding Braden's thigh with clean cloth taken from his own supply kit. "I've been happy the whole while, too."

Frankie studied the doctor closely. "How did you know I was a time-traveler like you?"

At last Gilford favored her with a smile. A rather nice one, as a matter of fact. "I'm a doctor. After only one look at you, I knew you'd grown up in a world where there was relatively clean water to drink, healthy nutrition, excellent medical care, and the like. Most of the people around us, in case you haven't noticed, are rather fragile creatures."

Frankie still held Braden's hand, and unconsciously she cradled it between her breasts. "What of the Duke? He's certainly nothing like them."

Gilford smiled at Braden, who had drifted off to sleep. No doubt the herbs the doctor had administered were responsible for that. "No, he isn't. He's a misfit, like you and me."

Frankie liked Gilford, despite their getting off on the wrong foot earlier, and it was a great comfort to know she was not the only one who'd ever found herself in the wrong century. "Are there others?" she asked.

"Other time-travelers?" Gilford was using the last of the wine to wash Braden's blood from his hands. "Almost certainly. If it happened to us, then surely someone else has experienced the same phenomenon. You, however, are the first such sojourner I've had the good fortune to meet." He summoned Alaric, who had been hovering at a little distance throughout the procedure, and sent him off for men to carry Braden upstairs. "You've been very careless so far, Francesca," the medical man scolded after Alaric hurried away on his mission. "These people fear what they do not understand, and what they fear, they destroy. You must guard your tongue, in the future, and try not to be so brazen."

Frankie felt faint and gripped the edge of the table to

steady herself. "I'm no fool, Doctor—I don't want to be hanged, or burned at the stake, and I promise I'll be more careful. At the moment, though, it's Braden I'm worried about—is he going to make it? How long will he be laid up with this injury?" She held her breath while she waited for Gilford's answer.

The portly time-traveler sighed again and folded his bulky arms. "Sunderlin will recover, I'm sure—he has the personal tenacity and physical strength of a mountain goat. And my guess is, he'll be up and walking about on that leg within a day or two, though I'd much prefer that he rest."

Frankie was torn, feeling both joy and terrible desolation. Braden would get well, that was wonderful. But if he truly was back on his feet in a matter of days, he would still participate in the tournament in a week's time. And that meant he would die.

"You're his doctor! Can't you order him to stay in bed until he's had a chance to mend?"

Sadly Gilford shook his head. "No one keeps this man from doing exactly as he wishes," he said.

Frankie confided in him about her encounter with Merlin that day, and told of the dire prediction the magician had made, but only in the barest detail. She felt drained; so much had happened, just since she'd opened her eyes that morning, that it seemed she'd lived a whole decade without taking a breath.

Alaric returned with two big men, and they carried Braden to his room. Frankie sat with Braden until midafternoon, then, satisfied that he was sleeping comfortably, went off to get some fresh air and some perspective on the situation.

She was drawn to the chapel, which she found by trial and error on the ground floor of the castle, well away from the Great Hall and the usually busy kitchen. She was not a particularly religious person, but a spiritual one, and sitting in that small chamber, with its rough-hewn benches, rows of unlit candles, and towering wooden cross, was like nestling in the soul of God.

"Show me what to do," she whispered, clasping her hands together tightly in her lap. "Please. Show me how to save Braden from the sword."

No ready answer came to Frankie, and yet she was restored by the mystical peace of the place. It seemed then that there was indeed a solution, and that she would find it.

After an hour she went back to Braden's chamber and found him sitting up in bed, drinking ale from a wooden mug. His color was better, but his mood was sour indeed.

"Why, Francesca?" he demanded hoarsely, virtually impaling her with his sharp gaze. "Why did you interfere with the fighting that way? The distraction could have gotten me killed."

Frankie kept her distance, even though she knew instinctively that Braden would never hurt her. "I told you I was sorry. And I was coming to—to warn you about something."

Braden's brows knitted together for a moment as he frowned. "Warn me? About what?"

She swallowed. This was not going to be easy. Braden probably wouldn't believe her story, and she didn't blame him. "I met a wizard today—his name was Merlin. He said you were going to be killed a week from now, fighting in a tournament."

Braden refilled his cup from a jug on the table next to his bed and took an audible gulp, then filled his mouth again, so that his cheeks bulged. He swallowed once more, and his voice came out sounding raspy when he spoke. "A wizard," he repeated with irony.

Frankie's temper flared when she heard the quiet annoyance and thinly veiled pity in his tone. "Yes."

The Duke was not looking at her when he spoke again. "Alaric was with you. Did he see this man of magic, too?"

Braden's manner told Frankie it was Alaric's presence he was concerned about, not the wizard's. Despite her frustration, and her fear, she felt a little thrill of pleasure at the realization that Braden was jealous.

"No," she answered, gaining confidence. "Alaric didn't see anything. He was frozen, between one heartbeat and the next, and freed only when Merlin permitted it."

Braden reached out suddenly, grasped her hand, and squeezed. His face was filled with an anguish Frankie suspected was unrelated to the wound in his thigh. "Francesca," he whispered, "promise me, please, that you will not speak thus, of wizards and the like, to anyone but me."

She sat down on the edge of his bed and smiled softly. In those moments Frankie was filled with immeasurable joy and equally unfathomable sorrow, for it was then that she grasped the terrible, wonderful miracle that had occurred. She was in love with Sunderlin, and that love was an eternal thing, meant to outlive both of them.

She smoothed Sunderlin's rumpled, dusty hair back from his forehead. "I do promise to try, Braden," she said gently. "But I'm impulsive, and sometimes words are out of my mouth before I know I was even thinking them."

Braden lifted her hand to his lips, sent a charge of emotion through her merely by kissing her knuckles. "You and Gilford were saying very strange things today," he recalled after some moments had passed. "He has always refused to explain his odd talents and beliefs. Will you refuse as well?"

Careful not to bump Braden's injured leg, Frankie made a place for herself beside him, resting her back against his shoulder, turning her face into his neck. "I'll tell you everything," she said. "But I'm so afraid, Braden. So very afraid."

"Why?" He entangled a finger in one of her curls, twisted with an idle gentleness that somehow stirred her heart. "I know there's something different about you, but I'll not declare you angel *or* witch, and I promise I'll protect you from the whole of the world if need be."

Frankie was touched to the core of her spirit. Why, she wondered sadly, couldn't she have met this man in her own time, where they might have had a happy life together? Here, they had a mere week to share.

She sighed, settled closer to Braden, and began to talk. She told him about Seattle, and other modern cities. She described flying to New York in a jumbo jet, and then crossing the Atlantic the same way, to land in London. Braden listened to the whole story, in what was probably a stunned silence, never interrupting.

Frankie spoke of her trip to the village of Grimsley, the Medieval Fair that was held there every year, for the tourists, her attempt to rent a costume, the glimpse she'd caught of Merlin through the shop window, her unscheduled trip through time.

When it was over, Braden shifted both himself and Frankie, so that he could look deep into her eyes. "How could one person devise such a tale?"

Tears brimmed along her lower lashes. "I'm not making anything up, Braden," she said. "It's all true. And I saw that same wizard again this morning, like I told you. He said you were supposed to be born in my time, the future, but there was some sort of mistake and you ended up here. And you're going to be killed in a tournament next week, unless you call it off."

His face hardened, and Frankie saw in his light brown eyes both bewilderment and the desire to trust her. "I cannot do such a thing. I am not a coward, and I won't have the whole of England saying I heeded the words of a witch!"

Frankie wriggled off the bed and stood, disappointed and stung even though she'd known he wouldn't readily believe her story. "All right. You're a hardheaded, arrogant, opinionated *male*, and as such you aren't about to listen to reason. Well, that's just fine, but I don't intend to hang around here, caring more with every day that passes, only to see you run through with a sword!"

She would have turned and fled the room then, and maybe the castle and the village, too, but Braden caught hold of her hand and held it fast.

" 'Caring more with every day that passes,' is it?" he asked in a low, teasing voice. "Confess, witch—are you falling in love with me?"

It was worse, Frankie admitted to herself. She'd already

fallen. But that didn't mean she had to let Braden know. "Of course not." She thought fast. "Alaric is more my type."

"What?" Braden snapped the word, and his color, so good a moment before, had gone waxen again.

Frankie looked away, biting her lip. She couldn't say any more; the lie was too profound, the truth too holy.

"Look at me, Francesca," Braden ordered gravely.

She looked, not because of his command, but because she was hungry for the sight of him. And she despised that hunger, even as she succumbed to it.

"Whatever you are, witch or angel," Braden said, "you've managed to cast an enchantment over me. I must have you, no matter what else I gain or lose. In you I will plant my children, and all my hopes of joy and passion."

Frankie stared at him, dumbfounded, wondering at the new universe that had sprung to life inside her, a vast expanse of love for this one man.

He smiled and caressed her cheek, then pushed her off the bed, where she scrambled to get and keep her footing.

"Summon Mordag," he said, gesturing toward the bell-pull. "I would have him fetch a priest."

# Five

Frankie recovered some of her aplomb only after she'd given the bellrope a good yank. "Braden, stop and think. We can't be married—we're from different universes! Besides, you don't even know me, really, and I don't know you, either."

"Happens all the time," Braden said, settling back on the pillows and folding his great arms. "My mother came from the North to be wed to my father—the first time they laid eyes on each other was at the ceremony." He hoisted himself from the bed, and Frankie winced as he flexed his injured leg. "That marriage went well enough."

Frankie ignored the comment. "Shouldn't you be lying down?"

Braden was walking back and forth over the rushes, his jaw set, his face colorless as he dealt with the inevitable pain. He did not reply, except to pinion her with a brief, fierce glare.

Mordag appeared soon enough, bowing and scraping and plainly alarmed that his master was up and about so soon after sustaining a wound. He chattered away in Old English and distractedly Frankie wondered why she could understand Braden and Alaric, but not the ordinary people.

Braden told Mordag to go into the village and bring back the priest, but before that, he was to send up women servants to groom "the lady" for a wedding.

"I haven't agreed to your proposal yet, you know," Frankie pointed out, somewhat shakily. "You're being a bit hasty, don't you think?"

"No," Sunderlin answered succinctly. His color was returning now, and he moved more easily. "Even now my son and heir may already nestle in your womb. There will be no question of his legitimacy."

"It's equally possible that there is no child," Frankie reasoned. "We've only—we've only been together once, you know."

Sunderlin smiled. "Once is often enough. I'm sure that's true even in your faraway world."

Frankie gaped at him for a moment, then blurted out, "You believe me, then?"

He came to her, fondly lifted a tendril of her chin-length hair, rubbed it between his fingers, and let it fall back into place. "At first," he reflected with a bemused grin, "I thought you had been shorn in some asylum while suffering from a brain fever. But reason tells me that you are too sound, not only of body but of disposition, to have been through such an illness." Braden paused, sighed, kissed her forehead. "Yes, I think I believe you, Francesca, though I don't claim to understand how such a thing could happen."

Frankie laid her head against Braden's chest, felt his hands come to rest lightly on her shoulder blades. She was almost as confused by the suddenness and depth of her feelings for Sunderlin as she was by the knowledge that she had indeed traveled through time.

"Take me to London," she said in a desperate bid to spirit Braden away from Sunderlin Keep and the tournament.

"Please, darling—as soon as we're married."

Braden curved a finger under her chin, lifted her head so that he could look directly into her face. "I will be happy to take you to London, there to present you at court. *After* the tournament."

An overwhelming grief surged up inside Frankie, and she marveled because at the same time she felt a powerful, greedy joy. "Do you wish to die?" she demanded angrily, leaning back in his arms but not quite able to leave his embrace. "Why else would you ignore such a warning?"

He sighed, and she saw the pain of his physical injury flicker in his eyes. "I cannot run away from what has been given me to do," he said with gentle reason. "It is a matter of honor. Besides, if my death has been ordained by the powers of heaven as it would seem, it will do no good for me to flee to London."

Before Frankie could offer further argument—and even then she knew it would be fruitless to try anyway—several female servants came to collect her. She was taken to a smaller chamber down the hall, where a large copper tub had been set before the fire.

Frankie had a bath, her hair was washed and brushed, and then the women dressed her in a slightly musty-smelling but nonetheless beautiful white velvet gown. She went back to the master chamber to fetch the wreath of dried flowers she'd brought with her from the other time, and there was no sign of Braden.

He awaited her in the chapel, pale and grim, and yet with a fire burning in his caramel eyes as he watched her come toward him. He had to be in serious pain, but he'd learned to transcend it, probably through his training as a knight.

What are you doing, Francesca Whittier? Frankie's good sense demanded, even as she hurried up the narrow aisle to stand beside her future husband. This man isn't real— he's a ghost, a pile of moldering dust lying in some crypt!

Frankie shook her head slightly and sent the ghoulish thoughts scattering. Braden was a miracle, and he might well be taken from her all too soon, either by the sword or by her own unexpected return to the modern world. She would live breath by breath and heartbeat by heartbeat, cherishing every moment she was given to spend with Braden.

The priest was a friar, straight out of a storybook, and Frankie didn't understand a word he said. She simply mumbled and gave a slight nod whenever he turned an expectant look on her. All too soon the romantic, strangely magical ceremony was over, and Braden bent his head to place a light kiss on Frankie's mouth.

She lifted her eyes to meet his, inwardly stunned at the power and breadth of her love for him. It was as if it had always existed within her, a vast plain of the spirit, infinite and rich, only now discovered.

Tears brimmed along her lashes; she gave a little cry of mingled sorrow and joy, and threw her arms around his neck. This caused a twittering among the few guests, but

Frankie didn't care. Every second was a pearl of great price; not one would be wasted.

Braden smiled, shook his head, as if marveling at something too amazing to mention aloud, and tugged gently at one of the ribbons trailing from her crown of flowers.

Frankie had expected that she and her groom would return to the bridal chamber straightaway, and she was unabashedly ready. Instead, however, a celebration of sorts was to be held in the Great Hall; musicians and mummers and jesters had been commandeered from the village fair, and there were mountains of food.

Despite the festive air of the place, Frankie had no illusions that the people of Braden's world accepted her as their mistress. She saw in more than one pair of eyes that she was still feared, still suspected.

While Braden held court at the head table, enjoying the toasts and guarded congratulations of his men-at-arms, Gilford approached Frankie and took her elbow lightly in one hand.

"Come with me," he whispered urgently. "Now."

Frankie didn't want to stray too far from Braden's side, but she was alarmed by the doctor's earnestness. They slipped into a small courtyard, tucked away behind the Great Hall, where bees bumbled and buzzed among blowsy red and yellow roses.

"If you know a way to get back to the twentieth century," Gilford whispered after making certain they were alone, "you'd best be about it. There's talk among the servants and the others that you've bewitched the Duke somehow—they're blaming you for his wound, and they say no power less than the devil's own could have made him marry you." The doctor took both her hands in his own and squeezed. "Please—do not tarry in this place. If you can't will yourself home somehow, then we must smuggle you out of the keep and hide you somewhere."

She opened her mouth to protest, but Gilford never gave her a chance.

"Frankie," he said, "these people are terrified of you. They want to burn you as a witch."

"Braden would never allow it!" Frankie said, but she was cold with fear there in that warm, fragrant garden.

"Sunderlin may not be around after the tournament, if your wizard is to be believed. I beg of you, Frankie, save yourself both heartache and a truly terrible death if you can."

She pulled her hands free of his and hugged herself, but that did not still the trembling. "Merlin did say something about thinking long and hard of my own time, as if that would make me go back. He also said I could end up at any stage of my life—"

"Do it, then."

Frankie shook her head. "No," she said. "I'm here now, and there must be some reason for that. I'm going to see it through."

Gilford sighed heavily and gestured toward the west. "At least let me take you to the nunnery, just beyond the fells, where you'll be safe. I can enter and leave the keep whenever I wish, and you could hide in my cart, under some straw or blankets."

For a moment Frankie considered the idea. In the end, however, she discarded it because it meant being parted from Braden, even by a short distance.

"I'm staying," she said, starting around Gilford to return to the celebration. After all, she was the bride, and her handsome groom awaited.

Gilford caught her arm. "That is a very foolish decision," he bit out. His fingers cut into the tender flesh on the inside of her elbow. "I beg you to reconsider."

Frankie looked down at her white velvet dress, and when she raised her eyes again, her vision was blurred with tears. "I must get back to my husband," she said softly. Then, reluctantly, Gilford freed her, and she hurried back into the Great Hall.

Strong as he was, Braden had had an especially hard day. After only a few boisterous toasts, each followed by a tankard of ale, he began to yawn. It was a relief to Frankie, who had been feeling more alienated from the guests with every passing moment, when he signaled that it was time for them to leave the festivities.

Once they were in their chamber, and the ever-present Mordag had been sent away, Frankie gave her bridegroom an unceremonious push toward the bed. Her reason was anything but romantic. "You need to rest," she scolded "You're dead on your feet."

Braden limped to the bedside, sat down gingerly on its edge, then stretched out with a low groan of mingled relief and suffering. "Now, there's a memorable saying. I suppose someone is going to write that one down someday, as well as the remark about the serpent's tooth."

Frankie smiled and bent over her husband to kiss his forehead. He looked very handsome in his clean blue leggings and purple silk tunic, even though the bandages on his thigh made for an unsightly bulge.

"Someday," she agreed. "I love you, Braden. Whatever happens to us, please remember that."

The groom reached up, touched the side of the bride's nose with a fingertip, then yawned again. "I'll just rest a while now, Duchess, then we'll enjoy the traditional consummation."

Frankie laughed, though she felt as much like crying. "What a poet you are, Braden Stuart-Ramsey, Duke of Sunderlin."

He grinned, though his eyes were closed, and only moments later he was snoring.

Frankie sat beside him for a time, trying to assimilate his presence somehow, as if it were medicine to her soul, and then went out onto the crude stone terrace. There, she had a view of the village, and the stream flowing through it like a wide ribbon of shining foil in the sunshine.

Standing high above the moat, which was filled with stinking, stagnate water, Frankie again considered her plight. Never before had she had a keener sense of what was meant by the phrase, *living for the moment*. She had nothing else—no past and, perhaps, no future. Just this precious wrinkle in time, where she and Braden were tucked away together.

When Braden stirred, after an hour or so, Frankie went back inside the chamber, removed her improvised wedding dress and the wreath of dried flowers, and lay down with her husband. Slowly, and with great reverence, the Duke introduced his Duchess to pleasures even sweeter and more fiery than those she had known before.

It was the next morning, when Braden had gone back to oversee the sword practice despite his wounded leg, that

Frankie saw the wizard again. She was sitting in the hidden garden, the one off the Great Hall that Gilford had taken her to the day before, when she suddenly looked up and found Merlin standing in front of her.

On a man of less commanding presence, the magician's robes and pointed hat might have looked silly, but he carried them off with a flourish.

"So you've married the Duke," he said, arms folded. "That was very foolish, indeed."

Frankie's heart had shinnied up her rib cage and made the leap to her throat, she'd been so startled by the magician's sudden materialization in the garden. Now the organ sank back to its normal place—or perhaps a little lower. At the same time she lifted her chin in a gesture of polite defiance.

"I love Braden."

"Perhaps," Merlin conceded, "but as I told you before, this is not meant to be. An error was made at the Beginning, yes, but what is done is done. Sunderlin shall perish, ere the week is out, and you must go back where you belong before you are executed for sorcery."

"By thinking long and hard of home?" Frankie sounded sarcastic, she knew, but she couldn't help it. She was terrified and confused, and those elements combined to make her tongue sharp. "What is this, the Land of Oz? Shouldn't I just click my heels together and say—"

"Enough," Merlin broke in, exasperated. "Time is a creation of the mind. Your other life is not at the end of the universe; indeed, it is so close you could reach out and touch it. Think of your own world, Francesca. Think of it!"

His words enchanted her somehow; she recalled Seattle,

with its hills, its busy harbor, its bustle and energy. For the merest fraction of a moment, she saw flashes of old brick around her, heard the horns of taxicabs as they bumped over the streets in Pioneer Square. For one tiny portion of a single heartbeat, she was back there, standing on the corner of Yesler Way and First Avenue South, only a stone's throw from her shop. A little more concentration, just a little, and she would truly have been there, as solid and real as the old brick building she knew so well.

Still, Frankie's heart was with Braden, and she followed it back in a single cosmic leap. She was perspiring, cold and sick, as she sat clutching the edge of the ancient stone bench in the garden of old roses, struggling to stay long after the need had passed.

"Fool," Merlin said, but in a kind tone. Then, as quickly as he'd appeared, he vanished into the soft, misty air of the morning.

Frankie braved the kitchen after that, there purloining a basketful of various foods from beneath the cook's disapproving nose, and ventured cautiously to the practice grounds. This time, heaven be thanked, she did not surprise Braden into being stabbed. In fact, he was on the sidelines, calling out instructions to other combatants, and when he sensed Frankie's presence, he tossed a smile in her direction and then came hobbling after it.

Even with a limp, she thought, he was a magnificent man. She pictured him in jeans and a half-shirt as he moved toward her, then in a perfectly tailored three-piece suit. Both prospects were delicious.

"I've brought the stuff for a picnic," she said. "We can sit under those maple trees on the far side of the grounds."

Frankie had half expected Braden to refuse her invitation, but instead he took the basket from her and started toward the place she'd chosen for their picnic.

An idea was forming in her mind, and as they ate, she told Braden more about modern-day Seattle. While keeping herself as detached as possible, lest she be snatched back, she tried to make her husband see the buses and cars, the paved roadways, the concrete and steel buildings that loomed against the sky. Her theory was that, if he could imagine the place, perhaps he could also go there somehow, with her. After all, Merlin had once said that Braden truly belonged in that other world, and not in the much cruder and more dangerous one around them.

They lay side by side in the grass for a time, once they'd eaten, and Braden plucked a dandelion from the grass and tickled Frankie's chin with its ghostly down. "I wish I could make love to you right here," he said hoarsely. "We are, of course, being watched."

"Of course," Frankie agreed sadly, catching his hand in hers, squeezing tightly. "Oh, Braden, won't you please call off the tournament? For me?"

He raised her knuckles to his mouth, brushed his lips across them in a caress as light as the passage of a butterfly. "I'm sorry, Francesca. I would do almost anything for you, but I cannot abandon my honor as a man."

Frankie was suddenly flushed with conviction, frustration, and fear. "Your *honor*? Good Lord, Braden, what is honorable about suicide? That's what this is, you know, because you've been warned and you still insist on fighting!"

He smoothed her wind-tousled hair back from her face.

"I can do nothing else, beloved—this is who I am. Besides, I am among the best swordsmen in England."

She closed her eyes tightly, seeking some inner balance, and then nodded. There was no use in arguing; that was clear. Braden was as set on following his path as she was on following her own.

They finished their meal of cold venison, dried fruit, and even drier bread, and then Braden insisted on going back to the field of practice. While Frankie could certainly see the sense in his desire to be as expert a swordsman as possible, she wished there were no need for fighting.

It was a brutal time in history, she thought as they walked back together, her hand tucked into his. And yet, Frankie had to admit, her own era was fraught with peril, too. Each had its pestilences, its widespread poverty, its violence and prejudice. The differences were really pretty superficial.

Now that she'd had a chance to compare the two, however, Frankie knew with a certainty that she preferred her own niche, far away in the tempestuous nineteen-nineties. The only hitch was that she would have to leave Braden to get back there.

Frankie stopped, shading her eyes from the sun and watching as her husband moved haltingly, and yet with that profound confidence of his, toward the field of practice. He must have felt Frankie's gaze, for, although he did not look back, he raised one hand in a gesture she knew was meant for her.

Inside the keep Frankie made her way through cool, shadowy passageways until she reached the chapel. There she sat alone on the bench closest to the wooden cross beside the altar, her hands folded.

The next few days passed in much the same manner as that one had. Braden practiced incessantly, refusing to rest, and Frankie prepared a picnic meal for their noon repast. In the afternoons she sat in the quiet sanctuary of the chapel, offering wordless petitions, prayers of presence rather than pleading.

The nights, ah, the nights. Those were the most delicious, the most bittersweet, the most glorious and tragic times of all.

Braden and Frankie loved until they were gasping and exhausted, until their bodies rebelled and tumbled into the dark, bottomless well of sleep. Always, when the morning came, they loved again.

Day by day, knights and nobles from other parts of the country arrived, with pageantry and fanfare, some housed within the keep, others pitching brightly colored tents outside the walls. The summer fair would soon culminate in a tournament that, according to Gilford, had been a local tradition since the time of William the Conqueror. It was even rumored that the king himself, His Royal Majesty, Edward III, might put in an appearance.

Frankie cared about none of this. When she awakened to the sound of trumpets that morning just a week after her arrival, she knew her own personal Judgment Day had arrived.

# Six

The maidservants murmured among themselves as they attended Frankie that morning of the tournament. She was decked out in a lovely gown of rose-colored silk, trimmed at cuff and hem with fine lace. Her hair was brushed and then pulled into a French braid, with ribbon to match the dress woven in for ornamentation.

Frankie was not seeing her reflection in the looking glass affixed to the wall behind the dressing table. The sounds of the trumpets echoed in her ears, and her heart was pounding with a steadily rising fear.

This day, unless she found some way to prevent it, the man she loved more than her own soul would die. He would no longer exist, either in this world or the one she knew, and she found the thought unbearable.

It was a word snagged from the conversation of the sulky maids attending her that caught Frankie's attention.

"—witch—"

She rose from the bench where she'd sat and turned on the two women. Both lowered their eyes.

"What are you saying about me?" she demanded.

The reply came not from the servants, but from Alaric, who had entered the chamber unannounced and was now helping himself to a piece of fruit from a clay bowl on a table just inside the door.

"They're certain you're the devil's mistress," he said idly, his hand hovering over one piece of fruit and then another. Finally he settled on a speckled pear. "God be thanked for the Italians and their sunny orchards." Despite his cheerful manner, he spoke sternly to the maids, and they vanished, but not before casting looks of mingled terror and resentment in Frankie's direction.

Frankie was only slightly more comfortable in Alaric's presence. He, after all, was slated by the fates to take over the estates following Braden's death and destroy everything the family had built over the centuries.

"Braden isn't here," she said, keeping the breadth of Sunderlin's writing desk between them.

Alaric ran his dark gaze over her, then sighed. "What a lovely, lovely thing you are, Francesca. My brother is a fortunate man."

Frankie said nothing; she knew Alaric had not come to praise Braden. Perhaps he'd even known all along that his elder brother was already out greeting visiting nobles and their knights.

After taking a bite from the pear and wiping the juice from his mouth and chin with a forearm, Alaric set the core aside and regarded Frankie in silence for a time. Then, hands resting on his hips, he said solicitously, "Poor Francesca.

This, I fear, will not be a good day for either you or my dear brother."

She clutched the table's edge, felt herself go pale, and yet kept her chin high and her eyes fiery with rebellion. "Why do you say that, Alaric?" she dared to ask. "Are you plotting against Braden, and thus against me?"

Alaric chuckled. "There is no plot," he said. "But I sense danger, the way one sometimes senses the approach of a storm in otherwise perfect weather. I have a cart ready and waiting at the south gate, Francesca. It's not too late to escape."

"And leave my husband? Never."

"How is it that you've become so attached to him in such a short time?" Alaric inquired with what sounded like genuine puzzlement. He shrugged when she didn't reply, and went on. "True, Braden is much-praised as a lover. But he is not the only man in the world who knows how to give a woman pleasure."

Frankie felt her cheeks turn crimson. As far as she was concerned, Braden *was* the only man in the world, period, for she wanted no other. And she wasn't about to discuss something so personal as her husband's sexual prowess with Alaric or anyone else. "I love him," she said honestly and with a certain quiet ferocity. "Now, please leave me. It's time I joined my husband."

Alaric did not leave; instead, he crooked one arm. "I know, milady," he answered. "I have been sent to escort you. The Duke is busy welcoming his guests, you see, and as a younger son, I am expected to serve as his emissary."

Frankie glared at her brother-in-law for a moment, keeping her distance. "There must be no more talk of my sneaking away in a cart," she warned. "No matter what happens, I will not leave Braden's side."

"Rash words," Alaric replied, not unkindly. "I hope you do not come to regret them."

With the greatest reluctance Frankie took Alaric's arm and allowed him to squire her out of the bedroom, along the wide passageway, and down the enormous staircase to the Great Hall. There, an enormous crowd had gathered, the women chattering, the children running in every direction, the men laughing together and hoisting pints of ale.

At Frankie's appearance, however, a buzz moved through the group, and then there was utter silence. It took all her courage not to cower against Alaric's side when every person raised their eyes to stare.

Alaric called out something to the people, and Frankie knew he was presenting her as the new mistress of Sunderlin Keep even though she didn't comprehend the actual words. The room seemed to quiver for a moment, with that special kind of silence that indicates strong emotion. Then, here and there, a tradesman or a knight or a squire dropped to one knee and lowered his head in deference to the Duke's bride.

The women eyed her narrowly, far more suspicious than the men, but some of them executed grudging curtsies as she passed with Alaric.

It was something of a relief when they passed beneath the high archway and onto the castle grounds.

Colorful tents dotted the landscape, inside the walls as well as out, and one could not turn around without seeing a juggler or a pie merchant or a musician or a nobleman in grand clothes. Frankie took in the spectacle—that could not be helped—but she was too nervous to really appreciate what she was seeing and hearing.

Where was Braden?

Alaric took her to the field of practice, where a long, fencelike structure had been set up, along with a grandstand of sorts and still more tents. Keeping Frankie close to his side with a certain subtle force, Alaric explained that the wooden wall was called a tilt, and that it was designed to keep the horses from colliding during the joust.

Frankie was shading her eyes from the morning sun and searching the crowd for Braden. She thirsted for the sight of him, yearned for the sound of his voice.

But Alaric did not seem anxious to find his brother. He gestured toward the drawbridge, which lay open across the moat. It was packed with travelers coming in and out, on foot, in carts, and on horseback.

"It would be easy to pass through unnoticed, milady," he said. "We have only to exchange those rich silks of yours for a peasant's rags and muss up your lovely hair a bit—"

Just then Frankie spotted Braden. He was standing in a circle of men, smiling, and as she watched, he threw back his magnificent head in a burst of happy laughter. The sound struck Frankie's spirit like one of the spiked steel balls she'd seen in the chamber where weapons were kept.

She pulled free of Alaric, despite his attempt to hold her, and set off toward her husband. It was probably a breach of some masculine code for her to stride right up to him that way, but Frankie was past caring about such things, if she ever had. Her only plan—and a pitifully thin plan it was, too—was to hover close to Braden throughout the day and somehow protect him.

On some level Frankie knew this would probably turn out to be an impossible feat, but she had no other choice but to try. She could not simply abandon Braden to the death the fates had assigned him, even to save her own hide. If the worst happened, she wanted to hold her love in her arms as he passed from this world into the next, and give him whatever comfort she could.

Just the thought filled her eyes with tears.

Braden saw her and pulled away from his circle of friends to greet her with a husbandly kiss on the forehead. With one hand he held her shoulder, with the thumb of the other, he brushed the wetness from her cheek.

"This day will pass, beloved," he told her quietly. "Tonight, you and I will celebrate my victory together."

Conscious of Alaric standing nearby, Frankie shivered. "Who is your opponent?"

Braden lowered his hands to his sides. "I don't know. Lots will be drawn before the competition begins." He offered her his arm as the trumpets sounded, evidently to mark the beginning of the first event. They were settled on a high wooden dais, in straight-back chairs, before he spoke to her again. "First, the joust."

Frankie sat stiffly, biting her lip, as men in heavy armor, mounted on spectacular horses, took their places at either end of the field. The tilt protected the animals to breast height, but the knights themselves were exposed to their onrushing opponent's lance.

Nothing in Frankie's high school performance of *Camelot* had prepared her for the sight of two men riding toward each other at the top speed their burdened horses could manage, long spearlike weapons in hand. The sound was even worse, and she bit her lip throughout, and only kept her breakfast down by the greatest self-control.

The events seemed interminable, but finally, in midafternoon, Braden left the dais to take the field, wearing his sword and a chain-mail vest. Frankie wished he were in full armor or, better yet, that he'd been born in the right time period in the first place and avoided this moment forever.

The people cheered as he took his place in the center of the action and unsheathed his sword. Sunderlin ignored the adulation; his gaze locked with Frankie's, and he seemed to be making a silent promise that he wouldn't let anything separate them.

Frankie's vision blurred; she lifted her hand. *I love you,* she told him in the language of the heart. *Forever and always, no matter what happens, Braden Stuart-Ramsey, Duke of Sunderlin, my soul is mated to yours.*

Braden's opponent was a large man, not as solidly built but clearly strong. He had a red beard and a Nordic look and Frankie thought uneasily of the Viking god Thor.

She rose out of her chair when the blades were drawn, stepped off the dais, and moved through the crowd as the swords were struck together in a sort of warrior's salute.

The cheers and calls of the spectators seemed to Frankie to roll from some great, hollow cave, and the air pounded like a giant heartbeat. Over this, always, always, rang the cruel sound of steel on steel.

She might have stepped right onto the field if Gilford hadn't grabbed her and hauled her back against his rotund torso.

"Are you trying to get him killed?" the doctor rasped, his breath whistling past her ear. "Did you learn nothing before, when Sunderlin was wounded because of your reck-lessness?''

The thrumming in her ears stopped; suddenly everything was crystal clear. Something had passed between the war-riors, and the crowd sensed the change and fell silent. The match had turned, between one moment and its successor, from sport to warfare.

Frankie almost screamed, so great and uncontrollable was her terror, but Gilford stopped her by pressing one meaty hand over her mouth and shaking her.

"You must not distract him!" he breathed.

Someone else did that, as it happened. Alaric rushed onto the field, shouting, and in that fragment of time Braden hesitated. It was enough for Thor, who plunged his sword straight into the Duke's abdomen.

Frankie felt the blow as surely as if it had been dealt to her. She shrieked in protest and furious grief, and somehow twisted free of Gilford's hold, stumbling as she raced onto the field and threw herself down beside Braden in the bloody dirt.

She was wailing softly, speaking senseless words, as she gathered him into her arms.

Remarkably he smiled at her, reached up to touch her face. "So you were right," he said softly. "It ends here. I'm sorry, my love, for not believing you."

Frankie sobbed when he closed his eyes, tried to shake him awake. It was no use, and she was like a wild creature when Gilford and another man took her arms and hauled her off Braden so he could be carried away.

The crowd had been stirred to rage by the spectacle, by

the unthinkable fall of their legendary leader, but it wasn't Thor they turned upon.

No.

One of the women pointed at Frankie. "Witch," she said. Others took up the cry. "Witch—witch—witch—"

"God in heaven," Gilford gasped, "it's happening. Come, Francesca, we must be away from here, quickly!"

Frankie was prostrate with grief; the damning words of the crowd meant nothing to her. She wanted only to sit with Braden, to tell him all the things she'd stored up in her heart, to hold his hand in case he would know somehow that she was there.

Alaric moved to join the others, who had encircled Frankie and the physician now.

"She knew this day would come," Braden's brother said clearly, gesturing toward Frankie. "She predicted it. Maybe she even made it happen with chants and magic!"

"Are you insane?" Gilford demanded of Alaric, holding tightly to Frankie, who was only half-conscious. He raised his voice, addressing the witch-hunters who surrounded them, looming closer and closer. "This is a mere woman, not a witch!" he cried. "She has a heart and soul, blood and breath, like any one of you!"

Frankie fainted at that point, only to revive a few moments later and find herself being forcefully separated from Gilford, her only defender.

"In the name of all that's holy," her friend begged, his face wet with sweat and perhaps tears, "release her! She has done nothing wrong!"

"Silence!" Alaric shouted. "Why do you defend her, Gilford? Are you in league with this—this mistress of the devil?"

"You are a traitor!" Gilford accused in return. "Mark my words, Judas Iscariot, the Duke will avenge this wrong, and God Himself will come to his aid!"

Someone came forward from the seething crowd and struck Gilford hard with a staff. The big man's knees buckled and he went down, and the sight shook Frankie partially out of her stupor. At last she realized what was happening.

She was dragged, kicking and scratching, to the whipping post, a horror she had not seen before, and thrust against it with cruel force. Her arms were wrenched behind her and tightly tied with narrow strips that bit into the flesh of her wrists.

For a few moments Frankie honestly didn't care whether she lived or died. After all, Braden was dead—he'd perished in her arms. If there was an afterlife, she might see him there.

As the villagers began stacking twigs around her feet, however, and as their eyes filled with unfounded hatred, it occurred to Frankie that she might be carrying Braden's child. It didn't seem fair that the infant should die before living.

Frankie fought hysteria as she searched the mob for one friendly face, one person who might dare to speak for her. There was no sign of Gilford—he had been overcome and perhaps even arrested—but Alaric soon approached, as if drawn by her thoughts.

"I warned you, Francesca," he scolded. No one would ever have guessed from his manner that he'd just seen his only brother die, that he was about to watch another human being burned alive. "You should have listened to me. I would have taken you away."

"You did it on purpose," Frankie accused, as the terrible realization dawned. "You weren't going to help Braden on the field; you only wanted to distract him so that his opponent could run him through!"

Unbelievably, Alaric smiled. "You might have been my duchess, after a decent interval had passed," he said. "How sad that you would never listen to reason."

Frankie spat at him, though until then her mouth had felt painfully dry. "I'll burn for a few minutes," she hissed, causing the mob to gasp in fear and draw back, "but you, Alaric Stuart-Ramsey, will suffer the flames of eternity for what you've done! *You are cursed!*"

Alaric paled, then his jaw hardened. "Bring the torches!" he cried.

Frankie watched in stricken horror as the pitch-soaked torches were lit and then laid to the dry twigs at her feet. She heard the crackle of burning wood, smelled the acrid smoke, saw the shifting mirage of heat rising in front of her like a wall.

Then she heard Merlin's voice, though she could not see him.

"Think of Seattle, Francesca," he said urgently. "Think of the big white ferryboats crossing Puget Sound. Think of those wonderful snowcapped mountains, and the hillsides carpeted with green, green trees. Remember your shop, and your cousin Brian, and your friends. Remember the Space Needle, and Pioneer Square, and the Pike Place Market—"

Tears rolled down Frankie's cheeks as she tilted her head back and remembered with all her might, with all her being.

She felt the flames begin to catch at her skirts, felt the horrible, choking heat . . .

"Seattle," said Merlin. "Seattle, Seattle—"

"Witch!" screamed Alaric, his voice hoarse and fading. Slowly fading, into the heat, beyond it. "*Witch* . . ."

There was no explosion, no sprinkling of magic dust. The shift was graceful and quiet.

Frankie's first realization was that it was cooler, that her hands were no longer bound. She opened her eyes and found herself staring into a shop window at her own reflection.

She was wearing a silk dress, torn and singed, and her face and hair were dark with soot. Taxis and pedestrians moved past, also mirrored in the dusty glass, and Frankie turned slowly to look.

Pioneer Square.

Frankie began to weep, stumbling through staring, whispering tourists, street people, and office workers, making her way around the corner.

The sign above her shop still read CINDERELLA'S CLOSET. Frankie sagged against the door, sliding downward until she was sitting on the worn brick step.

Passersby stopped and made a semicircle around her; Mrs. Cullywater pushed through, carrying a bag from a nearby bakery in one hand and wearing the key to the shop on her wrist, dangling from a pink plastic bracelet.

"Why, Miss Whittier!" the friendly old woman cried, dropping the bag and crouching. "What's happened? Merciful heavens, how did your clothes get into such a state. . . ."

Frankie drew up her knees, wrapped her arms around

them, and shook her head from side to side, unable to offer a sensible explanation.

SHE SPENT THAT NIGHT IN HARBORVIEW Hospital, under observation, but was released in the morning. A friend, Sheila Hendrix, brought jeans and a T-shirt and drove Frankie back to her apartment.

"I'll stay if you want," Sheila said. She was obviously worried, but Frankie didn't want to keep her. Sheila had a good job with a local advertising firm, and she had better things to do than play nursemaid.

"I'll be all right," Frankie insisted, and Sheila left.

The apartment was unchanged, except that everything was covered with a fine layer of dust and the plants were all desperate for water. Frankie made a ritual of small chores, but the place was small, only a studio, though it was attractive, and all too soon there was nothing to do.

Frankie sank onto her couch, gnawing at her lower lip. It was only a matter of time before the police would show up, wanting to know what she'd been doing, staggering through the streets in such a state, with her dress half burned off and her hair and face covered in soot. Given the bohemian nature of Pioneer Square, she could probably convince them that she'd been practicing to become a street performer.

What would be harder to explain, however, was her total lack of identification. Her passport, driver's license, and credit cards were all still in England, in the Grimsley Inn, where she'd left them before going to the medieval fair that first day.

She splayed her fingers and plunged them into her hair. Braden, she thought, with a sorrow so desperate, so all-encompassing, that it was crushing her. Oh, Braden. What do I do now? How do I go on without you?

Somehow, though it seemed an impossible thing to do, Frankie did manage to go on with her life. After a few days the police casually stopped by to ask what had happened, why she'd been wandering in the streets in a charred dress, and she told them she was into performance art. She didn't think for a moment that they believed her, but they had other concerns and didn't press.

Mrs. Cullywater stayed on to help run the shop, since Frankie was in a daze of grief most of the time, and it was that kind woman who called the inn in Grimsley and asked them to send back Miss Whittier's identification, along with her suitcase. Yes, the older woman assured the clerk on the other end of the line, Miss Whittier was fine. She'd left Great Britain under special circumstances and apologized sincerely for any concern her disappearance might have caused.

A month had passed since her dramatic return from England, and Frankie was sitting in her shop, watching lovers pass by on the sidewalk, hand in hand. She was sipping strong tea and feeling sorry for herself when a terrible crash sounded from the back of the shop.

Mrs. Cullywater, normally unflappable, was back there sorting a shipment of antique buttons, and she let out a scream that all but cracked the window glass. Frankie spilled her tea and overturned her stool in her haste to get to her employee.

The shop was small, and very narrow, and Frankie had

to make her way between counters of old jewelry, racks of both vintage and used designer clothing, and pyramids of hatboxes. When she burst into the storeroom, she screamed, too—not for fear, but for joy.

Braden was sitting on the floor, clad in his usual leggings and tunic, looking dazed and very pleased with himself. "God's knees," he said. "I finally managed it."

Mrs. Cullywater had collapsed into a chair and was fanning herself with an old copy of *Photoplay*. "Out of nowhere," she muttered. "I swear, he just appeared out of nowhere."

Frankie was kneeling on the floor, laughing and crying, fearing to close her eyes lest Braden disappear again. She flung her arms around him, held on tight, and sobbed because he was real, and because it was no dream.

"How—?" she finally managed to choke out. "Oh, Braden, I thought you were dead!"

He got to his feet, bringing Frankie with him. "Gilford was there to take care of me." Braden put his arms around her, held her loosely, so that he could look down into her eyes. "You should have heard the uproar, Duchess, after you disappeared right out of your bonds the way you did!"

Frankie reached up, tentatively touched Braden's face. "How did you get here?"

"Your wizard came to my room one night and told me to remember all the things you'd told me about your world. He said I might be able to get to you, since I was supposed to be born here in the first place. I failed any number of times, but I'm glad I kept trying."

Mrs. Cullywater edged around them and fled the shop. Frankie hoped the poor dear wasn't too frightened, but she did not go after the older woman. Any attempt to explain would, of course, have only made matters worse.

Braden bent his head, kissed Frankie lightly on the mouth, the way he always did before he made slow, sweet, thorough love to her. "For a time there," he confessed a moment later, "I thought the villagers might have been right about you. Who else but a witch could vanish the way you did? It was Gilford who set me straight and said you'd come back here."

Frankie remembered the insane anger of the mob and shivered, and Braden held her a little closer. "I thought they were going to kill him, too, because he tried so hard to save me."

Braden shook his head. "They gave him some bruises and scrapes, all right, but he was a healer. They needed him, and they knew it."

Frankie laughed, even though her eyes were glistening with tears. "How are we going to explain you to the modern world, Braden Stuart-Ramsey?"

He gathered her to him and kissed her in the way she'd dreamed of, remembered, mourned during the long weeks since their parting. "We'll worry about that later," he said. "For now, Duchess, I just want to hold you in my arms."

Not wanting to confront Braden with the strange sights and sounds of the nineteen nineties without some preparation, Frankie took him by the hand and led him through the alleyways to the rear entrance of her apartment building. They climbed the inside stairway and hurried along the hall to Frankie's door.

They were inside before Braden really began to absorb his surroundings. He touched the television set in curious bewilderment, and Frankie smiled. She would show him how it worked later; with the twentieth century rushing at him from every direction, his senses were surely approaching overload as it was.

"Where do you sleep?" Braden asked when he'd checked out the bathroom, where he immediately flushed the toilet, and given the kitchenette a quick examination.

Frankie was just standing there, leaning against the door and silently rejoicing. She was all but blinded by tears, and yet she couldn't stop smiling. That is, until she remembered that he'd suffered two grievous sword wounds in the space of a week.

She thrust herself away from the door and hurried over to him. "You're hurt—good heavens, in all the excitement, I'd forgotten—"

Quickly she removed the sofa cushions and folded out the hidden bed.

Braden stared for a moment, then crossed himself.

Frankie took his hand. "You need to lie down," she said.

He smiled. "What I need, Duchess, is for you to lie down with me." He pulled her close and kissed her in his old, knee-melting way. Gently he lifted her T-shirt off over her head and tossed it aside. "Strange clothes again," he teased, but he had no trouble removing her bra.

"Braden," she whimpered joyously as he cupped her breast in his hand, chafing a ready nipple with his thumb.

Sunderlin was fumbling with the snap on her jeans by then. "What manner of leggings are these?" he asked, but he didn't wait for an answer. Instead, he gently stripped away the last of Frankie's clothes and lowered her to the bed.

Frankie watched as her husband removed his own garments, things that probably belonged in a British museum, saw the scars on his belly and his right thigh. If anything, these imperfections made Braden even more magnificent. She held out her arms, and he fell to her with a low, hoarse groan of need.

"Your wounds?" Frankie asked, searching his eyes for some sign of the pain he had to be feeling.

Braden kissed her hungrily and at great length before answering. "My wounds will heal, now that I am with you again. For the moment, let there be no more talk of suffering, Francesca, or of trouble. We can think about our problems later."

Frankie arched her hips and deftly received him, delighting in the way he tilted his head back and moaned. "Much later," she agreed.

In that moment, somewhere far away and yet very nearby, a passageway between two eras closed without even a whisper of sound.